WORLDS APART . . .

"What could you possibly be afraid of?" Adrian asked.

"Myself. And you."

"Me? What makes me such a fearsome fellow?"

"It is not you, Adrian, but what you do to me. You make me look at things differently, make me think in new ways. I am not certain I want to."

He slipped his arm around her shoulder and drew her close. "Wasn't it Plato who said the unexamined life was not worth living?"

"I do not know. Remember, I do not have Greek—or Latin. That makes me feel stupid."

"You are not stupid, Rose. A gentleman's education is not necessary for a woman like you."

"An idle, spoiled aristocrat?"

He placed a finger on her lips. "Do you really think I wish to discuss the conjugation of Latin verbs with you?" Adrian wrapped his other arm around her waist and drew her even closer. "That is the very last thing I wish to do."

Their lips were so close, barely a breath apart. Her blue eyes were wide, dark, uncertain as they gazed into his.

"What do you wish to do?" she asked breathlessly.

"This." He brought his mouth down on hers.

SIGNET REGENCY ROMANCE
Coming in August 1998

Allison Lane
Devall's Angel

Nadine Miller
The Madcap Masquerade

Gail Eastwood
The Magnificent Marquess

The
Temporary Duke

Melinda McRae

A SIGNET BOOK

SIGNET
Published by the Penguin Group
Penguin Putnam Inc., 375 Hudson Street,
New York, New York 10014, U.S.A.
Penguin Books Ltd, 27 Wrights Lane,
London W8 5TZ, England
Penguin Books Australia Ltd, Ringwood,
Victoria, Australia
Penguin Books Canada Ltd, 10 Alcorn Avenue,
Toronto, Ontario, Canada M4V 3B2
Penguin Books (N.Z.) Ltd. 182–190 Wairau Road,
Auckland 10, New Zealand

Penguin Books Ltd, Registered Offices:
Harmondsworth, Middlesex, England

First published by Signet, an imprint of Dutton NAL,
a member of Penguin Putnam Inc.

First Printing, July, 1998
10 9 8 7 6 5 4 3 2 1

Copyright © Melinda McRae, 1998

All rights reserved

 REGISTERED TRADEMARK—MARCA REGISTRADA

Printed in the United States of America

Prologue

∽

England, 1812

Adrian Stamford sat in the far corner of the timbered taproom of the Scalded Goose, nursing a steaming mug of cider. The hot brew was well appreciated, for he'd been numb with cold when the carter set him down half an hour ago. With any luck, he might thaw out before he had to continue his journey.

Fortunately, the Bristol coach was late today.

Tramping feet and loud, boisterous voices sounded in the corridor; then the taproom door flew open, and a group of pink-coated and mud-bespattered huntsmen poured into the chamber.

Adrian edged closer to the fire, determined to ignore this end to his peaceful musings. The new arrivals paid him no heed, more concerned with making certain their ale arrived posthaste. But after the tapman scurried off, their interest wavered, and one man glanced in his direction.

The stranger looked away, then whirled around and stared at Adrian.

"By God, it's Alston!" the man said.

The room went suddenly silent. Adrian glanced up uneasily and saw everyone staring at him.

"How in the devil did you beat us here?" a tall, lanky man demanded. "Thought you went haring off after that stoat."

Adrian smiled. "I fear you have me confused with someone else."

Another hunter guffawed loudly. "Trying to run one of your rigs on us again? Don't think we'll fall for that twice. We're on to your little jokes."

"Even changed his clothes to fool us," another noted. He

leaned closer and plucked at Adrian's coat sleeve. "Did you roll some farmer in a ditch and take his gear?"

Adrian was well aware of the shabby nature of his coat; he wasn't going to subject his best garments to the wear and tear of travel. "I'm sorry, but I'm not the person you think I am. My name's Stamford—Adrian Stamford." He took a sip from his mug.

A stout man clapped him on the shoulder with such force that Adrian's cider sloshed onto the table. "And I'm George the Third. Give it a rest, Alston. Did you think to order food? We're starving."

The door opened, and Adrian heard booted feet crossing the floor, but the men clustered around him blocked his view of the new arrival.

"Standing around like a bunch of gogglehobs," the newcomer drawled in aristocratic tones. "Just like you rotters to leave me behind. I hope to God you've ordered something decent to drink."

The huntsmen turned en masse to confront their accuser, once again preventing Adrian from catching a glimpse of him.

The lanky man turned and stared at Adrian again, confusion etched on his face. "Alston?"

"It's a joke," one man said.

"A great jest on Alston's part."

"Who is jesting?" the newcomer asked.

"Look at him—he's the spitting image of Alston."

"No, he's not."

"The hair, the eyes . . . identical, I tell you."

One of the men leaned over the table and peered into Adrian's face. "By God, I think you're right."

Another man plucked Adrian from his seat and shoved him to the center of the room, leaving him face-to-face with the new man.

Adrian found himself staring into a familiar face—one that he saw in the mirror every day. Grey eyes, long, narrow nose, straight brown hair tinged with gold.

Except this was no mirror; it was a flesh-and-blood man standing before him.

"Good God!" the other man exclaimed. He gave Adrian a thorough head-to-toe perusal, then shook his head in disbelief. "It's uncanny. Who are you?"

"Adrian Stamford."

"I'm Alston." He held out his hand, and Adrian shook it. "Quite a strange quirk of fate, don't you think?"

"I've heard it said that every man has his double, but I never expected to meet mine," Adrian said, with a rueful shake of his head. "Particularly in a coaching inn."

Alston put a hand on his hip and regarded Adrian with a puzzled look. "Stamford, you say? Any relation to the Surrey Stamfords?"

Adrian shook his head.

"The Stamfords in Cheshire? The Sloan-Stamfords in Norfolk? The Stamford-Smedleys in Yorkshire?"

"My family comes from Essex," Adrian said.

"Amazing," Alston said, still eyeing him closely. He gestured toward the table. "Join us for a drink, won't you?"

The coachman's horn blew outside, announcing his tardy arrival.

"I must go," Adrian said, reaching for his greatcoat.

Alston put a hand on his arm. "Give me your direction. I'd like to look you up someday."

"I'm off to Buckleigh Manor—near Newton Abbot."

"Well, Mr. Stamford, of Buckleigh Manor, it has been a pleasure to meet such a well-featured man." He grinned.

Adrian managed a smile. He took a last gulp of his still warm cider, then headed for the yard to make sure his bags were loaded onto the coach. The innkeeper started to brush past him in the narrow hall, then came to a sudden halt, his expression turning anxious.

"Is everything to your satisfaction, Your Grace?"

Adrian opened his mouth to respond, then the import of the man's words hit him. *Your Grace.*

Good God. Alston. The *Duke* of Alston. Adrian whirled

around and started back toward the taproom, but the horn blared again, and he dashed out into the yard, barely in time to catch the Bristol Flyer.

He took one final glance at the inn as they pulled out of the yard, trying to decide if he liked the idea of looking like a duke's twin.

Chapter 1

Oh, what a tangled web we weave,
When first we practice to deceive!

—Scott, *Marmion*

England, 1816

The most noble Lady Rosemary Alicia Devering, younger—and only—sister to His Grace, the Duke of Alston, stamped her ladylike, satin-clad foot in a most unladylike manner.

"How could he do this to me?" she demanded of the two gentlemen before her. "He knows I cannot go to London without him. Think of the questions it would cause! Does he expect me to spend the entire Season trapped in the country?"

"I am sure there is nothing amiss, Lady Rosemary." The short, bespectacled man in the somber garb of a solicitor gave her a reassuring smile. "No doubt a letter explaining the entire situation went missing."

"More likely, it is Simon who has gone missing." Rose glared at the rotund figure of her uncle, the Earl of Felton. "Did he forget that his wedding is only six weeks away?"

The two men exchanged uneasy glances. "Is it possible that your brother might have communicated with someone outside the family?" her uncle asked.

"Are you referring to his rackety friends or his last mistress?" Rose asked acidly.

Lord Felton remained unperturbed by her outspokenness.

"I am certain we will hear from him eventually," the solicitor said, attempting to soothe her. "You both must be patient and wait."

"Patient!" Rose knew her voice had risen to an unbecoming screech, but she could not help herself. Simon's unexpected absence was nothing less than a disaster. They should have been in London a week ago, yet she was still here in the country, while everyone else was enjoying the Season in town.

She would not endure this exile any longer. "I will make my own plans," she announced. "I am not going to wait until Simon deigns to inform us of his intentions. I *shall* go to London by myself."

"Rosemary, you are not the only one who is in a fix here." Her uncle gave her a pleading look. "If anyone thinks something has happened . . ."

"Under the hatches again, Uncle? What was it this time—cards or horses?"

"Both," he admitted ruefully. "And unless—until—your brother returns, I do not dare show my face in the city."

"That is not my concern," she said stubbornly.

The solicitor stepped forward and cleared his throat. "Lady Rosemary? The situation is . . . um . . . a bit more desperate than we first explained. It is not merely that no one has heard from His Grace. He has failed to return from a hiking expedition in the Swiss Alps. There is some fear—"

"That is just the sort of thing Simon would do—break his neck on purpose in order to avoid taking me to London."

"Rosemary!"

She gave her uncle a chagrined look and a reassuring smile. "I know nothing could have happened to Simon. He's probably ensconced with some buxom milkmaid in a quaint Swiss chalet."

"There is the matter of his wedding . . ." the solicitor nervously pointed out.

"Which he will no doubt arrive for with mere days to spare. That would be just like him too, the wretch. Poor Juliet will not even be able to enjoy her own engagement."

"It is not Lady Juliet I am concerned about, but her father, Lord Ramsey," Felton said. "He might decide to call off the wedding if he discovers the bridegroom is missing."

"Cancel his daughter's wedding to the Duke of Alston?" Rosemary scoffed at the thought. "He is more likely to ride down St. James's Street naked, sitting backward on an ass."

"Ramsey's financial situation is perilous right now," Felton replied. "Juliet will do his bidding."

"Let her cry off, then. Simon can find another wife."

"But, Rosemary, you are forgetting the *will*."

She sank into a chair and sighed. He was right; she had forgotten about the will—her odious grandfather's intolerable, ridiculous, idiotic will. The one that said Simon had to marry Lady Juliet, or forfeit the unentailed part of the estate. Which amounted to over half their holdings—and most of their ready income. Without it, life would be very dull indeed.

She looked wearily at her uncle. "Whatever are we going to do?"

"I have already sent search parties to Switzerland. They will scour every inch of the country, looking for him. If Simon is there, they will find him. Meanwhile . . ."

"Yes?"

"I have a plan . . ."

Adrian Stamford sat at his scarred dining table, eagerly examining the bit of metal he had unearthed while digging this morning. He carefully scraped away the accumulated dirt that clung to the uneven edges. Was it a Roman brooch? The clasp to the heavy fur cloak of some ancient Briton?

Or a piece of garbage discarded by a farmer?

Before he could examine it further, he heard the scrape of feet on the cottage doorstep and the loud voices of the ten-year-old Topmore twins, Eddie and Freddy. Reluctantly, he set down his find and went to the door to greet his pupils.

Two more unstudious boys could not exist in all of England, and it was Adrian's unenviable task to attempt to drum enough Latin into their thick skulls so they could consider themselves gentlemen. He despaired of success. But as long as the squire was willing to pay for their lessons, Adrian would do what he could.

"Hullo," said Eddie—or was it Freddy? Adrian was never quite certain, thanks to the boys' deliberate attempts to mislead him. "We've got to hurry today because Papa's coming back from town and he's bringing us all sorts of presents."

From any other child, the remark might indicate wishful thinking, but the squire spoiled the twins abominably. Adrian only hoped it wouldn't be anything noisy this time—like the two drums they had received at Christmas—or dangerous, like the rabbit slings that appeared in January. They had tormented their tutor with both.

It became obvious after the first few minutes that today's lesson was not going well. The two lads fidgeted and squirmed, casting longing glances at the bracket clock on the mantel. It was a pity Adrian hadn't been hired to teach them arithmetic, or he might have been able to conduct a usable lesson. Tacitus could not hold their interest today.

When the unexpected sound of an approaching carriage reached their ears, it was all over. Before he could say "halt," they had raced out the door. Adrian followed at a more sedate pace.

The twins stood awestruck on the edge of the gravel drive, staring at an elegant traveling carriage. Its coating of dust could not hide the gleaming maroon paint beneath, nor the elaborate crest on the door.

It was definitely not the squire.

A groom climbed down and opened the door, pulling down the stairs. A round-faced, middle-aged man stuck his head out and examined Adrian with rapt attention. "Amazing," he said at last, shaking his head. "The likeness . . . You are Mr. Adrian Stamford, are you not?"

Adrian nodded in growing puzzlement.

"Good." The man climbed down from the carriage. "You are a difficult man to find, Mr. Stamford. I've been searching for you for some time, now."

Adrian saw that Eddie and Freddy were watching this exchange with round eyes. "Lessons are over for today," he said sternly. "Go home."

They regarded him with dismay.

"Didn't you say your father was coming home at any moment?"

That reminder overcame their reluctance to abandon the elegant vehicle, and they dashed off down the lane.

The visitor gave Adrian an impatient look. "Well, Mr. Stamford, aren't you going to invite me in?"

"But of course . . . I mean . . . who are you?"

"I will explain everything after some refreshment." The man snapped his fingers, and the groom appeared at his side. "Bring the hamper."

Mystified, Adrian led the way into the house.

He had no choice but to take the man into the tiny parlor. Adrian swept a pile of papers off the armchair and looked around for a place to put them. Unsteady piles of books teetered precariously on the window ledge; pottery fragments littered the tabletop. Finally, he carted his armload into the dining room and set the papers down on the table beside the twins' forgotten Latin grammars.

His visitor took in the disorder with a loud "harrumph" and sat down. The groom placed an enormous wicker hamper at his feet and withdrew.

The visitor pointed to the basket. "If you would be so kind, Mr. Stamford."

Opening it, Adrian discovered a bottle of brandy, glasses, a packet of biscuits, a squashed but still serviceable cake with white icing, assorted silver cutlery, and fine linen napkins.

"I'll take a drop of brandy now," his guest said. "We can enjoy the rest of the repast after we've talked."

Adrian poured a glass and at the man's nod, poured another one for himself. He had the feeling he was going to need it. The sheer oddity of this visit filled him with a deep sense of uneasiness.

"Well," the man said, "you are probably wondering why I am here."

"True," Adrian replied. "You might start by telling me who you are."

"Felton."

Adrian regarded him blankly. Should that name mean something to him?

There was a trace of exasperation on the man's florid face. "*Lord* Felton."

Adrian nodded, still mystified. "Go on."

"I have a business proposition for you, young man." Felton glanced around at his chaotic surroundings and barely suppressed a shudder. "One that will pay you handsomely, I might add."

Adrian relaxed. The man, no doubt, was looking for a tutor for some noble scion.

"Do you recall an incident at a . . . hmm . . . traveling establishment a few years back? Something about a bit of mistaken identity?"

Even after all this time, a cold chill crept up Adrian's back at the remembrance of that eerie encounter with the Duke of Alston. He had never forgotten it.

"Ye . . . es," he replied, his uneasiness returning.

"That young man was my nephew. Frankly, Mr. Stamford, I—we—need your help. An unusual circumstance has arisen and you are the very man to help us set things to right again."

More confused than ever, Adrian took a sip of brandy. Very good brandy, he noted. "The duke wants me to help him?"

"Ah, so you do know to whom I am referring." A smile creased Felton's pudgy face. "Yes. The duke is abroad at the moment—on a matter of the greatest urgency, national security, the fate of the realm, that sort of thing. Because of the delicate nature of his business, it is critical that no one knows of his absence."

Adrian waited impatiently for the man to come to the point.

"It has been suggested, in light of the striking resemblance between yourself and His Grace, that you take his place, so to speak, for a short while."

The glass slipped from Adrian's hand and hit the floor with a thud, the brandy spreading out in an amber puddle, filling the room with its strong perfume.

Adrian stood up. "You want me to *what*?"

Felton motioned for him to sit. "Please, hear me out. It is merely a minor masquerade, filling in for His Grace until he returns from abroad."

"Filling in where? And how?"

"Well, it is rather imperative that His Grace be in London this spring. There is, of course, his presence in the Lords to be dealt with—but that's a minor affair; he doesn't take that responsibility seriously—and providing an escort when needed for his sister—"

"His sister?" Adrian glared at the man. "You want me to carry on this pretense in front of his sister?"

"Oh no, no, not at all. She will know the truth, of course. How else could we manage?"

"Indeed," Adrian said. It was a mad scheme—and he did not like it one bit. Surely, there were other ways to cover the duke's absence—ways that did not involve him.

"In return for your cooperation, we are prepared to offer you the heartfelt gratitude of His Grace's family." Felton looked pointedly at the ragged draperies hanging alongside the window. "And a generous compensation."

Adrian was not fooled. The man's unfailing politeness made him suspicious. Something more complicated was going on here.

"Why can't you simply explain that the duke is ill, or staying in the country?" he asked bluntly.

His guest looked highly uncomfortable. "Well, there is the matter of the duke's intended bride. She does not wish to be denied her engagement parties. Your task will be to escort the lady about town until he returns."

"Will there be anyone in London who does not know?" Adrian asked.

Felton ignored his question. "We will, of course, make you acquainted with the duke's habits, tastes, his intimates, and his activities." He took a quick breath. "You are of a similar size, so you may avail yourself of the duke's wardrobe and—"

"I am not going to do it."

The earl stared at him in disbelief. "But . . . but you must!"

With deliberate provocation, Adrian took one of the elegant linen napkins from the hamper and proceeded to mop up the spilled brandy. From the corner of his eye, he watched the earl, who was regarding him with a look of growing panic.

"I'm sorry that you came all this way for nothing," Adrian said, tossing the sodden napkin into the hamper. "But I really have no desire to participate in such a scheme."

"I did not wish to have to take this course." The earl's expression hardened as he withdrew a folded paper from his greatcoat. "I had hoped that words alone would convince you. But since they did not, I was ordered to show you this." He handed the letter to Adrian.

With a deep sense of foreboding, Adrian broke the seal, unfolded the paper, and scanned its contents.

"To our loyal and dutiful subject, Mr. Adrian Stamford. You are hereby requested . . ."

The signature at the bottom looked like chicken scratchings, but there was no mistaking that it spelled out George. He didn't need the feathered seal of the Prince of Wales beside the signature to convince him.

Adrian glanced up. A look of smug satisfaction shone on the earl's face.

Adrian reflected. They could not do anything to him if he refused—political prisoners were no longer clapped into the Tower. But the Prince himself had requested his assistance . . .

There had to be more to the story than the earl had revealed. Why else would the Regent be involved? Adrian might be walking into a highly awkward situation—if the letter was genuine. He could not find that out without asking the Regent himself—a highly unlikely prospect. But surely, a duke would have the opportunity to speak with the future king . . . A slow grin spread across his face.

Adrian had always been drawn to mystery—why else did he spend so much time digging for the relics of Britain's ancient inhabitants? This situation looked as puzzling as an unearthed heap of broken pottery.

He knew Eddie and Freddy would not mind having a holiday from their lessons. And once in London, Adrian would have the opportunity to pay a personal call at the offices of the Antiquities Society, and perhaps persuade them to pay attention to his discoveries. He glanced at the earl.

"How long do you expect the duke to be gone?"

"Eight weeks at the most."

Two months. Adrian had no pressing obligations. There was no reason he could not take the time. And the absurdity of the whole plan appealed to his sense of humor. He, Adrian Stamford, would be mingling with the highest ranks of the British aristocracy. A grand and glorious joke.

"I will do it."

The obvious relief on the earl's face told Adrian that his instincts were correct. They needed him badly. How long would it take before he discovered the whole story?

The earl stood. "We can leave as soon as you are ready."

"It should not take me more than a few days to settle my affairs," Adrian said.

The earl gaped at him. "Days? My good man, I hope to be back on the road within the hour."

"I cannot walk away like that," Adrian protested. "I have students—"

"We will send someone to deal with them. Latin it is, I believe, that you teach?"

Adrian nodded.

"We will have someone here within two days to take over your charges. All you need to pack is a small bag—the duke's possessions will be at your disposal."

Shaking his head at his folly, Adrian went off to pack.

The earl delayed their departure long enough for Adrian to leave a letter with the squire, explaining the situation, along with the key to the cottage for the replacement tutor. In a short time they were on the main road, galloping straight into Adrian's strange future.

It was a pleasure to travel in the ducal carriage. Adrian almost sank into the heavily padded, velvet upholstery. Matching

curtains hung beside the windows next to lamps that would il-
luminate the interior at night. He leaned back into the comfortable seat, wondering anew about the man who had such luxury
at his fingertips.

Adrian appreciated the luxury even more when the earl explained they would be traveling through the night, stopping
only for dinner and the changes of horses. "Time is of the
essence," he explained.

Adrian doubted that the *real* duke ever had to sleep in his
carriage.

He was tired, dirty, hungry, and thoroughly out of sorts when
the carriage pulled off the main road early the next evening and
turned down a narrow but well-kept country lane. It rolled to a
stop in front of a neat, brick Jacobean house.

"This is one of the duke's lesser hunting boxes," the earl explained as Adrian stared out the window. "We thought it would
be a good place to begin your training."

A good place to hide him, Adrian thought. In case he was not
up to the task.

Heaving a sigh of trepidation, Adrian climbed down from the
coach. The "lesser hunting box" would swallow his own small
cottage whole. He followed the earl into the flagged entry hall.
Felton darted off through a side door, leaving Adrian standing
awkwardly, wondering what would happen next. The earl had
not been forthcoming with any details.

Adrian heard footsteps on the stairs and turned in time to see
a dark-haired beauty racing down them.

"Simon!" she cried and flung herself at him.

With a wide smile at this unlooked-for pleasure, Adrian wel-
comed her with open arms.

Chapter 2

∽

"I should box your ears!" Rose wrapped her arms about her brother's waist. "Do you realize how many engagements I have missed in your absence?" She squeezed him tightly, then tilted her head, taking in his disordered appearance. "Really, Simon, it's most perturbing . . ."

Her voice trailed off as she looked more deeply into those clear grey eyes. Then her arms fell to her sides, and she took a stumbling step backward.

This man was not her brother.

She examined him with a mixture of disbelief and fascination. In appearance, he could be Simon's twin. He had the same gold-tinged brown hair, the long, narrow Devering nose, the tall, lean form of her brother. Yet now that she knew, she saw subtle signs of difference—the awkwardness of his stance, the flush of embarrassment on his face from her mistaken greeting, the nervous clenching of his fingers.

Three things one would never see in Simon.

"You must be Mr. Stamford," she said at last.

He bowed.

Her uncle stepped forward, his face reflecting delight at her confusion. "He even had you fooled, didn't he?"

"I wasn't expecting you to arrive so soon," she said, miffed at the trick he had played on her.

"We traveled through the night," Felton explained. "And I, for one, could use a bite to eat. Order us some food, girl."

Rose turned, and the men followed her to the front parlor, the only decent room in this drafty old house. Rose could not wait to get back to a more civilized atmosphere. But that depended entirely on Mr. Stamford and his training.

She still entertained doubts about Uncle's plan. Was it really possible to turn an ordinary man into a duke in the space of a few short weeks? Her future, and Simon's, depended on a country schoolteacher. She must have been mad to agree to this.

Rose rang for a servant and ordered a cold meal to be sent up, then sat down. Uncle pointed Stamford to a chair and sat down across from him.

"It was a tiring journey," Felton observed. "I'm too old to be jolting about the countryside all day in a carriage."

Rose was unable to keep her gaze off the man who looked so like her brother. He sat stiffly erect in his chair, looking ill-at-ease.

How was it possible that he so closely resembled Simon? Was he the descendant of some unknown by-blow of a long-dead ancestor? Or merely a strange quirk of nature?

Whatever he was, it was her job to teach him the manners and ways of a duke. The sooner she started, the sooner they could all get out of this miserable excuse of a house.

"I am grateful that you have come to our assistance, Mr. Stamford." She flashed him a welcoming smile. "I assume that my uncle has explained what it is that we require of you?"

The man nodded. "I'm to do my duty to God, King, and country by pretending to be your brother."

Rose smothered a smile. Her uncle had undoubtedly laid it on thickly. "Yes. Unfortunately, we do not have a great deal of time to prepare you, Mr. Stamford, and if we are to successfully carry out this masquerade, your performance must be perfect."

His grey eyes darkened for a moment, then resumed their previous amiable glint. "I'll do my best."

A tray of food arrived, and the two hungry men ate in silence, leaving Rose to contemplate the work ahead of her. She must fill his head with family history, and acquaint him with her brother's likes and dislikes, habits and vices. She needed to check if Simon's clothes fit him, and if not, to have them altered.

Then came the most daunting prospect—making him familiar with the ways of Simon's world—and hers.

Watching him eat, Rose realized she needed also to examine his table manners, his ability to carry on a conversation, his skill on the dance floor . . .

"Do you know how to dance, Mr. Stamford?"

He looked up from his plate and shrugged. "Nothing more complicated than a simple country dance, I'm afraid."

"No dancing for you, then. We'll put out that you've injured your ankle."

"What?" Amusement twinkled in his grey eyes. "You will deny me the chance to dance the scandalous waltz?"

She gave him a dampening look. "I think you have plenty of other things to learn, Mr. Stamford."

"Please, call me Adrian. I'll think you're one of my students if you keep calling me 'mister.' "

"Your name is *Simon*." She firmly corrected him. "Our situation here is isolated, but we dare not take any chances. You must act as if that name is your own."

He regarded her with a haughty expression. "To be proper, you should call me Alston."

A chill swept through her. He sounded exactly like Simon when he was trying to dampen someone's pretensions. "*That* name is for everyone else. I call my brother Simon."

"And what does he call you?"

"Brat," her uncle interjected.

Rose quelled him with a sharp look. "Rose."

"What kind of mission is your brother on?" Stamford asked, pushing his plate aside.

She looked at him, puzzled. "Mission?"

"His diplomatic mission," Stamford explained. "The reason I am filling in for him."

"Simon is not on any diplomatic mission. He is hiking in Switzerland."

"I'm confused." Stamford glanced at her uncle. "Is the duke on a secret diplomatic mission or not?"

Rose couldn't suppress her laughter. "Simon? A diplomat? Oh, that's rich."

Felton glared at her. "Lady Rosemary is not aware of her brother's activities for the government."

"It sounds like you should get your stories straight," Stamford said with an annoying smirk.

"This is not a laughing matter, Mr. Stamford. Futures are at stake, here."

He darted her a wounded look. "I thought you intended to call me Simon."

Rose threw up her hands in exasperation. "If you cannot take matters seriously, Mr. Stamford, I am not sure that we can use you."

He looked chastened. "I will try to restrain myself. I do wish to help."

The earl set down his fork and scanned the room. "Rose, where's my after-dinner brandy?"

"How should I know?" she snapped at him with irritation. "You've been here before—where does Simon keep it?"

Felton looked blankly at her. "Don't recall, as a matter of fact."

Rose scowled. "Go find Hobbes, then. He will know."

Her uncle stood and motioned for her to join him. "Come with me, my dear. You will need to know this as well." He nodded to Stamford. "We'll be back shortly."

Once they were in the hall, the earl regarded her eagerly. "What do you think?"

"He certainly looks like Simon. But as for the rest . . ."

"I have faith in your ability to turn him out right."

Rose laughed. "Faith, and a desperate need. Don't worry, Uncle, I have no desire to be poor any more than you do. What was that taradiddle you fed him about Simon being on a diplomatic mission?"

The earl cleared his throat. "Ah, I prepared a little story, complete with supporting documents, in case Mr. Stamford was not immediately eager to come."

"You lied to the poor man?"

Her uncle spread his hands defensively. "We both agreed he was our only hope . . ." His expression sobered. "I assume there has been no word from abroad?"

She shook her head. "Not a word."

"Then I will be leaving in the morning. I must get back to town to smooth out some of the details and pave the way for the 'duke's' return."

Rose stared at him in alarm. "You are going to leave me here alone with him?"

He shrugged. "I wouldn't call it alone. The servants are here."

"But we don't know a thing about the man. He could be a murderer—or worse."

"He teaches Latin to trumped-up farmer's sons—how dangerous can he be? Besides"—Felton smiled cheerfully—"I know what a good shot you are. Keep a pistol by your side, and you'll be safe enough."

Tossing her head in irritation, Rose returned to the parlor.

Stamford stood in front of the mantel, hands clasped behind his back, staring at the portrait on the wall. He glanced toward the door as she entered.

"Did I pass the first test?"

His frankness startled her. Then she reminded herself he was well aware why he was here.

Stamford pointed to the portrait. "One of the family, I presume?"

"My grandfather," Rose replied. "The fifth duke."

"That must mean I am the seventh."

At least he can add. That gave him a definite advantage over some other noble peers.

"I will tell you all about the family at a later time. There are more important things you need to know. Now—"

"How old are you?" he asked.

She started. It wasn't what she expected him to ask. "Two and twenty."

He raised a brow. "And still unwed?"

Rose felt the heat rise to her cheeks. What she did with her life was *her* business—certainly not his. "That is none of your concern. Now please, Mr. Stamford, do pay attention. You were born on the twenty-seventh of August at the family estate in Berkshire, where our parents resided. That house is called Brompton. You grew up—"

"Couldn't you have written this all out?" he asked. "I can read, you know."

"It is written out—what do you think I have been doing for the last se'nnight? I thought you might like to have a *brief* introduction first."

"Carry on, then, my lady."

"Rose."

He grinned again, showing even white teeth. "Of course, *Rose*. Do continue to tell me about my life."

Unnerved by his irreverence, she raced through the rest of her recitation. She didn't intend him to remember all of it, but wanted to take this opportunity to examine him more carefully, to take his measure, to decide if he was capable of carrying out this extraordinary task.

He interrupted her several times with questions, which pleased rather than irritated her. It demonstrated he had a quick intelligence.

Once or twice she glanced at him, and forgot for a moment that he wasn't Simon. Then something in his expression, or a gesture, startled her back to reality.

"Now, Simon's favorite club is—"

"Enough." He held up his hand in protest. "I cannot absorb any more tonight."

Rose glanced at the clock, surprised to find she had been talking for over an hour. Suddenly, she felt exhausted.

"You are right—it is late. We can start again in the morning. I'll show you to your room."

Adrian followed Lady Rosemary up the stairs and down the narrow, paneled hall to the bedchambers.

The room she led him to was probably small, to a duke, but it was enormous by Adrian's standards. A large canopied bed dominated the room, festooned with heavy brocade curtains and tasseled ties. He suppressed a shudder. He did not relish sleeping in that museum piece. If this was an example of the duke's personal tastes, his opinion of Alston dropped a notch.

She bade him a curt good night, and he was left alone.

Adrian sat gingerly on the edge of the enormous bed and pulled off his boots. Then he lay back, hands behind his head, and stared at the faded canopy above him.

What sort of mess had he gotten himself into? He must have been truly bored with his life to think this was going to be a lark.

Lady Rosemary might be viewed as every man's dream, with her dark hair, rosy lips, and shapely curves. But he wasn't sure the woman beneath was as attractive.

He had already formed his quick opinion of her—she was spoiled, arrogant, and accustomed to having her every whim obeyed—qualities he disliked, particularly among the aristocracy. She treated him with icy condescension, as if he were a small child or a dim-witted adult.

Adrian did not relish having to spend the next few weeks in her close company. He would not do anything to tweak her sensibilities—unless she really deserved it. But if Lady Rosemary thought he was going to bow and scrape before her, she was sadly mistaken.

He was certain they hadn't told him the entire story. He sensed a hidden desperation in both Rose and her uncle. Adrian vowed to discover the truth—after all, that was one of the reasons this whole crazy proposition had intrigued him.

A sane man would bolt.

He grinned wryly. No one had ever called Adrian Stamford sane.

He'd stay—for a while, anyway—and play the game of learning how to be a duke. Lord knew, it would be far more enjoyable than trying to beat Latin into the Topmore twins' thick skulls. And the Antiquities Society awaited him in London. The Duke of Alston might be able to accomplish a great deal more than plain Mr. Stamford.

A slow smile spread over his face. He just might enjoy this experience after all—if he could find a way to tear down the high wall of Lady Rosemary's aristocratic hauteur.

*   *   *

In the early morning darkness of her gloomy bedchamber, Rose vaguely heard the sounds of a carriage on the drive. Drowsily, she realized it must be her uncle, leaving for London. She rolled over and went back to sleep.

She awoke again at a much more reasonable hour and breakfasted in her room. After dressing with the clumsy assistance of a local girl hired for the occasion, she descended the stairs, ready for a long day of instructing Mr. Stamford in the ways of a duke.

Rose half expected to find him waiting for her in the front parlor. To her chagrin, she realized she had not made any provisions for his breakfast. He probably had no idea how to ring for a servant—or had he been too afraid to try?

She hoped he had wandered through this rabbit warren until he found the kitchen. Annoyed with herself for not making plans for this morning, and annoyed with Stamford for not waiting for instructions, she made her way to the antiquated kitchen at the rear of the east wing.

The kitchen was deserted. Rose thought to ring for Hobbes, but decided against that action. She would find Stamford herself.

Rose peeked into the ground-floor rooms, where the dust lay as undisturbed as it had on the day of her arrival. With increasing irritation, she trudged up the stairs to explore the first floor.

The first traces of apprehension niggled at her mind when she failed to find Stamford in any of the rooms.

Then she laughed. Of course. He was still sound asleep in his bed. But even a duke could not sleep all day. They had work to do.

She marched back up the stairs and rapped loudly on his door. Receiving no answer, she pushed the door open and stepped into the master bedroom. That hideous monstrosity of a bed stared back at her, its counterpane smooth and unruffled.

Stamford was not there.

Rose stood in the doorway, staring at the empty room. Where was that man?

She ran back downstairs, her panic growing with each step. She threw open the door to the parlor, the library, every room on the floor until she was running frantically from room to room, but there was no sign of Stamford.

Think, she told herself, pressing her fingers against her temples. Where might he go?

For a walk? The grounds were not particularly interesting or vast. He did not know the area; surely he would not strike out for a walk across the fields.

Unless he was searching for the nearest coaching stop.

She raced back upstairs to the bedroom and threw open the wardrobe, looking for the small portmanteau he had brought with him. It was not there.

Rose sank into a chair, gripped by despair. He had bolted, and all their plans were ruined. She would not be able to hide Simon's disappearance, Lord Ramsey would grow restive and cancel the marriage, and most of her brother's holdings would be lost. Her life would change forever.

This was all Uncle's fault, of course. Instead of staying to help her, he had raced off to town as soon as he could and left her to deal with this man. Stamford had given no indication of his dissatisfaction last night—how was she to know that he'd run off at the first opportunity? And now there was no way to get him back. She didn't have a carriage, and even if she found one, she had no idea where the man lived.

But if Stamford was gone, she was not going to stay here alone. She had to find a means to get away herself. There was a man at the stables; he would know where she could hire, borrow, or even steal a vehicle to take her to London.

Furious at Stamford's ill-treatment of her family's generosity, she stormed down the stairs and out the front door, heading for the stables at the rear of the house.

Returning from the stables, Adrian rounded the corner of the house and crashed headlong into the woman running toward him. He grabbed her arm and steadied her.

Rose's eyes widened in shock. "You!" she gasped.

He lifted an amused brow. "You were expecting someone else?"

"Where have you been?" she demanded, her voice shrill. "I have been looking all over for you."

"Thought I'd bolted, did you?"

"No!" Her unnecessary vehemence was an admission. "We need to get to work."

"Fine with me." He fell in step beside her, and they walked back to the house.

"Where were you?" she asked.

"Out for a walk," he said. "This looks like a fine holding. Are there any Roman ruins in the area?"

"How should I know?" she snapped. "I've never been to this godforsaken house before."

"A pity," he said calmly. "I suppose the servants might know something."

"You are not to talk to the servants," she said.

"That might make my life a bit awkward. Surely, you don't expect me to do everything for myself?"

Rose gave him an exasperated look. "I mean don't talk with them unnecessarily. And certainly not about Roman ruins. Simon would never concern himself with anything like that. These people don't know him well, but we don't want to arouse any suspicions."

"What *does* your brother concern himself with?"

"Horses, gambling, *filles de joie*, and fine brandy."

Adrian snorted his derision. "He sounds like a respectable fellow."

"He's not—but don't worry, you won't have to adopt his vices. We'll put out that you've reformed in anticipation of your marriage."

"How responsible of me."

She glanced at him sharply, sensing his sarcasm, but his expression was one of bland innocence.

"This morning I want to check the fit of Simon's clothes. Then we will go over the family estates and properties. I have detailed plans of the London house. Then I will tell you about Simon's cronies and—"

He held up a hand. "One at a time, please. You don't want to befuddle me."

Her lips thinned, but she said nothing.

Once inside the house, Rose led him to another bedchamber, one less lordly than his own. The bed didn't even have curtains. A large trunk stood in the middle of the room. Rose opened it and pulled out an armful of clothing.

"Try these on first—they'll be the least of our worries." She shoved the clothes into his hands and then pointed to a small antechamber. "You can change in there."

Adrian stared at her with growing dismay. "Shouldn't your brother's valet take care of this?"

"Simon's valet is not here."

"Perhaps your uncle can help, then," he suggested hopefully.

She laughed. "Uncle left for London early this morning. Did he not tell you?"

Adrian smothered a grin. "Isn't it highly improper, leaving you here alone with me?"

"Why should it be? You are my *brother*, after all. I expect you to behave yourself."

"But am I safe from you?"

He left her staring at him, mouth agape, as he sauntered into the changing room.

One point for his side.

Adrian stripped to his drawers and pulled on one of the shirts she'd handed him. The fine and no doubt expensive fabric felt soft against his skin. Adrian pulled on a pair of buckskin breeches, fastened with pure silver buttons, he was certain. He had to give the duke credit—he had excellent taste in clothing. Of course, a duke could afford to have good taste.

Adrian opened the door and struck a pose. "How do I look?"

A tiny line creased her brow as she examined him critically, stepping close to tweak at the cuff and run her hands down his side, checking the fit of the shirt against his torso. The motion tickled, and he twitched.

"It will do," she pronounced. "I fear you are a trifle taller than Simon." Without warning, she stuck her fingers into the waist-band of his breeches. "And narrower through the waist. These will have to be altered."

Before he could open his mouth to protest, she was on her knees before him, running her hands across his hip and down one thigh, gathering the excess cloth with pins.

Adrian bit down on his lower lip to contain his reaction to her touch. Was she so naive that she had no idea what her hands were doing to him? Or did she think he wouldn't dare have such thoughts about the sister of a duke?

From the little he knew of her, the latter was most likely.

She stepped away, and he sucked in a relieved breath. Rose handed him a plain yellow waistcoat, which he donned and but-toned, and then a dark jacket. Once again, he stood for her in-spection.

Rose carefully smoothed the fabric over his shoulders, eyeing him carefully. "You are thinner. But the shoulders fit, so I don't think anyone will notice. If the buttons are moved—"

To escape her hands, Adrian took a step forward and felt the sharp prick of a pin against his thigh.

"Ow!"

"Careful," she warned and turned back to that ominous trunk. What was she going to come up with next?

Evening clothes—black silk breeches, a silver embroidered waistcoat, long-tailed coat, white silk stockings. The sort of things one wore to a formal ball, or the opera—or an audience with the Prince of Wales.

A sudden chill swept over him—a reminder that this was more than a casual lark. These people were deadly serious about the role they wanted him to play—and expected him to be too.

Adrian wondered if his sense of the absurd had finally got the best of him.

Chapter 3

As she surveyed the dining room the following evening, with its wobbly table and mismatched chairs, Rose realized it was ridiculous to attempt to emulate an elegant dinner party in this atrocious house. There was barely enough china and plate to set the table for two, and she'd been forced to use a sheet as a table cover. Whatever did Simon and his friends do when they were here?

Judging from the ample supply of glasses, she doubted they ate much at all. No wonder he always looked so ragged at the end of the hunting season.

Nevertheless, it was imperative that she observe Mr. Stamford's habits at the table, so she knew how much work lay before her. He would not be familiar with the nuances of formal dining, but she hoped he could at least handle a knife and fork.

Once again, the enormity of the task ahead threatened to overwhelm her. She had tried to think of everything Stamford needed to know, but how could she impart a lifetime of knowledge and training into a few short weeks?

Rose told herself he didn't have to be perfect. She and her uncle would strive to keep him out of awkward situations. As long as Lady Juliet and her father thought he was Simon, the others did not matter. After all, he only had to pretend for a little while. Simon would arrive long before the wedding.

The door opened. She turned and forgot to take a breath.

Stamford stood silently in the doorway, dressed in Simon's

evening clothes, looking every inch like the duke he was sup-posed to be—handsome . . . elegant . . . aristocratic.

Except for his sloppily tied cravat. When they found him a valet, it would have to be a man who could tie a fashionable knot. Stamford obviously did not know how.

"I'm not late, am I?" He did not look the least bit apologetic.

Rose exhaled, realizing she'd been holding her breath. "Not at all." She gestured at the table. "You sit at the head, of course."

Brushing past her, he pulled out his chair and sat down.

"It is customary to wait for the ladies to be seated first," she said.

He scrambled to his feet. Rose walked slowly to her own chair, on his right, and sat.

Rose took the small bell from beside her plate and shook it. Hobbes must have been waiting outside the door, for he entered at once, carrying the heavy soup tureen. He set it on Stamford's left and filled their bowls. Rose gritted her teeth to keep from chastising the ancient retainer when he slopped soup on the cloth. She was here to teach Stamford, not the servants. Hobbes bowed and left the room.

"I assure you, the service will be better in London," Rose told Stamford.

He grinned. "It makes me feel like a helpless dolt to have someone fill my bowl for me."

"You'll grow accustomed. Now, watch what I do." She lifted her spoon, dipped it into the bowl, and took a dainty sip.

"Looks easy enough."

He imitated her motions exactly, and Rose relaxed. He could manage soup, at least. She dipped her spoon in her bowl.

Stamford made a loud slurping noise. Rose winced and fixed him with a reproachful glare. He returned an abashed look.

"Sorry."

Had there been a hint of mischief in his eyes when he'd said that? Rose glanced quickly at him, but his face was a mask of bland innocence. She must continue with her instruction.

"Now, it is important that you divide your conversation

equally between your partner on the left and the right, whether you are at the head or the side of the table."

"What if they don't wish to talk with me?" he asked.

She laughed. "You are a duke, remember? *Everyone* will wish to talk with you. Now, when we are in town, I will do my best to keep you abreast of the latest *on-dits*, which you can share with ladies."

"Will any of them have an interest in Roman ruins?"

"Why are you so fascinated with Roman ruins?"

"Actually, it's not the Romans per se, but the people who were here before them." He leaned forward, his expression eager. "Tacitus did not say much about them, but they had a flourishing culture when Caesar and his legions arrived. I collect artifacts."

"A very commendable pastime," she replied. "But one which the *ton* will regard with supreme disinterest. Remember, you are *Simon*, not plain Mr. Stamford."

"There are several noble patrons of the antiquarian societies," he protested.

"Not among my acquaintances—or Simon's." She rang the bell again for the next course.

Rose shuddered as Stamford jabbed his fork into the slice of meat and sawed at it with his knife. She started to offer a gentle correction when his grip on the fork slipped and the meat shot off the plate onto the floor.

He cast her an embarrassed look. "The meat is rather tough," he said and bent to retrieve the piece.

"Leave it," she snapped.

Stamford straightened in his chair and plucked another slice from the serving plate—using the point of his knife.

Rose shut her eyes. This was worse than she could have imagined.

While Stamford eagerly ate all his food, Rose picked at hers. The roast was overdone, the vegetables nearly raw, the pudding scorched. It did not seem to bother him in the least.

He saw her looking at him and smiled. "Excellent food. The cook has a way with carrots."

Rose dropped her gaze to her plate. The exquisite efforts of her French chef would be wasted on this man.

"Can I pour you more wine?" he asked. "Or must I ring for Hobbes to do that?"

"A gentleman may refill a lady's glass." She nodded approvingly. At least he had a few social graces.

He reached for the decanter, dragging his sleeve through the pudding.

"You have pudding on your sleeve," she informed him through gritted teeth.

Stamford glanced at his coat. "So I do." He grabbed a corner of the table cloth and wiped it away. "Is that better?"

Too dismayed to even speak, Rose merely nodded.

He started pouring wine into her glass.

"Wait, stop!" Rose cried. He was filling it far too full; it was going to spill—a red stain spread over the sheet.

"Oh, dear." He grabbed his napkin and began dabbing at the liquid. "I hope you have a good laundress here."

"Glasses should never be more than half full," she said curtly.

"I am terribly sorry." He looked at the brimming glass. "Shall I spoon out some of the wine?"

"Perhaps you think I should lean over and slurp the excess off the top?" Rose demanded heatedly. She pushed back her chair, tossed her napkin onto the table, and strode toward the door.

"Aren't we having dessert?" he called after her.

Rose stalked to the parlor—that wretched, cramped room where the chimney smoked, rats nibbled on the wainscoting, the furniture was filled with lumps, and the windows rattled in the merest breeze. She sank down into the chair nearest the paltry flames, furious with her uncle, with Simon.

It was impossible. How could they have thought they could take a country bumpkin and turn him into a duke? Simon, despite his faults, was flawless in his charm and elegance. That oaf in the other room belonged in a stable, not the finest dining rooms in London.

*   *   *

Adrian realized he had carried the joke a bit too far, but it was hard not to retaliate against the subtle digs she directed at him at every turn. She seemed to think that no one raised outside her oh-so-noble household had a clue about how to get on in the world.

From the first, she had assumed the worst about him. Of course, he hadn't done anything to disabuse her of that notion, either. But it was so easy to ruffle her equanimity . . . and so amusing.

However, he did not want to anger her to the point where she sent him away. He must behave himself—for a while. Adrian grabbed his wineglass and went in search of Lady Rosemary, intent on soothing her ruffled feelings.

He spent a boring two hours the next morning, listening to Rose describe every detail of her brother's past. Adrian's head ached, and he wished to God he'd never heard of the Duke of Alston, his sister, or anyone remotely connected with the family. No one could pull off such an elaborate masquerade. He'd be unmasked the moment he set foot in London.

A scratching sounded at the door.

"The Reverend Toombs is here, Your Grace," the deaf Hobbes shouted.

"Tell him we're not in," Rose said hastily.

Adrian saw the apprehension in Rose's eyes, and he leaped at the chance to relieve the tedium. He flashed her a wide smile.

"Now, Sister, that would be rude. The man has come all this way to see us; surely we should grant him a few moments of our time."

She looked at him with undisguised alarm, but he ignored her. Adrian turned to Hobbes and said loudly. "Please, send him in."

"What do you think you're doing?" Rose hissed the minute Hobbes retreated. "Are you trying to ruin everything?"

"You wouldn't want it said that His Grace, the Duke of Alston, was rude to a man of the cloth, would you?" He gave her an ostentatious wink. "Obviously, he knows we're here, or he wouldn't have come."

"You're not ready to act as Simon."

"From what you've told me of your brother, I doubt he's well acquainted with this fellow. I should be able to fool him easily. And if not, what harm can he do you?" Adrian shrugged off her concerns. "He's just an obscure country vicar."

She scowled at him.

Adrian smiled inwardly. Perhaps this was the way to deal with Lady Rose—stay one step ahead of her. As long as she didn't know what he intended to do, she could not stop him.

"The Reverend Toombs," Hobbes yelled from the doorway.

Adrian languidly rose, adopting the posture he imagined the disreputable Duke of Alston would take.

"Your Grace, it is such a pleasure." A short man in cleric's black rapidly crossed the floor, his face beaming. He grasped Adrian's hand and shook it with enthusiasm. "And such an honor for the neighborhood."

Adrian smiled politely. "Let me make you acquainted with my sister, Lady Rosemary."

The vicar nodded at Rose, but kept his attention focused on the duke. "And the timing of your visit, Your Grace—so fortunate."

Adrian took his seat, motioning the vicar to a chair. "Rose, dear, do ring for tea. How is my visit fortunate, Reverend?"

"Why, the roof! Surely, you've heard of our campaign to replace the roof at St. Efflam's. Why, once it is known that a man of your stature stands behind the campaign, donations will come flooding in."

"Ah," said Adrian. "The church needs a new roof, does it?"

Toombs nodded. "It's been leaking for years, but that last storm did it in. Took quite a beating last winter, it did."

Adrian steepled his fingers. "Why, Reverend Toombs, I am appalled that you have not brought this to my attention before."

The man flushed. "I did try to speak with you during your last visit, but due to the . . . um . . . nature of your guests, I did not feel it would be quite appropriate for a man of the cloth to—"

Adrian waved a hand. "I quite understand. It would not have done. But I am here now in the respectable company of my sister and would be most delighted to help you."

From the corner of his eye, Adrian saw Rose waggling her fingers at him, trying to capture his attention, but he pointedly ignored her. She wanted him to act as her brother, didn't she? He would play the duke with a vengeance.

"How much money has your campaign raised?" he asked.

"At present, the amount is a little over 150 pounds, Your Grace." Toombs smiled apologetically. "We've barely begun the fund."

"Still, a splendid start. Splendid. I should like to add to it." Adrian looked questioningly at Rose. "A worthy cause, don't you agree, Sister? Just the sort of thing for a *duke* to interest himself with."

"I see nothing amiss with a *donation*," she said stiffly.

"Good, good. Well, my good fellow, how much do you need? Five hundred? A thousand?"

Rose coughed sharply. Adrian struggled to suppress his laughter at her dismay—and her inability to object. "Do you wish to say something, Sister dear? Am I being too nip-farthing? Should I make it guineas, instead?"

"I believe five hundred pounds is a laudable amount." Her voice was firm. "You do not wish to give too much, else no others will wish to donate. And it should be a community effort, isn't that right, Reverend Toombs?"

He nodded eagerly. "You are most generous, Your Grace."

Hobbes pushed through the door, carrying the tea tray. Adrian looked at Rose. "Please, do the honors of pouring, my dear."

"Will you be long in the neighborhood, Your Grace?" Toombs asked.

"Yes," he said.

"No," Rose blurted out.

"What my sister means," Adrian said, with a calm smile, "is that we will not be staying here as long as she would like."

"But long enough to join our little congregation for services on Sunday, I hope."

"Oh, assuredly," Adrian said. "My sister and I will be in attendance." He stifled a laugh at the look of smug satisfaction on the vicar's face.

As soon as the vicar left, Rose gave Adrian an outraged look. "What do you think you are doing?"

"Why, playing my role, of course." He adopted an expression of wide-eyed innocence. "Did I do all right?"

"You could have ruined everything!" she snapped at him.

"You are taking a simple visit far too seriously. This is not London—and he is not the archbishop. It was the perfect opportunity to practice my role on an uncritical audience."

He smothered his mirth as he watched the warring emotions flit over her face. She simply did not know what to do with him when he stepped out of the narrow role she had assigned him.

At last, she gave him a grudging smile. "You did sound and act exactly like Simon—except, of course, for your generous offer to the roof fund. I can't imagine Simon ever doing such a thing. You shall have to watch your charitable impulses, or you will give the game away!"

Adrian grinned broadly. He had won another round.

To placate her, Adrian remained on his best behavior for the next two days, hoping to lull her into a sense of complacency. He committed long lists of names to memory, studied plans of the duke's London house, and wondered anew why it was so important that the duke be in London this spring.

"One thing to remember about Simon—he detests strawberries," Rose said. "So for goodness' sake, do not heap your plate with them at a midnight supper."

Adrian moaned aloud. "I love strawberries. Do you really think anyone would even notice?"

"It could be something that simple which unravels our entire plan."

"I could claim I developed a taste for them in order to please my intended bride. We can tell her to support the story."

Rose started coughing.

His eyes narrowed with suspicion. "What is wrong?"

"What exactly did my uncle tell you about Lady Juliet?"

"That she is going to marry your brother this spring, and she wants me to escort her about London until he returns."

"She does not know about you."

"Does not . . ." His eyes widened in horror as he realized the meaning of her words. He jumped out of his chair. "She does not know? You intended me to play this game with your brother's wife?"

"*Future* wife."

Adrian ran a hand through his hair while he tried to think. This changed the whole situation. He did not mind fooling London society. But to act the attentive suitor to a woman he had never met?

He looked straight at Rose. "I will not do it."

"Of course you will. Juliet will not suspect."

"How can she not suspect?" he demanded. "She's in love with your brother. She's bound to notice."

"In love?" Rose gave a short, harsh laugh. "Love has nothing to do with their engagement."

"Why does she want to marry him, then?"

She regarded him curiously. "Why ever wouldn't she? Simon is a duke."

"Is her father pushing her into this? What if she is in love with someone else?"

"I doubt Juliet would be willing to give up the chance to be a duchess, even for love." Rose responded dryly. "And even if she did, her father wouldn't allow it."

"Good God, can you people really be that mercenary?"

"Simon is a duke. And the future of a dukedom is much too important to leave to chance—or the vagaries of the heart."

"Does your brother want to marry her?"

She shrugged. "He asked her."

"I don't see how you can expect me to fool her. She will brand me as an impostor immediately."

"Don't give her *too* much credit." Rose's cheeks dimpled.

"Beautiful and brainless?" he asked with dismay.

"Beautiful, brainless, and *rich*," Rose explained.

"It always comes down to money, doesn't it?" Fresh indignation rose within him. "Is that why you haven't married yet? You haven't found someone rich enough to suit your needs?"

She paled, and Adrian felt a twinge of guilt at his harsh words, which he quickly brushed aside. It was one of the reasons, after all, why he despised the aristocracy. Family position and money were far more important than love, or mild affection.

It was the life Rose had been born to, and she accepted it. But Adrian almost felt sorry for her. Did she ever feel constrained by society's restrictions? Was that why she had not married?

He looked at the woman sitting across from him, sitting regally erect in her chair, and grinned to himself. It was hard to picture Lady Rose as a rebel. No, if she hadn't married, it was because she had not received an offer from a man she deemed worthy of her. No doubt she was holding out for a prince.

Adrian sighed and sat down again. "If you intend me to fool Lady Juliet, you are going to have to tell me a great deal more about her."

Stamford's words haunted Rose as she prepared for bed. *You haven't found someone rich enough to suit your needs?*

What did he know about her needs and wants? He thought her life was solely devoted to pleasure. He had no idea what it was like to be born to a life of wealth and privilege, where one was hemmed in on all sides by rigid rules, from which there was no escape. For a woman, marriage was not freedom.

She stared thoughtfully at her reflection in the mirror. Was that what Simon was doing now—trying to escape? Rose shook her head. It was different for men. Simon might not be free to marry as he wanted, although she doubted he cared, but marriage did not have to be a major part of his life. For a woman, it was everything.

And Rose had not found a man she liked—or at least

trusted—enough to take charge of her life. Unwed, she had much more control over her life.

Yet she knew that situation could not last much longer. Simon paid no attention to it, but others—like her uncle—did. The time was not long in coming when he would talk with Simon, and the two of them would pressure her into taking a husband.

A husband chosen from the limited options available to her. One rich enough, with a grand enough title, to be worthy of the sister of the seventh Duke of Alston. She could already guess what names would be on that short list, and she didn't relish the thought of marrying any of them.

Once Simon married, it was inevitable. She'd lose her home, after all. And what better place for her to go than to her own husband's house?

And if Simon failed to come back, she wouldn't have any choice at all.

So Mr. Stamford had no right to act so high and mighty at the thought of marriages arranged for reasons other than love.

She shrugged and pulled the pins from her hair. What did she care what Mr. Stamford thought? He was, after all, an employee. Pretending to act as her brother didn't mean that he had a brother's right of concern for her. Rose knew she should feel supremely indifferent to what he thought of her.

But for some reason, she did not.

Chapter 4

Adrian tossed fitfully in his bed, seeking an elusive sleep. This casual lark was starting to look a lot more complicated than he had first anticipated. Finally, bowing to the inevitable, he climbed out of bed, donned a robe and slippers, and headed downstairs. If he could not sleep, he might as well read.

He caught a faint whiff of smoke as he entered the parlor, and tensed before he remembered Rose's continual complaints about the smoking chimneys. No doubt she had sweeps coming daily to the London house. He lit another candle, carried it over to the chair, and pulled out his tattered copy of Tacitus.

He was several pages into the narrative when he realized that the smell of smoke was growing stronger. Puzzled, Adrian quickly crossed the room and pulled the door open, taking a deep breath.

There was no question—the smell was stronger out here. He felt the first twinge of alarm. Had a burning candle been left untended?

He walked slowly down the hall, the smell of smoke growing stronger with each step. He halted suddenly outside the kitchen, horrified to see wisps of pale grey curling under the door. Something in the kitchen was on fire.

His heart pounding, Adrian tried to think. He had to get everyone out of the house.

Wishing he had a lantern, Adrian cupped a protective hand around his candle and raced up the stairs as quickly as he dared. He skidded to a halt outside Rosemary's door, twisting the handle, but it was locked. He pounded on the wood with his fist, yelling her name.

"What is it?" her sleepy voice answered from inside.

"There's a fire," he shouted. "Help me wake the others."

Within seconds, she was at the door. Adrian stared at her, momentarily forgetting his mission. In her lacy white nightgown, her dark hair hanging long and loose, she no longer looked the proper aristocrat. Eyes still misted with sleep, she stared back at him in alarm.

Alarm.

"There's smoke coming from the kitchen," he said, recovering his wits. "Where are the servants?"

She pointed to the ceiling. "Upstairs."

"Can you wake them? I'll get a groom from the stables. We may be able to stop the fire if we hurry."

She nodded quickly and brushed past him toward the back stairs. Adrian raced to his room, pulled on breeches and boots, and dashed down the stairs again. Already, smoke drifted through the hall. He tore out of the house and raced to the stables, where he roused the groom.

"Fire in the house," he shouted. The groom was at his heels as they raced toward the pump in the yard. Grabbing a bucket, Adrian filled it, then dashed to the rear of the house. Seeing no sign of flames through the window, he grabbed the door handle, twisted, and pushed.

A searing blast of heat hit him full in the face, and he leaped back. The groom ran up beside him and flung water at the flames now shooting out of the doorway. Adrian grabbed his own bucket and tossed the water into the burning kitchen.

He prayed Rose and the others were out of the house. He wanted to stop and make sure, but he could not leave the groom to fight the fire alone. Two men, working together, might have a chance to save the house. He darted back to the pump.

Adrian shouted aloud with relief at the sight of Rose standing there. All the servants, shivering in their bedclothes, stood with her.

"Search the stables for more buckets—bins—any sort of

container that can hold water," Adrian commanded. "Fill anything you find." He grabbed his own bucket and ran back to the house.

With a sinking heart, Adrian saw that they were making little headway against the flames, which had taken secure hold of the kitchen. With more men, they could attack from the other side, perhaps containing it to this one room. But Hobbes and the women were no help. It was only Adrian and the groom against the growing inferno.

Rose staggered toward him, struggling with an overflowing bucket. Adrian skidded to a halt. It was the last thing he'd expected to see—a duke's daughter carrying water—and he felt a stab of admiration for Lady Rose. He grabbed the bucket from her and flung the water into the kitchen.

He wanted to thank her, but there was no time for anything but the endless race from door to pump and back again as they carried out their one-sided struggle against the flames. His lungs burned, his eyes stung from smoke and sweat, but still he ran and filled and ran and tossed.

A shout came from behind him, and he glanced at the house. Flames flickered in the first-story windows, and Adrian realized that they had lost. There was no way they could save the house now.

Stubbornly, he shoved his bucket under the pump and grabbed the handle, but a hand on his wrist stopped him. He looked up into Lady Rose's dirt-streaked face.

"There is nothing more any of us can do," she said. "Let it burn."

He turned back to the house, unwilling to admit defeat. "We have to try."

The sharp crack of shattering glass echoed across the yard, and they both jumped. Three more windows quickly snapped from the heat, and Adrian accepted the inevitable. The house was gone. They could only wait and watch its death throes.

"We should wet down the stables," he said, signaling the groom. "A stray spark could set them alight."

Even from the distance of the stables, the heat from the burning house grew almost unbearable. Sparks shot from the inferno. Most lit on the ground, now wet and muddy, but some carried to the outbuildings. Adrian watched anxiously, letting out a sigh of relief when they fizzled out on the dampened timbers.

A huge crash sounded, and he started. Whirling around, Adrian saw the roof on the far wing collapse in a shower of flame and sparks.

Watching, he was filled with a sense of awe. If he forgot what was burning, it was a majestic sight as the old house surrendered to the flames. The noise was deafening—the sharp shatter of window glass, the deeper thumps as large beams collapsed. And behind it all the steady roar of the flames, growing louder as they inexorably ate their way through the building.

He glanced at Rose, standing beside him, her features glowing in the bright glare. Her face was streaked with dirt and soot, and she did not look at all like the arrogant daughter of a duke.

Adrian walked to her side and put an arm around her shoulder, hugging her.

"You were magnificent," he said.

With a sudden loud crash, another section of roof collapsed, shooting a fresh spray of sparks into the air. One landed on Rose's skirt, and the cloth started smoking. Adrian lunged at her and beat out the ember with his hands. Sharp pricks stabbed at his neck; sparks landed on his skin. He felt someone tug at his arm, and together they stumbled away, slipping and sliding on the wet ground until they reached the cool grass at the far edge of the yard.

Adrian sank onto the grass, pulling Rose down beside him, and they watched, unable to tear their gazes away, as the house slowly fell in on itself.

Every muscle in his body ached, and his skin stung where sparks had scorched him, but when he saw the other four members of the household huddled next to the barn, he knew the pain was worth it. They had all survived.

"Simon," Rose said with a shaky laugh, "is going to be rather angry with me for burning down his house."

"Simon," Adrian reminded her, "is sitting beside you and knows that you saved the servants and made a valiant effort to save the house as well."

She looked at him and smiled faintly. "As if I had much choice—after you abandoned me in there."

He grinned back. "I woke you up, didn't I? I knew you would get out."

"Simon will be perturbed, but thank goodness there wasn't anything of value in the house."

Adrian, remembering the silver, china, heavy Queen Anne furniture, and the intricate wood moldings, did not agree with her, but it wasn't his house. No doubt, to Alston, it wasn't much of a loss.

"Ho there!" A strange voice shouted at them. "Is everyone all right?"

Adrian could just make out the shadowy shape of a cart coming across the lawn. He scrambled to his feet.

"We saw the flames," the man said, driving closer. "Looks like we're too late to help."

"There wasn't much any of us could do," Adrian said.

The cart halted, and the man handed the reins to the boy beside him and stepped down.

"Everyone out?"

Adrian nodded. "We saved the stables, and that was about it."

The man shook his head. "Shame, 'tis. Was a good house. Guess that means we won't see any more of the duke."

Behind him, Hobbes cleared his throat. "If Your Grace would pardon me, perhaps we can make some arrangements for the ladies."

The farmer's eyes widened as he stared at Adrian. "Your Grace? Be you Alston?" The man pulled off his cap. "Beggin' yer pardon, then. We didn't know you were in the area. I'm Samuelson. From the near farm. We can take the ladies right enough. The missus can provide for them."

"I believe my sister would be more comfortable at the vicarage." He turned to Rose. "Will that do for the night?"

"Only if you stay with me," she replied.

"I should remain here," Adrian said.

"There's nothing more anyone can do, Your Grace," the groom said. "I can stay on and keep an eye on the ruins, make sure they don't spark up. You may as well try to get some sleep."

The man was right. Nothing more could be done here. The fire would burn itself out. And surely the duke would make the effort to see that his staff—and more important, his sister—were safely settled.

A sudden wave of exhaustion swept over him, and the thought of sleep—in any kind of bed—sounded like the most wonderful thing in the world.

They helped the ladies into the back of the cart, giving them stable blankets to wrap around themselves against the chill. The farmer ordered the lad into the back and gave Adrian the place of honor beside him.

"Nasty business, fires," he was saying.

Too tired to speak, Adrian could only nod his agreement. Every muscle in his body screamed a protest at the cart's jouncing progress.

What would happen now? Beyond the immediate need for shelter and clothing, there was the other "matter"—his impersonation of the duke. They'd brought him here because of the isolated location; that sanctuary was now gone. Would it bring an end to their plan as well? Adrian knew he was not ready to go to London. What would Rose do with him until he was? Find a new house in which to hide him? Or send him home?

His adventure might be over before it even started.

He was surprised to discover that he felt regret at the thought. He honestly looked forward to going to London and pulling off a hoax on the aristocracy. And he wanted to see if the Duke of Alston could make more headway with the Antiquities Society than plain Mr. Stamford.

Instead, within a few days he'd be back at Buckleigh Manor with Eddie and Freddy.

He glanced over his shoulder at the huddled figures in the

cart. Rose's actions tonight had been nothing short of surprising. He hadn't given her any choice when he left her to wake the servants. But instead of standing back and watching their efforts, she had worked as hard as anyone to fight the flames. She was dirty, disheveled, and exhausted when she ordered him to give up the fight.

He had never expected that of her. But he was learning that Lady Rosemary was not fitting neatly into the role he'd assigned her. She had thoroughly confounded him tonight.

She was the real reason he wanted this adventure to continue. He wanted to discover more about this intriguing woman.

Rose sat shivering in the back of the cart as it bumped down the lane. Only now, when the struggle was over, the battle fought and lost, could she look back and see just how close to disaster they'd come. If Stamford had not awakened her . . . She shuddered at the thought.

The house was a rattrap, and she did not consider its destruction a loss. Whether Simon would agree with her, she didn't know, or care. She might have died there tonight. They all might have died.

Stamford had fought the flames heroically. He had no reason to care if the house burned to the ground, but he'd valiantly struggled to save it. She would make sure that Simon learned of his efforts and rewarded him for it.

And after tonight, she did not think that Stamford would have any difficulty taking on the role of duke. He had an innate sense of command.

She started when the cart stopped moving. Blearily, she peered out and saw they were at the vicarage. Strong arms lifted her out of the cart and set her on her feet.

"Can you walk to the house?" Stamford asked.

Rose nodded and took a step, but her legs buckled beneath her. Stamford swept her up into his arms, and she gratefully clung to him as he carried her into the house.

A woman—the vicar's wife, no doubt—met them at the door and instantly ushered them upstairs. Stamford set Rose gently on the bed, then retreated before she could even thank him. The vicar's wife fluttered about her.

"Oh my poor dear, such a terrible thing to happen. And such a lovely house it was. You must be devastated." She wrung her hands in dismay.

Rose was too exhausted to answer her. She was filthy and reeked of smoke, but all she could think of was sleep. Rose allowed the woman to play maid, and before she was even aware, she was enveloped in a massive nightgown and tucked between the cool, clean sheets.

Chapter 5

❧

Rose pulled the pillow over her head, trying to drown out the sound of the chirping birds. She wanted to sleep and—

Her fingers released the pillow, and it fell to the floor. Rose rolled onto her back and stared in growing bewilderment at the plain, whitewashed ceiling. Where was she?

Memory flooded through her. The fire. Simon's hunting lodge, burned to the ground. The jolting trip to the vicarage. The soft, welcoming bed.

And she also remembered Stamford, and the comforting feel of his arm around her as they watched the pyre—a shared moment of sympathy and understanding.

What had she been thinking? Now, in the bright light of day, she knew that relaxation of the barriers had been a momentary lapse on her part, brought about by shock and exhaustion. She had to make that very clear to him. She did not want Stamford to think that anything had changed. She was a duke's daughter. He was a Latin teacher.

She raised up on an elbow and looked around. The room was plainly furnished with a dresser and small table. Rose wrinkled her nose. Her skin and hair reeked of smoke. Suddenly, she could not wait to get into the bath and scrub every inch of her skin until she felt clean again.

Her aching muscles protesting, Rose eased out of bed and looked for a bellpull to summon a servant, but did not see one. How was she going to gain someone's attention and order her bath readied? Someone should have made arrangements for a maid to assist her when she awoke.

Grumbling at the indignity, Rose grabbed the quilt from the bed and wrapped it around her, then padded barefoot into the hall. The house sounded ominously silent. With growing annoyance, she cautiously descended the stairs.

She was halfway down a dark corridor when the vicar's wife emerged from a room. Her face broke into a warm smile.

"Are you up so soon, my lady? Poor dear, I thought you would wish to sleep all day."

"Is my maid here?" Rose demanded.

Mrs. Toombs smiled. "The poor girl was quite overcome last night. She was delivered to her parents' house."

"Then perhaps your girl could help me . . . ?"

"My girl? Oh, you mean Sarah. She's off to the village. But don't you worry, my lady, I'll have everything ready for you in a trice. I've the bathing-tub set up in the kitchen, and all it needs is for the water to heat."

The kitchen. The meaning of the words hit Rose with a jolt. She had to take a bath in the kitchen, just like a servant or a country farmer. Rose thought longingly of her huge marble bathing-tub at Ashbridge, filled to the rim with hot water, the fragrant steam rising and filling the room with the scent of lavender and rose petals.

"His Grace went over to the house to see if anything can be saved," Mrs. Toombs continued. "What a terrible thing! It is a miracle that no one was trapped inside. And the duke—fighting the fire with his own hands! Such a brave man."

"Indeed," Rose said, trying to keep her voice even. No one had apparently mentioned *her* efforts.

"You go back upstairs, and I'll come for you when everything is ready," Mrs. Toombs said.

With a gracious nod, Rose turned to go, but ruined the elegance of her exit by tripping over the trailing end of the quilt.

Rose reminded herself that this was all Simon's fault. He would be facing her considerable wrath when he finally returned home.

Back in the privacy of the room, she tossed the quilt back onto the bed and glanced about for her clothes.

Then she remembered—she didn't have any clothes. She'd fled the house in her night robe and gown, and the rest of her things were now a charred pile of ash. Dresses, shoes, stockings—even her corsets.

She had absolutely nothing to wear.

Mrs. Toombs burst into the room without bothering to knock.

"I've water on the stove heating for your bath and the kitchen will soon be warm as toast." She held out a dress of a shiny brown kerseymere. "This should fit you well enough."

The dress, which was obviously built along the same ample lines as the nightgown that enveloped her, was the ugliest gown she had ever seen, and Rose shivered at having to wear such a thing. But she had no choice. She was at the mercy of this woman's appalling taste in clothes.

Rose forced a smile. "You are so kind, Mrs. Toombs."

The woman beamed at her faint praise. "Now, you wait a few more minutes and then come along to the kitchen—down the far end of the hall and turn to your left, and I shall have the bathtub all ready for you."

She scurried out of the room.

Rose looked again at the brown dress lying across the bed and shut her eyes.

What was she going to do now? About Stamford, Uncle's plan, London. The fire had destroyed their refuge, and Stamford was not ready to go to town.

She blinked. There was only one alternative—to go home. Home to Ashbridge, the ducal seat in Hampshire.

Taking Stamford there posed a risk, but this whole crazy plan was a risk. It would work if she managed things carefully. And really, it would be much easier to teach him how to emulate her brother in the ducal atmosphere of Ashbridge. She could finish his training there.

The more she thought about it, the better Rose liked the idea. It would be much more pleasant for her as well to be back in civilized surroundings. It had been hard to emulate an aristocratic life in that horrid hunting lodge of Simon's. At Ashbridge, Stamford would be surrounded by ducal majesty, reminding him every minute of the role he had to play.

And remind him of the differences between them. Last night's lapse into familiarity would soon be forgotten.

The biggest challenge would be to make Stamford familiar with the layout of the house and its contents before they arrived. She did not want him gawking at the paintings and sculptures like the crowds on public day. And he would have to be able to identify the main staff with ease.

Rose estimated it would take at least two days to reach Ashbridge. Two days to fill Stamford's head with floor plans, names, schedules, and habits—a tall order.

Could he do it?

She no longer doubted his ability—but his attitude puzzled her. Which was the real man? The buffoon who had disrupted dinner the other night with his comic antics, or the man who had taken charge at the fire? Or the man who had carried her in his arms into the vicar's house?

The buffoon was an easy man to deal with. The firefighter would have no trouble emulating Simon. But the kind, considerate man frightened her. He would be all too easy to like. And she did not want to like him.

There was too much at stake for her to take a personal interest in Stamford. In less than a fortnight, she had to turn him into a worthy imitation of Simon. The cost of failure was too great. She would not let anything get in the way of her success.

As long as Rose avoided glancing down at her dress, she felt remarkably refreshed after her bath. With a cup of soothing tea in her hand, she sat in the front parlor and realized that she actually felt almost civilized again.

Now it was time to turn her attention to the immediate problem—getting the two of them to Ashbridge as soon as humanly possible.

She did not even know the location of the nearest coaching

house where they could hire a vehicle. Rose thought longingly of the elegant, thickly cushioned, and well-sprung carriage that had brought her here, but it would take too long to send to Ashbridge for it. They would have to rely on a hired coach for their transportation.

She wished Stamford had thought to consult with her before going over to the house. Their travel arrangements could already have been made. Now, she must traipse after him and send him on his errand.

The vicar willingly drove her over in his small gig. Rose smelled the acrid odor of smoke before they turned down the tree-lined drive to the house, but she still was not prepared for the shock she felt at the sight of the blackened timbers and charred rubble that was all that remained of the house. The partially collapsed chimneys stood like sentinels over the ruins.

Rose felt a stab of queasiness at the thought of being in that house last night, sleeping peacefully, with no knowledge that something horrible was about to happen. If Stamford had not discovered the fire as early as he did . . . she shivered with remembered terror.

Stamford was standing near the ruins when they drove up. Rose waved to him, and he walked over. He was dressed in clothes as ill-designed as the ones she wore, but somehow, on him, they didn't look quite so bad.

"Not much left, is there?" he asked with a rueful look.

Intent on her mission, Rose frowned. "I realize you are *devastated* by your loss, Simon, but there are more important things to worry about. You need to hire a coach to take us to Ashbridge."

"Ashbridge?" His eyes widened with surprise. "You want to go *there?*"

She gave him a warning look and nodded. "I think that is the best place for us, don't you?" Rose cast a warm smile at the vicar. "I feel terrible about the impositions we are making on you and your dear wife, Reverend Toombs. If you could drive my brother to the nearest coaching inn, he can make the arrangements for us to be on our way."

"No trouble, no trouble at all." The vicar smiled agreeably, no doubt delighted to have someone as important as the Duke of Alston in his debt.

"How do you propose to pay for this carriage?" Stamford asked her bluntly.

Rose frowned. In her haste to get away, she had not given that a thought. "Once you explain the circumstances, I am sure they will be willing to help you."

Stamford laughed. "Not likely. They'll want hard cash for a carriage. Better that you send a note to Ashbridge and wait for our own vehicle to arrive."

"No! I want to go home *now*." She looked imploringly at the vicar. "You will be with him. Surely, you can make them understand."

"I shall do my best," the vicar said.

Stamford climbed into the gig. They let Rose off at the vicarage, then drove off to find a coach.

The next hours passed in excruciating tedium. The vicar's wife seemed to think that it was her Christian duty to make sure that Rose did not have a moment's peace, and regaled her with the family histories of everyone in the parish, the state of the year's crops, and every tidbit of gossip that had come her way in the past year. Rose wanted to press her fingers to her temples and scream "Enough!"

Instead, she nodded and smiled politely, and tried to think of a horrible enough punishment for Simon to adequately compensate her for what she was suffering on his account.

She eagerly leaped to her feet the moment she heard Stamford's voice in the hall.

"Well?" she asked when he entered the parlor.

"All the arrangements are made," Stamford said. "But we need to return to the inn as soon as possible. Are you ready to go?"

She nodded eagerly. Rose was so relieved to know she was on her way home she didn't even stop to wonder why the carriage wasn't coming here.

Mrs. Toombs's generosity knew no bounds, and she presented Rose with a plain chipstraw bonnet and a dark grey cloak for the journey. The only advantage to these, Rose thought, was that no one would ever recognize her in them.

They squeezed back into the gig and drove to the nearby village of Broughton, where the vicar halted in front of a small inn. Stamford handed her down and thanked the vicar again for his assistance. After he drove away, Rose glanced around at the empty yard.

"Where is our coach?" she asked.

Stamford squinted at the sun. "We're a bit early, I think. It should be along shortly."

Rose had a sudden, horrible thought. "What are we traveling in?"

Before Stamford could answer, she heard the trilling notes of the coachman's horn, and her worst fears were confirmed. The bright red coach of the Royal Mail came into view.

She whirled on him. "The Mail? You expect me to travel on the common stage?"

He looked entirely nonplussed at her outburst. "You said you wanted to get home as quickly as possible."

"There is a difference between traveling quickly and torture," she said. "This simply will not do. I must have a private carriage."

"There aren't any," he said bluntly. "At least none that anyone is willing to hire to a stranger without a penny to his name, whether he calls himself the Duke of Alston or George the Third. The vicar was kind enough to pay for our tickets."

Rose glared at him. "I will not travel this way."

"Fine. Walk back to the vicarage and wait there. *I'll* go to Ashbridge by myself and send a carriage back for you."

"You wouldn't dare go there on your own."

"Try me."

The determined look in his grey eyes made her hesitate. Then his expression softened.

"I know this is not what the elegant Lady Rosemary is accustomed to, but it is the only option available to us right now. And the fastest way to get us to Ashbridge."

"But what about all the things you need to know before we get there? I can't be explaining it to you in front of the other passengers."

"We'll find a few moments of privacy. All you have to do is get me into the house. I can hide in my room until you can prepare me."

Rose shut her eyes and took a deep breath. The sooner they got on a coach, the sooner she would be home. Stamford would be at her side; his presence would protect her from the worst impertinences.

And riding in a coach with other passengers was somehow less unnerving than the thought of being alone in one with Stamford for two days. They would have to maintain formality now.

She gave him a resigned look. "I do not have much choice, do I? And think how I can horrify my friends in London with the tale!"

He nodded approvingly, and Rose actually felt pleased with herself until the reality of what she had agreed to sank in.

To Adrian's relief, there were two other passengers in the coach when it stopped. He feared if they had been alone, Rose might reconsider her acceptance. She was too circumspect to air her irritation in public.

He handed Rose into the coach, took his seat beside her, and nodded at the other passengers. Rose slowly inched away from him and huddled in the corner. He fought back a laugh. She would appreciate having this much room if they picked up more passengers.

Adrian felt pleasantly surprised at Lady Rose's acquiescence, however reluctant. He'd half expected a hysterical scene. Yet after seeing her efforts at last night's disaster, he should not have been surprised. Although it was quite clear that by today she'd reverted to her old, high-handed ways. However, that she was sitting next to him inside the bright red Mail coach meant she was willing to be reasonable when it suited her purposes.

To his relief, their traveling companions were not inclined to talk. He was exhausted. He'd caught only a few hours of sleep last night before awakening with the dawn. He didn't know why he'd gone to inspect the ashes of the duke's hunting lodge—he knew the house was totally destroyed. He certainly wasn't going to climb through the rubble, looking for anything that might have survived the heat—silver, or china perhaps. From Rose's attitude toward the place, there wasn't much of value in it—or at least, of value to the duke.

The duke. Adrian had stood there, mouth agape, when Rose announced they were going to the ducal seat in Hampshire. Hadn't they brought him to this out-of-the-way spot precisely to avoid that?

He must be doing something right if Rose was willing to risk taking him there. Adrian knew he would have to give a flawless performance at the house, but really, it shouldn't be too difficult.

It did mean he would have to watch his teasing of Rose—except when they were alone. In a house like Ashbridge, with an army of servants, that would not be often. But after last night, there was no reason for him to continue acting the dim-witted fool. She would know it was a sham.

Going to Ashbridge meant that he was fully committed to this masquerade. He would not be able to withdraw now.

Adrian did not want to. He might have taken this whole thing on as a lark; a chance to see the vaunted aristocracy from the inside. He was more eager than ever to find out the full story behind their desperate need for him. And he relished the idea of spending more time with Rose.

But at the moment, his main concern was getting the two of them to Hampshire. He patted the pocket of his coat, where the coins the vicar had given him for meals clinked lightly. For once Adrian was grateful to men who toadied to an aristocratic title.

There were some advantages to being the Duke of Alston.

*   *   *

The mail coach rounded a corner, and the sleeping Stamford slumped against Rose. She attempted to push him back to his own side of the seat, but he was a deadweight against her. She tried to shake him awake.

"Let the poor man sleep, dearie," said the plainly dressed woman—a tradesman's wife, perhaps—who sat across from her. "He looks to need it."

Rose sniffed and shook Stamford again. She didn't need someone who traveled on the Mail telling her what to do. And she had no intention of playing pillow for Stamford.

To her thorough irritation, he simply would not wake up. Finally, with a sigh of frustration, she sat back and allowed his head to slump against her shoulder. She sat rigidly at attention, unable to relax.

It reminded her too much of that companionable moment they had shared at the fire, when she'd enjoyed the comfort of his arm around her. It had only been the shock of the moment that made it feel welcome. Today, the situation was entirely different. He should not be touching her.

Stamford continued to sleep soundly until they arrived at the next stop.

"Dinner," the coachman announced as he pulled open the door.

Stamford lifted his head and looked around sleepily. "Where are we?"

"Who knows?" Rose snapped. "The man said something about dinner."

Stamford stretched. "Good. I could eat an ox."

He climbed down and turned to offer his hand. At least he hadn't forgot *all* the social niceties.

"I suppose it is too much to hope that there is a decent menu here," she said as they stepped through the doorway.

"It's all you will get until morning, so I wouldn't be too choosy," Stamford warned her.

"At least bespeak us a private dining parlor."

He laughed. "My dear lady, apart from the fact that we do not have the money for a private parlor, this is the Mail. You have twenty minutes to eat and get back on the coach, or they will leave you here." He pushed open the door to the dining room and held it for her. "I suggest you hurry."

Her head held high, Rose swept past him with a flick of her revolting brown skirt.

The dinner, as she had anticipated, was miserable—either overdone or undercooked—and she did not have nearly enough time to finish eating before the passengers were chased out of the inn and back into the coach.

Traveling through the night was as dreadful as she had imagined. To her growing disgust, Stamford seemed to have no problem sleeping. But why should he—with her shoulder to lean on? They'd picked up another passenger at one stop, and they were now crowded three on the seat, so there was no escaping him.

She closed her eyes and tried unsuccessfully to will herself to sleep. But every bump in the road, every lurch of the coach jolted her into full awareness. She could not remember a more miserable night in her entire life.

Rose was exhausted, dirty, and thoroughly out of sorts when the Mail pulled up to the designated breakfast stop. She stood on the carriage step, surveying the muddy yard with utter loathing. Stamford held out his hand to help her down, but she batted it away. Despite the poorly fitting clothes he was wearing, he looked disgustingly cheerful and refreshed. As well he should—he had slept all night.

Rose stalked into the inn, ignoring Stamford as he followed at her heels.

"I suppose breakfast will be as inedible as last night's dinner?" she asked as they took their seats in the dining room.

"Probably," he responded with a cheeky grin. Rose wanted to slap him for looking so cheerful.

Thankfully, there was bread and butter and jam so she was able to ignore the foul-smelling plates that were passed up and down the table. But soon the smell of kippers grew so malodorous that she grabbed a second slice of bread and fled outside.

Crossing the yard, she tripped over the ill-fitting dress and fell to her knees. Her hands went out to break her fall, and her bread went flying, landing with an audible plop in a muddy puddle several feet away.

Rose scrambled to her feet, took one look at her mud-splattered dress and hands, and burst into tears.

It wasn't fair!

"Oh dear, did we have an accident?"

She whirled on Stamford. This was all his fault. He had forced her onto the Mail, forced her to endure the miserable ride, the loathsome food, the horrid passengers. She had taken all she was going to from this odious man.

"You are enjoying this, aren't you?" she demanded. "Go ahead, admit it. You think this is a great joke. Make life miserable for Lady Rosemary." She brushed back a strand of straggling hair. "Well, I give in. You have succeeded. I am hungry and dirty and tired and covered with mud, and I have never been so miserable in my entire life. Are you happy now?"

He pulled out a handkerchief and began daubing at the mud on her dress. She jerked out of his grasp, felt her foot slip on the slick ground, and sat down heavily.

Stamford laughed aloud.

Something inside Rose snapped. Men like Stamford simply did not laugh at her. She grabbed a handful of mud and flung it at him. "There—see how you like that!"

The mud landed just beneath his shoulder, splattering his chin with dirt.

She reached for another handful of mud, but before she could throw it, he lunged forward and grabbed her arm, jerking her to her feet. Rose tried to pull away, but his grip was like iron.

"I am sick and tired of you acting like a spoiled princess," he said harshly. "So you have to travel on the Mail. There are people for whom that would be the height of luxury. The food may not be the best, but at least it is food. Do you have any idea how many children in London go to bed hungry every single night?"

She stared back at him, livid. "How dare you talk to me like this!"

"It's about time someone did. I doubt anyone ever said no to you in your life. And that's your problem, *Lady* Rosemary. You're spoiled, arrogant, and selfish, and give no thought to anyone's comfort but your own. You've been waited on hand and foot from the day you were born, treated like royalty, and it's gone to your head. Money and a title do not make you a superior person."

Her jaw dropped open at his unbelievable tirade. "May I remind you, Mr. Stamford, that you are my *employee*. You may not speak to me like that."

"Fine. I quit." He pulled a few coins from his pocket and slapped them into her hand. "Your seat on the Mail's paid through to Ashbridge. Here's some money for your next meal. It has been a most illuminating experience, and I hope that our paths do not cross again."

He stalked off toward the inn.

Rose stared after him, aghast. He wouldn't dare leave her here, alone like this.

Would he?

"Wait!" she called after him.

He halted and turned toward her, arms crossed over his chest. "Why should I?"

She swallowed hard. He was being thoroughly unreasonable, but she did not have time to point that out to him now. Already, the passengers were filing out of the inn. In a few moments the Mail would leave, and she had to make sure he was on it with her.

She forced the words out. "I am sorry."

He remained at rigid attention. "For what?"

"Do you need a list? Just accept my apology, and let's be gone. The Mail is leaving."

He glanced over at the coach and nodded in agreement.

"Well?" Rose glared at him in exasperation. "Come on, then."

Stamford did not move, and Rose's panic grew.

"I am . . . I am sorry for throwing mud at you."

"That's a start."

"And . . . and for complaining about the food. And for being tired and . . . and out of sorts. But you would be, too, if you hadn't slept a wink and had to wear this horrible dress and bonnet and—"

To her surprise, he suddenly grinned. "Good enough." Grabbing her hand, he pulled her toward the coach and shoved her up the steps. He landed with a thump on the seat beside her as the attendant slammed the door and the coach lurched forward.

All the other passengers stared at them wide-eyed. Rose slanted a glance at Stamford. Mud speckled his face and chin and the front of his jacket. He looked ridiculous.

Rose burst out laughing.

He looked at her curiously, as if uncertain of her mood, but he must have seen her amusement as he, too, chuckled.

"You have a spot of mud on your cheek," he said and dabbed at it with his handkerchief.

"And you have mud there." She took the cloth from him and swiped his chin, then glanced down at her filthy skirts. "And I have mud everywhere!" This sent her off into another gale of mirth.

The other passengers looked at her as if she were a lunatic, but Rose did not care. She did make an amusing picture in her bedraggled state.

Stamford leaned close and whispered in her ear. "I take back some of the things I said, Lady Rose. You can be a trooper when you try."

She looked at him with surprise, and he winked broadly. Rose hesitantly smiled back.

Stamford was not such a bad person after all.

Chapter 6

❧

Late in the afternoon, the Mail dropped them at Little Burton, the nearest coach stop to Ashbridge. The innkeeper instantly recognized his noble neighbors, said nothing about their unusual appearance, and sent them off in his best carriage.

Now that they were almost at the house, Adrian's misgivings about his ability to play the duke in front of the family servants resurfaced. But he was determined not to let Rose know.

"We do not have much time," Rose said as the carriage pulled away from the inn. "I will draw up floor plans after we arrive, but you need to learn the basic layout."

"That will be easy," he said with a light grin. "I walk in, order everyone about in the proper ducal manner, and march off to my room."

"Not quite. Now, the butler is Mr. Markham—he will be the only one who is not in livery. As for the footmen . . ."

Adrian tried to pay attention, but he sensed Rose felt nearly as nervous as he did. She talked rapidly, her eyes growing dark and intense. Was she regretting her decision to bring him here?

He should reassure her. She had been subdued, almost penitent since he'd wrung that apology from her this morning in the inn yard. He knew it had been hard for her. He doubted Lady Rose had ever apologized to anyone before.

Adrian reached across the seat and gave her hand a comforting squeeze. "I will make a grand duke—I promise."

She still looked doubtful. "This is not a country vicar you

have to fool," she reminded him. "Half the staff have known you since you were in short coats."

"And they would not dare to remind me of that," he replied with his most arrogant look. "Remember, I am the *duke*."

That won a smile from her.

The carriage turned down the entry drive, and he peered out the window, eager to catch a glimpse of the house. To his disappointment, they approached from the side, and all he could see were neat lawns and manicured gardens.

He knew Rose would not let him hang out the window to look, so they were nearly at the door before he caught a glimpse of the building.

It was a massive house, the central building of beige Hampshire stone with pavilions on either end. The formal Georgian facade looked almost plain . . . cold. Yet from what Rose had told him, the interior was lavishly decorated. He felt a sudden stab of panic at the thought of walking into such a palace and affecting an attitude of bored indifference.

Already, it was hard not to stare at the bewigged and liveried footman who held open the coach door. Taking a deep breath, Adrian descended the steps, then held out his hand for Rose. He pretended not to notice the footman's startled look at the sight of their disheveled appearance.

A smile of pure delight crossed Rose's face when her foot struck the graveled drive.

"Home at last," she breathed softly. Gathering up her skirts, she raced up the front stairs. Adrian hurried to catch up.

Another footman stood at rigid attention beside the open front door. Rose swept past him into the entry, and Adrian feared she would desert him in her excitement. But then she turned and grabbed him by the arm.

"Stay close to me," she whispered.

He barely heard her as he took in the incredible grandeur of the entry hall. The ceiling—encrusted with cavorting nymphs peeking from behind feathery clouds—had to be forty feet high, at least. A massive, gilded chandelier hung from the distant ceiling. When all the candles were lit, it must have glowed like the sun. Straight ahead, a wide marble staircase led to the upper floors.

Rose jabbed him in the side. "Quit gawking," she hissed. "Your Grace!"

A surprised voice came from his left. Adrian glanced toward a man dressed in black. It must be Markham, the imperious butler.

The man's expression looked pained. "Your Grace, we were not expecting—"

Adrian slipped on his mask of ducal arrogance. "A slight mishap in Cheshire," he said. "We are back here for a time. See that our baths are prepared immediately."

The butler looked startled at the command, and Adrian realized he must have said something wrong. But what? He looked helplessly at Rose.

"The hunting lodge burned to the ground, and we escaped with only our nightclothes and little else," Rose explained. "We have no luggage, no maid, no valet. So if you would be so kind as to take care of matters . . . ?"

The butler nodded. "Of course, my lady. Mrs. Fletcher will know an appropriate candidate to assist you. And if Your Grace would be so kind, I would be honored . . ."

Adrian did not need Rose's warning glance. The butler knew Simon far too well to allow him to act as valet.

He spotted another footman standing at attention by the door and pointed to him. "I can use that footman."

The butler looked aghast. "Your Grace, forgive me, but he is our newest footman. I hardly think—"

"He will do." Adrian held out his arm to Rose. "May I escort you to your room, Sister dear?"

She took his arm, and they started up the enormous main stairway. As they climbed, he ran his hand over the rich wooden handrail, which was polished to a glasslike luster. How many hours did servants devote to that single task each day?

What must it be like to live in a place like this? It was beyond anything he could have imagined. Just as he caught a glimpse of one priceless art object, another came into view. A gilt-framed landscape caught his eye, only to be supplanted by a bust of a laurel-crowned Roman, which gave way to the carved detailing over a doorway. He wanted to stop and examine each one, yet knew that displaying even the briefest interest would be a mistake.

Rose seemed supremely oblivious to her opulent surroundings as she led him toward the wing housing the family apartments. The transition was marked by a set of carved double doors; the corridor beyond narrowed.

Adrian's attention was focused on a painting of the Italian countryside when he literally bumped into Rose, who had halted outside a door.

"Do be careful," she said.

"Sorry."

"Your room is at the end of the hall," she reminded him. "Stay there until I send for you. And do not let the footman stay long—dispense with his services as soon as possible."

"I will be fine," he assured her with a confidence he did not entirely feel.

"Just do not leave that room." She entered her bedroom and closed the door swiftly before he had a chance to get a glimpse of the chamber beyond.

He turned away and strode down the hall, his sense of impending doom rising as he neared the large door at the end of the corridor. If Alston's room at that hunting lodge had bordered on regal splendor, what must it be like in this palace? Taking a deep breath, he pushed open the door, steeling himself to look.

To his surprise, the duke's bedroom was pleasantly decorated in a refined style, completely unlike the room at the lodge. The bed hangings were staid green velvet, the ceiling plasterwork painted white, without any leering cherubs or angels.

Adrian heaved a deep sigh of relief.

He quickly scanned the rest of the room—bed, dressing table, wardrobe, chairs, night table, all in dark mahogany. The public sections of the house might leave him awestruck, but in this room, he could relax. It was a *room*, not a museum piece.

A knock sounded on the door, and the footman stepped into the room.

"I'm here to be your valet, Your Grace," he said with obvious nervousness.

The poor lad didn't look a day over eighteen. No wonder the butler had been so horrified at Adrian's choice. The real duke would not have given the most junior footman a second glance, but for Adrian, he was the perfect answer to a number of problems.

"What is your name?" He smiled, trying to set the lad at ease.

"Roberts, Your Grace."

"Do you want to play valet for me?" Adrian asked.

The lad's face broke into a smile. "Yes, Your Grace, it would be an honor."

Adrian wondered why he was so eager to take on such a major task, then he remembered Rose's explanations—the personal valet of the duke held a place above all the other servants in the household, except for the butler and housekeeper. Adrian realized he had given this young man a singular honor—and probably put the butler's nose out of joint as well.

Adrian didn't know if he'd been clever, or incredibly stupid.

"Have my bath readied," Adrian said, striving to sound ducal.

Roberts nodded and headed instantly toward the door on the far wall. Adrian let out a relieved breath. At least he knew where to go.

After pulling off his boots, Adrian circled the room while he waited for his bath, pulling open drawers and inspecting their contents. In the carved dresser he found fine linen handkerchiefs—each embroidered with the ducal monogram—and stockings in plain and colored hues. There was a drawer for gloves, for neatly folded smallclothes, for nightshirts and caps.

He had just turned to explore the desk when Roberts reentered.

"Your bath is ready, Your Grace."

"Good." Adrian followed him through the doorway into what he assumed was the bathing chamber.

He almost gasped aloud at the sight inside. A massive marble tub sat against the far wall, a permanent fixture in the room. Adrian stared at it in growing amazement. He had never seen anything like it. It was large enough to bathe an entire household.

And it was all for him. Through the mist of steam rising to the ceiling, he saw it was filled nearly to the brim with clean hot water. This was a kind of luxury he had never envisioned.

He finally realized what it truly meant to be a duke.

Roberts stood at attention, looking at him expectantly. Adrian realized he intended to undress his master.

That was too much. Adrian would probably have to submit to such ministrations eventually, or it would seem odd. But he could not deal with that now, when he was so overwhelmed by his surroundings.

"You may lay out my clothes," Adrian said in a dismissive tone. Roberts nodded and went back to the bedroom.

Adrian hastily undressed, fearing Roberts would come back too soon, and stepped into the tub. It was long enough that he could stretch out full length and completely sink into the water. It was a pure, sybaritic delight. He took a gulp of air and sank beneath the surface.

He reemerged for air, then suddenly wondered if Rose had an equally luxurious bath. Was she lying naked in her bath, her skin turning a rosy pink from the heat of the water?

It was an audacious thought, but he could not banish the vision from his mind. He still treasured his memory of how she had looked the night of the fire, when she came to her door in her night rail, sleepy eyed, with her hair tumbling over her shoulders.

Would she have that hair pinned up now, to keep it out of the water? Would a few loose strands have escaped, curling in the steam?

Adrian firmly told himself that this was Lady Rosemary Devering he was daring to think about, the daughter of a duke—a woman who until two days ago he was not even certain he liked.

But that was before he'd seen her resolution and determination in combating the fire, and her unexpected vulnerability as she sat crying in the mud of an inn yard. Now he wanted to see her rising from her bath like Venus rising from the sea.

Which could present a problem if he ever expected to be comfortable in her presence again. Adrian reminded himself that he was here to play the duke—and Rose was the duke's sister. All his thoughts of her should be brotherly. He dare not think of her like this.

To divert his thoughts, he grabbed one of the bottles from the shelf beside the tub, removed the stopper, and sniffed. He gagged at the strong, floral scent. Alston bathed in this? Adrian was not going to carry his ducal masquerade that far. He tried to put the bottle back, but the smooth glass slipped from his wet fingers and landed with a plop in the tub, spewing out its repellent scent.

Adrian grabbed for the bottle, but the damage was done. His bathwater reeked—and no doubt, he did, too.

At least he did not have to worry about staying away from Rose—she would not dare to come near him now.

Rose stretched out in her bath, breathing in the familiar scent of the heated rose and lavender oils that drifted through the steam. This was what she'd longed for, dreamt about, ever since setting foot in that stupid hunting lodge of Simon's. She would revel in the sheer pleasure of the luxuries she was accustomed to, and forget, for a few moments, the pressing matters before her.

But unwillingly, her thoughts turned to Stamford and the things he'd said to her this morning. "Spoiled," "arrogant," "selfish," he'd called her. He had caught her in a weak moment, when she was miserable from traveling, lack of sleep, and hunger. It had been a shocking display of peevishness on her part to throw mud at him, but he had no right to laugh at her misfortune.

She would show him that his estimation of her was wrong. She did think of others. Look at what she was already doing for him. He seemed to have forgotten that.

Stamford was not going to look down his nose at her.

Later, wrapped in her favorite robe and sitting in front of the dressing table while the housekeeper's niece brushed her hair dry, Rose thought about the days ahead. Their arrival had gone smoothly, thank goodness.

It was obvious that her biggest problem would be to keep Stamford from gawking at the house and its furnishings. He had behaved like a visitor on public day when she took him up the grand staircase. As a reminder, she had jabbed him in the side with a well-placed elbow, but that was not a permanent solution.

She particularly didn't want him exploring the house on his own. Rose needed to keep him occupied until she had the time to take him on a full tour. It wouldn't do to have him get lost and ask a servant for directions.

The library would be a safe place for him today. He would find something there to hold his interest—he was a scholar, wasn't he? She could draw up the house plans for him, answer his questions, and remind him again that he was playing the role of duke, not visitor.

The library would be useful for another reason—she did not want to deal with the formality of eating in the dining room tonight. They could have a simple dinner served on trays. They would have no need to leave the room all evening. By the time they did, she would have Stamford better prepared for life at Ashbridge.

She scribbled a hasty note to Stamford, advising him to meet her in the library precisely at half past six, and not to dress for dinner. She did not know what he would make of that command, but his valet would know which clothes to set out for him.

Clothes. Rose looked at that hated brown dress, draped over a chair, and wished she could fling it onto the fire. Instead, she ordered it to be cleaned and thought about a suitable gift of thanks to send to the vicar's wife. A shawl, she decided. A gift that was useful, but not personal.

Rose took great delight in going through her closet while she decided which dress to wear this evening. Did she feel like silk or muslin? Pink crepe or green merino? She finally settled on an afternoon dress of patterned blue muslin, with slippers to match.

It was such a joy to wear a dress that both fit and looked good. Rose admired her reflection in the floor-standing mirror before she grabbed her shawl and headed for the library to meet Stamford.

To her surprise, he was there waiting for her, even though she was early.

"You found your way here, I see," she said.

He shrugged. "T'was easy enough. You told me the layout."

He leaned against the mantel, dressed in Simon's clothes—fawn breeches, top boots, dark blue coat. Even his cravat looked acceptable. To her amusement, he twirled a quizzing glass on a chain, then peered at her through the eyepiece.

"You're looking more the thing," he drawled in a languid, aristocratic tone.

"So are you." Rose settled on the settee and arranged her skirts in an artful drape, exposing just a hint of ankle. She wanted to look her best for him tonight. He had certainly seen her at her worst this morning. "Wherever did you find that glass?"

"In a drawer."

"I am sorry to dampen your enthusiasm, but Simon never uses it. You will have to put it back."

With a grin, he tucked it inside his waistcoat.

"I thought you might want to inspect the library," she said. "While you do that, I will start drawing the maps for you."

"This is quite a room." He prowled the perimeter, eyeing the hundreds of volumes crowded upon the shelves. Once or twice he took down a volume and thumbed through it.

"Simon rarely comes in here—books are not to his taste—so it will not do to spend too much time here," Rose informed him. "I thought you would find it less intimidating than the saloon tonight."

He smiled. "Thank you."

"How did the footman do as your valet? The way you deflected Markham's offer was masterful."

"I'm not eager to keep up the pretense in front of him any more than I have to," Stamford confessed as he sat in a chair facing her. "Roberts, the footman, seems suitably in awe of me. He won't question anything I do."

Rose sniffed the air. "What is that smell?"

"Me." Stamford turned red. "I dropped a bottle of scent in the bath."

She waved away the invisible fumes. "I cannot believe Simon has anything so foul."

He grinned. "Neither can I."

Rose pulled a traveling writing box onto her lap and spread out her papers. "Now, the center section of the house, as I told you, houses the public rooms, which won't be in use while we are here. Saloon, grand dining room, the red drawing room . . ."

He did not ask a single question until she had gone over the entire house, and she feared he was not paying attention. Had it been a mistake bringing him here? Was he having second thoughts about the role he was to play?

Stamford took the maps from her, folded them, and stuffed them into his pocket.

"These are good, but I would like to see the place firsthand, as well. If you do not want me stopping to gawk at every picture and carved head, you need to show me the whole of it," he explained.

He was right. He had to be comfortable in his surroundings.

"I intend to do that," she said. "But we need to have a good excuse, else the staff will wonder."

"Tell them I lost at the gaming tables and need to sell off a few priceless heirlooms." He grinned at her.

Rose gave him a withering look.

"I know. I want some suitably expensive gift to present to my future in-laws."

"That's it!" Rose said excitedly. "You want a description of all the rooms to present to Lady Juliet. No doubt she will want to redecorate after she moves in."

He jumped to his feet. "Let's get started."

She stared at him. "Now? You must be joking. I have no desire to traipse through this house until I've had a good night's sleep. We can have a quiet dinner here in the library and then retire early. You can save the exploring until tomorrow."

To her surprise, he actually looked disappointed.

"I thought this room would hold your attention for a few hours," she said gently. "There are cabinets full of all sorts of strange things at the far end of the room. My grandfather was quite a collector."

She saw the gleam of interest in his eyes and knew that she had deflected him from the idea of an immediate tour of the house. Good. All she wanted to do was sit quietly. She had more lists to make for him—names of the servants, a plan of the outbuildings, a listing of some of the more valuable art objects in the house.

"Good God!" he exclaimed in a loud voice as he peered through the glass. "Do you have the keys to the cabinets?"

"Markham does." She rose and walked to his side. "What have you found?"

He pointed to a curved metal bar at the back of the shelf. "Look at that torque. It has to be British. Do you know where it came from? Did your grandfather keep records of his collection?"

Rose shrugged. "I don't know."

"Well, someone must. Who maintains the library? Does your brother employ a secretary or a librarian?"

"I do not think anyone has worried about these things since my grandfather's day," she responded dryly. "If anyone knows, it will be Markham, but I do not want to ask him."

"You must." His eyes were dark with excitement. "Please? I need to know about this torque. I must know where your grandfather acquired it."

"Simon would not be interested in that sort of thing."

"*Simon* has developed a sudden interest in ancient antiquities," he said, glaring at her. "Call the butler. Now."

"Let it wait until tomorrow, when you have had more time to settle in."

He waved his hands in the air, frustrated. "Why can't I make you understand? I have been trying to find something like this for years. I want to hold it, touch it, find out where it came from."

"Is this tied to your interest in Roman ruins?"

"Yes." He nodded vigorously. "The Romans usually built on or near existing habitations. Where there are Roman ruins, there are usually pre-Roman ruins—and the chance to find something like this." He stared through the glass. "Just look at the silver work! It was made by a master."

Rose debated silently. Markham might think it odd, but he would hand over the keys without question. And knowing of her grandfather's meticulous obsession with detail, he had kept the type of records Stamford wanted. Markham should know about that, too.

Rose pulled the bell cord. "We can always say you are looking for a gift for Lady Juliet."

She wanted to do this for Stamford—to show him that she was not totally selfish. If giving him access to her grandfather's collection of oddities would do that, she would willingly give him the opportunity.

Chapter 7

Adrian could hardly contain his excitement while they waited for the butler. He would give anything to get his hands on several of the pieces in that case, even if only to examine and sketch them. Why hadn't Rose told him that her grandfather collected artifacts?

Because they meant nothing to her.

Why should they? She had a house full of exquisite art and priceless antiques that the world valued far more than the primitive relics of some ancient Britons. Her grandfather's collection was regarded as oddities, nothing more.

When the butler appeared, Adrian remained in his chair, fearful to betray his keen interest. He let Rose make the explanations.

"I would like the keys to the cabinets," she said, smiling sweetly at Markham. "Simon thinks Lady Juliet might be interested in one or two of the knickknacks."

Markham crossed the room and unlocked the glass doors. Adrian wanted to spring out of his chair and grab the torque. Instead, he crossed the room with studied nonchalance.

"Is there a catalogue of the collection?" he asked. "I should like to let the lady know exactly what she is getting. I would hate to give her some insignificant trinket by mistake."

The butler went to the bookshelf behind the desk and pulled out a ledger bound in red leather.

"Your grandfather kept meticulous records of his collection," he replied. Adrian sensed a subtle undertone of condemnation in those words. Obviously, the present duke was not so meticulous.

"Markham, we would like to have dinner brought here in an hour," Rose told him.

The butler looked taken aback. "In the library? The dining room is all prepared, my lady."

"We will not dine there tonight," Rose said with a note of finality in her words. Adrian admired the way she did that— daring the butler to contradict her. Markham merely bowed and left the room.

"Poor man." Rose laughed lightly. "He doesn't quite know what to do when his employers take on such strange whims."

Adrian barely heard her. He pulled open the cabinet door and drew out the torque. On close inspection, it was an even finer piece than he'd first thought. The curved metal band was made of burnished bronze, incised with an intricate design. The knobbed ends were worked in silver.

Whose neck had it once graced? An ancient prince? Or a druid priestess? No one would ever know.

Rose came up beside him and peered around his shoulder. He held out the torque to her. She gave it a quick glance, and her indifferent expression told of her lack of interest.

"It is not very fancy, is it?"

"Fancy? This is the finest metalwork I have ever seen. Do you realize how old it is? This piece could have been made before Caesar and his legions even set foot on Britain."

"Is it worth a great deal?"

He gave her a disdainful look. "It's priceless." He walked to the desk and flung open the ledger. "I wonder where he got it."

As the butler had said, the fifth duke was meticulous in documenting the objects he'd collected over his lifetime. The ledger was divided into sections by type of art—paintings, sculpture, ceramics. Adrian flipped through pages, looking for a category that would encompass ancient British artifacts.

He found it at last, toward the end of the listings. He ran his finger down the page, looking for a description of the torque. Ah, there it was.

One brass and silver torque, age unknown, probably pre-Roman. Turned up by a plow on Swithern's field.

"What—where—is Swithern's field?" he demanded of Rose.

"That's part of the home farm," she said.

"Here? That field is here?" His whole body tingled with excitement. "This says the torque came from that field. I have to look. There may be more things there."

"You can't go out there. Simon would not be caught dead in the fields—unless he was crossing them during a hunt."

Adrian would not let her deny him this chance. It would be sheer luck if he found anything as exquisite as this piece, but there might be other objects—something, anything—still in that field.

"Simon's turning over a new leaf in anticipation of his marriage, remember? No one needs to know what I'm doing there. I'd just like to inspect the field."

She looked at him thoughtfully. "I suppose it would be all right. We can ride out there tomorrow." Rose glanced at him anxiously. "You do ride, don't you?"

Adrian rolled his eyes. "Yes, I can sit a horse. Although it makes it hard to carry a shovel."

"A shovel? Oh, no, you are not going to do any digging out there. Absolutely not."

"But how can I tell if anything is there if I do not dig?"

"There will be no digging," she said firmly, before grabbing one of her interminable lists. "If you could divert your attention back to your task for a few moments, there are more things you need to know . . ."

With a sigh, Adrian closed the ledger and went back to his chair.

They ate a quiet dinner, while Rose continued to explain about the house, the servants, and the daily life of a duke. Finally, she declared that she was tired, and it was time for them both to go to bed. Adrian agreed without protest.

To his surprise, Roberts was sitting on a chair outside the

bedroom. When he saw Adrian approaching, he jumped to his feet.

"What are you doing here?" Adrian asked.

"Waiting to help you prepare for bed, Your Grace."

"Oh, for God's sake." Adrian shook his head. "I can get undressed by myself. Go to bed."

Roberts looked so disappointed at his dismissal that Adrian relented slightly. "I will need you in the morning, however."

"Would you like me to wake you, Your Grace?"

Adrian groaned inwardly. Couldn't these people do anything for themselves? "I will ring when I want you."

As soon as he was safely in his room, he pulled off his jacket and ripped off the restricting cravat. He had not been able to get that torque out of his mind all evening; tomorrow he would be able to see the field where it had been found. The thought of exploring a known site made him giddy with excitement.

Thank God he'd been able to persuade Rose to let him go. Tonight, dressed in a fashionable gown, with her hair arranged in an elaborate style, she looked once again like the aristocratic Lady Rose—the one who'd treated him with such condescension at the hunting lodge.

The Rose who was the daughter of a duke—not the Rose who'd hauled buckets of water to fight the fire; or the Rose who'd flung mud at him in an inn yard.

Or the Rose he'd fantasized about in the bath.

They had certainly reached a new level of ease with one another, but she had made it quite clear, in her attitude and manner tonight, that she was willing to unbend only so far. They were still from two different worlds, and he needed to keep that uppermost in his mind, no matter how difficult he found it.

It was the only way he could survive.

Adrian awoke at an unconscionably early hour and chaffed at the knowledge that he could not immediately ride to the home farm. He would have to wait until Rose arose at her usual languid hour. Then she had to dress and eat breakfast. It would be noon, at least, before they started out.

What was worse, she would not let him poke around with a shovel. How could he know if there were still artifacts at the site if he couldn't dig? He had searched Alston's room, looking for some tool that might work, but the duke's elegant penknives were not going to be much help.

He needed something small, like a trowel, that he could slip into a coat pocket without drawing attention. With it, he could at least probe the surface of any interesting spots he found. Rose couldn't complain about *that*.

Where was he going to get one?

Adrian pulled out her sketch of the estate grounds, trying to remember where the greenhouse was located. There, behind the west wing. There should be trowels aplenty there.

Dressing quickly, Adrian forgot all about ringing for Roberts. He memorized the route he needed to follow to get out of the house and headed down the corridor.

No one—well, no one except two parlor maids and a scurrying footman—saw him as he left. Adrian lived in terror of encountering the butler without Rose at his side. He feared Markham would ask him a question that he had no idea how to answer.

He walked down the drive, then cut across the lawn toward the back of the house. The strong fragrance of roses reached his nose as he came around the corner. He saw a gardener working among the bushes and almost gave him a friendly wave, then stopped himself. Adrian had to remember that he was the duke, and dukes did not wave at their gardeners.

When he reached the glass-enclosed greenhouse, he was forced to circle halfway around before he finally found the door. Pulling it open, he stepped into a foreign world.

A moist, steamy heat enveloped him, filled with the strange smells of exotic flowering plants and the rich scent of fresh dirt. Wiping the moisture from his brow, he looked around. Actual trees grew in pots the size of a hogshead of beer. Delicate vines twined around tall poles, with fragile flowers poking out from the leaves. Smaller potted plants sat on waist-high shelves.

He stepped forward, staring in amazement at the sheer size

of the place. Plants he'd seen only in books stood on either side of the aisle.

"Your Grace!"

Adrian saw a roughly-dressed man bearing down on him. So much for demonstrating ducal aplomb—now he'd been caught gawking in the greenhouse.

"I need . . . a trowel," Adrian said.

The man looked puzzled. "A trowel, Your Grace? Is there a problem? One of my men will take care of it."

"No, no, no problem. A strange whim of my sister's." He gave the man a conspiratorial smile. "She wishes to have a trowel."

The gardener still looked puzzled, but he hurried toward the back of the building, coming back shortly with the desired instrument. It was damp—the man had obviously given it a good scrubbing.

Adrian took it from him. "Thank you." He pointed to a large plant with long, sharp-edged leaves. "What is that?"

The gardener blinked. "That is a pineapple plant, Your Grace."

"Ah. Odd-looking thing, isn't it?"

"Yes, Your Grace."

Adrian realized he should retreat before he displayed any more ignorance. He waved the trowel and backed out the door. "Thank you again."

The cool air outside felt refreshing after the stifling heat. Now all he had to do was wait for Lady Rose to drag herself out of bed and lead him to the home farm.

He passed a gardener trimming the shrubbery, who tugged at his forelock as Adrian walked by. The action chilled him. The duke might be the man's employer, but he only deserved respect, not the obsequiousness of a serf.

The thought disturbed him all the way back to the house.

As soon as she breakfasted and dressed, Rose sent a footman to bring Stamford to the morning room. To her dismay, he was not to be found.

Had he dared to go to the home farm without her? The thought struck her with horror. That meant he had gone to the stables alone, and talked with the grooms, who knew Simon well. He would have had to ask directions to the home farm. Too many chances to make a bad mistake.

Why couldn't the man follow her instructions?

She paced the room in frustration, trying to decide what to do next. Perhaps he had given his valet some indication of his plans. She reached for the bellpull.

The door opened, and Stamford walked in, looking calm and unruffled.

"You were looking for me?"

"Where have you been?"

"I was exploring the greenhouse." He looked chagrined. "Do you know I have never seen a pineapple plant before?"

"I thought I told you not to go *anywhere* without me."

"No harm done." He smiled brightly. "Are you ready to go?" Frowning, she rose.

"Say as little as possible at the stables," she warned him as they walked toward the buildings. "Tell the groom you want to ride 'Saber' and don't engage anyone in further conversation."

"What if they want to talk with me?" he asked with an innocent look.

She pointedly ignored his question.

To her relief, everything went smoothly at the stables, and they were soon mounted and riding toward the home farm.

Rose observed him carefully as she rode beside him. He did not look as if he would be quite the neck-or-nothing rider Simon was, but Stamford knew how to handle himself on a horse. Watching him now, dressed in Simon's clothes, riding Simon's favorite mount, she could almost imagine that he *was* her brother.

With a sudden start, she realized that, without her noticing when or how, Stamford had easily slipped into his ducal role this morning. There was even a new air about him—one of confidence and command. When they had walked through the house, he showed none of yesterday's wide-eyed gawking. And he had adopted just the right tone with the grooms at the stables.

She halted while he opened the gate into the lane leading to the home farm.

"Which field did you want?" she asked.

"Swithern's."

"That is off to our left. Keep to the edge of the field—no one wants you trampling the corn."

"Even if it's *my* corn?" he asked with a cocky grin.

She gave him a chastising look.

Soon they reached the edge of the next field, the division clearly obvious with the change in crop.

"Here we are."

He surveyed the field of ripening hay with obvious dismay.

"I can't see a thing with all that hay in the way," he said.

"What did you expect to see?" she asked.

"Well, something unusual. A rise or a track or a ditch that would have existed in olden times."

"The field has been under cultivation for as long as the Deverings have held the property," she said. "Anything like that would have been plowed under long ago."

"Why didn't you tell me last night?"

"It was all I could do to keep you from dashing off as it was. You never said what you were looking for."

"What about the other fields? Are there any with unusual formations?"

He looked so crestfallen, she wished she could ease his disappointment, but she did not know how. "None that I know of."

"Isn't there someone we could ask? You must have a steward to manage all this property. He would know."

"You may not go asking him," Rose said. "You are Simon, remember. He does not care about that sort of thing."

"What about one of the tenants, then? They probably know the land even better."

"Perhaps," she conceded, reluctantly. There probably was no harm in that. They would have no idea that he was acting oddly. "We could ask at Taylor's."

"Do they farm this field?"

"And most of the land on the home farm."

He bowed to her from the saddle. "Lead on, my lady."

She turned her horse around and started for the home cottage. No doubt they were chasing a mare's nest, but she wanted to keep Stamford in a good humor. Now that they were at Ashbridge, his cooperation was crucial. Once he discovered that there were no ruins in the area, he would forget about them, and they could get on with the more important job of increasing his knowledge of Simon's world.

Stamford suddenly urged his horse forward and took off at a gallop toward the line of trees at the far edge of the field.

"Where are you going?" she shouted. "Stop!"

He didn't heed her, but turned his horse toward the narrow gap that cut through the stand and onto the hill beyond. Rose urged her horse into a sedate trot and followed him, shaking her head at whatever new start had possessed him.

By the time she caught up, he was off his horse and staring, hands on hips, at the elongated hump in the middle of the pasture.

"How long has this been here?" he asked her eagerly.

She shrugged. "I have no idea."

He started pacing off the distance around the mound. Then he halted at the narrow end, dropped to his knees, pulled something out of his pocket, and started scrabbling at the ground.

"What are you doing?" she cried.

"Digging," he yelled over his shoulder.

"You can't do that. Stop at once. We have to go back to the house."

He ignored her and kept working. With rising anger, Rose brought her leg off the saddle hook and slid to the ground. She stalked toward Stamford.

"This is ridiculous," she said. "It is just a bump in the middle of the field. Probably some ancient rock that they have been plowing around for years."

"That's what I am trying to find out," he said.

She stared accusingly at the trowel in his hand. "That's why you went to the greenhouse this morning! To steal a trowel."

"To *borrow* it," he corrected. "But don't worry, the gardener doesn't suspect a thing, I told him *you* wanted it."

"What?"

"Oh, sit down and be quiet. This won't take long. If there is a huge rock under all this grass, I will find out soon enough. Although it would be a dashed sight easier if you'd let me bring a proper shovel."

Frowning, Rose sank to the grass. She would give him a few minutes—no longer—to finish with this silliness. They had important things to deal with today. Stamford needed to remember why he was here.

"Aha!" He let out a whoop of excitement.

"Did you find the rock?" she asked.

"Better than that—gravel." He held out a handful of pebbles. "I think this is a man-made mound."

"A mound of what?"

"Most likely a burial chamber."

"A burial chamber? Here? There was never a church in this part of the land."

He laughed. "This person was buried long before anything you would consider a church existed on this island." He began attacking the dirt with renewed enthusiasm.

Despite her reservations, he had aroused her curiosity, and she crept closer. "Do you really think so?"

"I pray so."

Maybe he really had found something that might be worth exploring. Rose would allow him this treat. "We can come back later."

He turned and gave her such a look of dismay that she laughed. "I mean with the proper equipment. The gardeners could bring their tools and—"

"No," he said. "I want to do this myself. Alone. I know this is your land, and anything I find belongs to you, but please"—he gave her an imploring look—"let me be the one to dig it up?"

Any objections she still held faded before the look of raw pleading in his face. "Goodness, if it means that much to you. But you will have to find a way to do it secretly."

"A shovel and a pick is all I need," he said. "I can walk over with them—it's not that far."

"You can do that tomorrow—if you attend to your studies today."

"I will be a model pupil," he promised.

"We should go back to the house. We have to make our inspection tour, and that will take time."

Sighing, he shoved the trowel back in his pocket and brushed the dirt off his knees.

"You are right." He helped her on her horse and then, with a long, wistful look at the mound, remounted and rode beside her back toward Ashbridge.

Adrian chaffed at having to wait until the next day to go back and start his excavations. He wanted to be out there tonight, digging by lantern light if he had to. But without Rose's help, he wouldn't be able to get the things that he needed. He was totally in her power now.

They ate in the morning room, then Adrian dutifully followed Rose as she led him through the house. She started with the public rooms, with their sumptuous decor and regal appointments. But what had astounded him yesterday appeared only mildly interesting now. His mind was focused on simpler ornaments from a much older era.

"Are you paying attention to anything I say?" Rose asked with obvious exasperation after he nodded amiably for the fifth time.

"Of course. This is the Crimson Saloon, so called because of the wall coverings, which came from Brussels. The room was entirely redone when your—my—grandfather succeeded to the dukedom and has been left in a careful state of preservation ever since."

She cast him a suspicious look. "You sound as if you have been reading a guidebook."

"I?" He regarded her with an innocent expression. She didn't need to know that he'd happened upon just such a volume in the library last night, and had studied it intently while she worked on her maps and lists. He wanted her to think he was paying rapt attention to every word she was saying.

"Oh, never mind. Let me give you a quick look at the dining room—we'll eat there tonight—and then I'll show you the rest of the family apartments."

"Don't forget the attics—and the servants' quarters."

"You don't need to look there," she said.

"I bet you and your brother thoroughly explored both places when you were young."

"Yes—when we were children. Neither place matters to Simon now. Now do pay attention . . ."

Adrian had to admit he was growing rather tired of it all by the time they came back to the private wing. He didn't see the need to examine each and every empty bedroom. They all looked the same.

Rose's room was the only one that interested him.

"We have not yet seen your room," he reminded her.

"Of course," she responded dryly, and pushed open the door. Adrian stepped inside.

It was a pleasant room—bright, airy, and feminine without being fussy. No gilded cherubs or flocked wallpaper here—the walls were done in a dark blue with white plasterwork. The curtains, bed hangings, even the chairs, were all upholstered in blue-patterned fabrics. Lady Rose was obviously fond of that color.

He crossed to the window and looked out. The view was of the park, looking toward the east and sunrise—a pleasant scene.

"A nice room," he said. He saw the door on the far wall and remembered his curiosity from the day before—did Rose have a luxurious bathing-tub like her brother's? He wanted to know—yet hesitated—a lady's bath chamber was a private matter. But she was showing him the room.

He headed for the door and pulled it open. He felt a strange lurch in his midsection at what he saw.

He had been right.

"Modern plumbing, I see."

"Simon's idea," she replied.

"Lady Juliet will probably be glad of that." He turned to exit. "Which room is to be hers?"

"This one, probably."

He looked at her, puzzled. "But this is your room."

"And it is my brother's house, and his wife will be mistress here."

"She will not throw you out of your own room, will she?"

"I probably will not be living here much longer, anyway."

Her words startled him. "Where are you going?"

"As Simon's unmarried sister, I would only be in the way. A house can have only one mistress. It would not be fair to Juliet for me to remain here."

"But where shall you live?"

"Oh, I will marry and have a house of my own."

"But I thought . . ."

"That I did not want to marry? I believe that was *your* accusation. Of course, I wish to marry."

He saw the glint of anger in her eyes. "What other future is there for a woman? I do not think I am suited for eccentric spinsterhood."

"So you will be looking for a husband while we are in London." The idea made him uncomfortable. He thought Rose would be constantly at his side, to ensure that he did not make any missteps. But if she had her own plans . . .

"Yes."

He forced a grin. "Well, remember that any potential suitors must present themselves to me first. As your *brother* and head of the family, you will need my approval to marry."

She laughed. "You do sound exactly like Simon."

"I thought that was the idea."

"Yes." A shadow crossed her face, and Adrian realized she must be missing her brother.

"I'm sure he will come home soon," Adrian said. "Probably

the day we arrive in London, and all your work will be for naught."

"I hope so." She looked at him again, and the mask of well-trained politeness had descended over her face again. "I will show you the rest of the floor."

As he followed her out the door, Adrian saw, for the first time, that Lady Rose might not be so enamored of her life as he first thought she was.

He was sure that in many households, a newly wed couple would gladly share their life with the groom's sister. But for someone like Rose, for whom this had been her house, her responsibility for so long, it would be a strong blow to hand over the reins of power to another. And hand them over she must; she was right—a house could not have two mistresses.

She was forced to find a husband—and a house—of her own. She could do little else.

And they both knew her marriage options were limited—only certain men were suitable for the daughter of a duke. The very fact that she had not yet wed meant that she must not be overly fond of any of them. But marry she must—and soon.

Adrian shrugged. It was the way of her class, after all. Marriages were not contracted for love, but for money. She had been raised with that knowledge. She could only hope to find a man who would generously share his wealth, give her a family to raise, and not cause a public scandal.

The very thought of such a marriage made Adrian shudder. His own mother had fled from just such an arrangement. He did not wish that on Rose.

But she had delayed marriage for as long as she could. Now she had to make her choice.

He hoped it would be a happy one for her. She deserved that much.

Chapter 8

∽

In the morning, after Rose finished discussing the day's menus with the cook, she went in search of Stamford. He had behaved with perfect composure at dinner last night, not giving a hint that he was unaccustomed to dining off the finest French porcelain and heavy silver plate, with dutiful servants hovering at his elbow. He had looked every bit the noble duke.

As his reward, she would make good on yesterday's promise and let him explore that mound.

Rose half expected him to be hovering at her elbow all morning, urging her to hurry through her duties so he could return to the field. In fact, after a time, his absence began to make her suspicious. What was he doing?

She grew more suspicious when she did not find him in either his room or the library. On a hunch, she walked out to the stables. Yes, the duke and his valet had been there at the crack of dawn and taken out horses.

Fuming, Rose raced back to the house. She knew exactly where Stamford had gone. And when she got her hands on him . . . She had told him not to go *anywhere* without her. He was deliberately ignoring her admonition. Again. She changed quickly into her riding habit, returned to the stables, and rode off after him.

Rose retraced their route of yesterday and guided her horse through the trees that separated the far fields. Even before she caught a glimpse of Stamford, she heard his voice, the clunk of shovel on earth—and the voice of another man, as well.

She burst through the trees and galloped up to the mound, reining in her horse as the two men turned and stared at her.

Stamford, stripped to his shirt, the sleeves rolled up, looked like a small boy caught with a stolen treat from the kitchen. Beside him, she assumed, was the valet he had enlisted as his accomplice in crime.

"Caught red-handed." Stamford looked properly sheepish. "I thought you would be busy all morning."

"*Simon.*" She put heavy emphasis on the name. "You know we intended to discuss the guest list for the wedding before you came out here."

He waved his hand in the air. "Oh, you know whom we should invite. If I find you've left anyone important off the list, I will add their name."

She glared at him. The man was impossible! He knew she did not dare upbraid him in front of the footman.

"Have you found anything interesting?" she asked icily.

"Not yet—but we are getting close." He held out his hand to her. "Stay awhile—you might be here for a big discovery."

"If she finds dirt exciting," the valet mumbled.

Stamford shot him a dampening look, and the man grabbed his shovel. Rose dismounted, and Stamford spread his coat on the grass for her to sit upon.

"As you can see, we have cleared off most of the covering at this end," he said. "It is definitely a man-made structure underneath, not solid rock. But I cannot tell yet if there is anything inside."

"What do you expect to find?" she asked, curious in spite of herself.

"Bones, most likely," Stamford replied.

Rose shivered and started to get to her feet. "No thank you, I do not want—"

He put out a hand. "Sit. I don't intend to disturb anyone's rest. I am looking only for the possessions buried alongside."

"Like that piece of grandfather's you were so interested in?"

He nodded. "I will never find anything that grand, of course, but there could be some simple necklaces of jet and amber, or even pearl. And tools of worked bronze, if I guess right."

She looked doubtfully at the grass-covered mound. "In there?"

"More likely the rubbish pile from some long-gone house," Roberts said.

Stamford spread his hands. "See what I have to put up with? My own valet, a skeptic."

He turned back to his shovel. "Of course, someone could have come along over the centuries and stripped the place bare. But it is worth a look."

As she watched him dig, Rose was struck by how intently he worked, mind and body focused on the task, much as he had been when going through her grandfather's ledger. She had never seen Simon so absorbed in a purposeful occupation. Stamford might share her brother's teasing humor, but he showed a far more serious side as well.

Of course, Stamford was a Latin teacher. She must expect him to be serious at times.

It did look as if he had uncovered something. As the two men continued to strip away the grass and dirt, she saw the piled stones lying beneath. Someone had built the structure, although she doubted it was the exotic grave site he anticipated. More likely a long-forgotten stretch of Roman wall—or a rock pile from clearing the field.

"Enough," Stamford said and stepped back. The grassy end of the hump was now gone, replaced by a wall of neatly piled stone.

"Is that it?" she asked.

He nodded. "Now we have to break through to the inside."

Roberts picked up his shovel and made to push it at the rocks, but Stamford caught his wrist. "Not like that—we could cave the whole end in, and then we would really have to dig."

Starting at the top of the wall, Stamford began testing the stones, checking for loose ones. Grabbing the trowel, he wedged it between a gap and pulled out a long, flat stone about twice the size of his hand. It left a small gap in the wall.

"What is behind it?" Rose asked eagerly.

"Can't tell yet." He pulled a few more stones free and then carefully stuck his hand into the widened gap.

"Empty space!" he cried in jubilation. He shoved his full arm into the opening, and Rose gritted her teeth, afraid the stones would fall, crushing his arm.

He quickly and carefully enlarged the hole. Rose came closer, caught up in the excitement of what he would find.

"How are you going to see what is inside?" she asked.

"Did you think I would not have prepared for that?" Stamford flashed her a wry grin. "Candles, my dear."

After some work, he cleared an opening the size of a dinner plate. Lighting a candle, he stuck it through the opening and peered inside.

Rose tried to look over his shoulder. "What do you see?"

"Nothing."

"Nothing?" She sat back on her heels in disappointment. "It's empty?"

"The floor is covered with rubble; it could be just rocks. I need to open the entire end before I can get a good look."

"Start to work then. I want to know!"

He cocked a teasing brow. "I thought you said this was a foolish waste of time."

Rose felt color rise to her cheeks. "I take it back, Simon. I would like to see what is inside."

"I should have something to show you by tomorrow."

"Tomorrow?" Rose looked at him with dismay. She wanted to find out now.

"Didn't you say you needed to work on the guest list for the wedding? I do not want to keep you from your task."

"That can be done later. I want to see what you find."

"It must be close to noon," Stamford said. "You must be hungry."

"Food?" Rose shook her head. "This is far more exciting. Send Roberts for something to eat. And lanterns, so you will have better light. Do you want more men to help dig?"

Stamford looked at her with a startled expression, then burst out laughing. "Rose, Rose, you never cease to amaze me."

She glared at him. "Why? Didn't you think I would find it interesting?"

To her annoyance, he did not reply.

Roberts departed on his errand, and Rose sat down on Stamford's coat again, watching as he carefully worked to widen the opening.

She envied him his passion for his work. Rose could not think of a single activity that would have absorbed her attention like this. She wondered what had sparked his interest. His father? A teacher?

"How did you become so interested in ancient ruins?" she asked.

"My father. He collected spear points when he was a lad and encouraged me to do the same."

"Did he dig things up as well?"

Stamford shook his head. "That is my particular interest."

"Is that why you are teaching Latin? So you can have time to dig?"

"Partly."

"Have you ever found anything valuable?"

"I am not interested in making money from this—I want to study these people—who they were and how they lived their lives. There is so much we don't know. Not very many men are interested in studying the ancient Britons. I correspond with a few of them. We trade information about our findings."

It sounded fascinating to Rose. Much more interesting—and useful—than following horse racing or the boxing matches, which were Simon's main interests.

"What do you do with the things you find?"

Stamford grunted with effort as he pulled out an extra large slab of rock, then inspected the opening. "There—that looks big enough to try."

Rose gave the hole a doubtful look. It did not look big enough for him to crawl through.

"Shouldn't you wait until Roberts comes back?"

"I just want to take a look." He lit another candle and holding it in front of him, he carefully crawled over the pile of rubble.

Rose's breath caught as he inched his way into the tomb. Soon, only the soles of his boots were sticking out. She felt a stab of fear. He should not be doing this by himself. What if something happened?

"Come back out," she cried.

"It's all right," came his muffled reply.

Rose crept closer, afraid, yet infected by his enthusiasm. She tried to peer through the hole, but she saw only his white shirt and the faint glow from the candle.

"Did you find anything?" she asked.

"Hang on, I'm coming out."

She moved away, watching his slow progress as he literally crawled backward through the opening. The top of his boots had just emerged from the hole when the stone walls on either side collapsed, covering his legs in a pile of rocks.

Rose screamed and grabbed for his foot. Coughing and choking in the swirling dust, she scrabbled at the still-shifting pile of rubble, trying to free his legs.

"Can you hear me?" she cried. The only reply was the sound of trickling dirt.

Terrified that he was trapped, Rose frantically shoved rocks aside. The rough-edged stones cut through the soft leather of her riding gloves, scratching her hands. She ignored the pain and dug at the pile. She had to free him quickly, but feared she would not be able to.

Please let me work faster.

Her heart leaped when she saw one of his legs move, then she screamed again when another section of wall collapsed. She scrabbled at the pile.

"Are you all right?" she cried. "Can you hear me?"

He groaned in faint reply.

"Don't move—I am digging you out as fast as I can."

She would never forgive herself if he was hurt. She was the

one who insisted that he continue working. If only she had made him wait until Roberts came back.

Stamford moved again, inching slowly toward her. His thighs, then his torso slowly emerged from the hole, covered with dirt and small pebbles.

"Tell me when I'm free," he gasped as he continued to crawl backward over the fallen rubble.

She watched anxiously until his head was free. "You are out!" She nearly cried with relief.

He slowly rose up and sank back onto his heels. His face was streaked with dirt, and a thin trickle of blood dribbled down his temple.

"You're hurt!"

He put a hand to his head and drew it away, looking with bemusement at his bloodstained fingers.

"Rock," he mumbled.

Rose grabbed his arm and pulled him back onto the grass, where he stretched out wearily.

"Lie still." Kneeling beside him, she took her handkerchief and dabbed at the cut. "You scared me." Her voice was quavering, but she did not care.

"I scared myself, too," he said.

"Does anything hurt?"

He groaned. "My entire body."

"Do you think anything is broken?"

Stamford carefully moved each limb and joint. "I think everything is all right."

"You need a doctor."

"It is not that bad," he said. "I will be all right in a few minutes. Just shaken up, that's all."

"Roberts should be back soon. I shall send him to bring the cart to take you home."

He groaned again. "I feel as if I have been run over by a wagon." He grabbed her hand, and she winched.

"What have you done to yourself?" Stamford took her bruised and battered hands in his.

"It is nothing." Rose pulled one hand away and brushed back

his dirt-streaked hair, then dabbed at the cut on his forehead again. "You are very lucky."

"Or damn unlucky. It will take more work to clear away that mess."

Rose stared at him, horrified. "You aren't thinking of going back in there?"

He nodded. "Of course I am. Only the one end collapsed."

"And what if the entire roof comes tumbling down the next time? You will be squashed flat."

"That might prove bothersome," he admitted, closing his eyes. "When your brother returns, he would literally have to come back from the dead."

"Oh, do be serious!"

Looking down at him, Rose realized that she had not given that complication a thought. She had only been worried about this particular man. She glanced down at his hand, still clutching hers, resting in her lap. An enormous sense of relief filled her.

"I intend to take better care of you," she said softly.

His eyes flickered open. "Rosemary for protection. I like that."

She shifted on the grass. "Rest your head on my lap, Mr. Stamford. You will be more comfortable."

"Adrian," he said, as he readjusted his position. "I think after all that you can call me Adrian." His eyes drifted closed again.

Adrian. Rose felt strangely protective about this interesting man. Was it because she'd played a hand in his rescue? Or sheer relief that he was now safe?

Or was it because she now thought of him as a friend?

The sound of approaching hoofbeats reached her ears. She looked up and saw Roberts emerge from the woods. Rose knew he should not see her and Adrian like this, then she remembered. Roberts thought this was Simon. He did not know it was really Adrian Stamford she sat guard over.

Roberts jumped off his horse. "What happened?"

"The end of the tomb collapsed. Simon was hit in the head with a rock. Go back to the stables and get the cart."

"I can ride," Stamford mumbled.

"No, you can't," Rose said sternly. "And send someone for the doctor. I want to make certain he is all right."

Roberts was back on his horse racing away before she could even draw another breath.

"Bully," Adrian said cheerfully.

"Fool," she replied.

"You want to protect your investment," he said.

"Exactly. So I expect you to obey without causing a fuss."

He lay his head back in her lap and closed his eyes again. "I don't mind. You know, for the first time, I really envy your brother."

Rose looked at him. "Why?"

"Because if I didn't look like him, you would not let me lie here with my head in your lap."

Had the man been reading her thoughts?

"It is only natural that your *sister* would want to comfort you," she said, trying to keep her voice even. She didn't want him to know how shaken she was—not only by the accident, but by the realization of how nice it felt to sit with him like this.

"Are you hungry?" she asked finally. "I could get something from your basket."

"Not if it means you will move," he said. "I am content to stay here."

"The cart should be here soon."

"I know."

"Adrian?"

He opened his eyes. "Yes?"

"I'm really very glad you were not badly hurt."

"So am I."

"What did you see inside—before the end caved in?"

He laughed. "Eager to add more loot to the family coffers?"

"No!" she protested with vehemence. "How could you think that. It is only . . . well, you did say you saw *something*."

"It looked like bones, mostly."

"You mean someone really was buried there?"

He nodded. "It could be a good find. But I won't know until I go back inside."

"Which you are not going to do until the doctor has said you may," she warned him.

"I'm fine," he protested. "Why, I would be cavorting across the grass if I wasn't so comfortable lying here like this."

His grey eyes caught hers. She held his gaze for a moment, then looked away, afraid he might see something more than she wanted him to in her eyes.

She liked him. In spite of, or perhaps because, he teased her and argued with her and refused to treat her with the deference she was accustomed to from others. Rose suspected he might be the only person in the country who would deal with her honestly.

She appreciated that.

But that was all it was—appreciation. Adrian Stamford was a country schoolteacher, after all. If he wanted to forget she was the daughter of a duke, she could not.

Voices sounded in the distance, and she saw the head groom riding toward them, followed by the hay cart. Rose smothered a smile. What a blow to a duke's dignity—carried to the house in a hay cart. Simon would have had a conniption.

Adrian, she knew, would find it amusing.

"They are coming." Rose instantly regretted telling him when he sat up to watch the cart's approach.

"I see I am to be carried back to the house in ducal splendor."

"The carriage could never get through the woods."

"I've traveled on worse than a hay cart before," he said with a grin.

"This is probably a first time for *Simon*." She gave him a wry look and they both laughed.

To Adrian's dismay, the doctor was waiting at the stables when they returned.

"I'm all right," he protested as he climbed down from the cart.

"He cut his head," Rose told the surgeon. "And was buried

under a pile of rocks. I want you to examine him and make sure he is all right."

"Your Grace, if we could go into the house?" The doctor beckoned him forward, and reluctantly, Adrian followed.

Half an hour later, after enduring an endless round of poking and prodding, the doctor pronounced him fit, treated the cut on his forehead, and advised him to keep out of rock piles in the future.

Adrian intended to ignore that command.

Bathed and dried, dressed in clean clothes, with an annoying piece of sticking plaster on his forehead, Adrian went to find Rose. He was surprised, since she was the one who acted so worried, that she had not been hanging over the doctor's shoulder during the entire examination. Perhaps she realized she could only push him so far.

But he was damn glad she had been there to save him. And he had liked the way she had cradled his head in her lap. That had been worth all the trouble and pain. For a short time, she had treated him like an equal.

He wondered how long that attitude would last. Had he really broken through her barriers, or was it only a temporary lapse on her part, brought about by the shock of the accident?

Only time would tell. But he hoped it would last. He was beginning to think fondly of Lady Rose.

Following a servant's lead, he went outside to search for her. He found her, eventually, in the rose garden, sitting on a stone bench beneath a flowered arbor.

"What are you doing out here?" She jumped to her feet when she saw him. "Shouldn't you be lying down? What did the doctor say?"

"He said that I am a healthy young man who can endure a minor bump on the head, and that you wouldn't waste so much time worrying about me if you had your own family to raise."

She paled and turned away. "Did he really say that?"

Adrian stepped toward her. "If it makes you feel better, he told me to stay out of ancient mounds."

"And will you obey him?"

"Of course not. I'm ready to go back."

"No!"

The adamant tone in her voice surprised him. "I don't intend to go alone—Roberts will be there."

She lay a hand on his arm. "Adrian, please. Not today. I . . . well, it was rather frightening to see you buried like that. I should like to be free from worrying about you for the rest of the day, at least."

Her words took him by surprise. She almost sounded as if . . . as if she cared about him.

Which was ridiculous. He'd frightened her, that was all. He'd almost frightened himself, in fact. If she had not been there . . .

"I haven't properly thanked you for rescuing me." He took her hand and strolled with her along the graveled path that wound between the beds of fragrant roses. "I am grateful."

She nodded. "I am glad I was there."

They continued walking down the path.

"What will you do with . . . with anything you find inside the mound?" Rose asked.

"Give it to you, of course."

"I mean, is there some society or group that would be interested in what you discover?"

"I am not sure." Adrian hesitated. Would she laugh if he told her his ambition? It might sound insignificant to a duke's daughter. But somehow, after today, he thought she might understand.

"I have been trying to get the Antiquities Society to print my articles about my discoveries in Wiltshire, but they keep sending me polite rejections. Perhaps with a new discovery . . ."

Rose stopped and looked at him, her eyes bright with excitement. "What if the Duke of Alston approached them . . . ?"

"Then the Duke of Alston will get credit for the discovery."

"Oh."

They continued walking. He gave her a sideways glance and saw her brow furrowed in concentration.

"Does the society have an office in London? Couldn't you approach them yourself when we are in the city?"

"I plan to do that. But they still may not be interested in the work of Adrian Stamford."

She grabbed his sleeve. "If you go to them with a letter from the duke, they are certain to pay attention then!"

He laughed. "You mean I should write my own letter of recommendation?"

"Exactly! I know Simon would not object."

Adrian regarded her thoughtfully. "Lady Rose, that may be the most practical suggestion I've ever heard you make."

To his surprise, she smiled at his praise.

Adrian felt a surprising surge of gratitude for her suggestion. Perhaps he had breached that wall of aristocratic reserve after all.

Chapter 9

〜

When Adrian walked out to the stables in the morning, he took one look at the group of men assembled there and turned to Rose.

"I am not taking this mob to the site," he said flatly.

She crossed her arms over her chest and gave him an equally stern look. "I do not want a repeat of yesterday's disaster."

"A disaster is what you will have with this many people milling about," Adrian protested. "Roberts may come if he wishes. The rest of the men can go back to work."

"Simon . . ."

Adrian heard her warning tone, but realized, with sudden glee, that there was nothing she could do to prevent him from doing exactly as he pleased. He was the *duke*, after all.

He pointed to the last man in line. "You—what's your job?"

"Assistant gardener Jacobs, Your Grace."

"So you know how to dig holes?"

The man nodded.

"You may come, Jacobs. The rest of you go back to whatever it is you are supposed to be doing." Adrian gave Rose a smug look. "Do you intend to come with us, Sister dear?"

"I wouldn't miss it for the *world*," Rose replied.

Adrian knew he would hear about his actions when they were next alone. But if all went as he planned today, that would be many hours from now.

He and Rose rode out to the site while Roberts and the gardener followed with the cart. Rose had ordered it filled with shovels, picks, food, and water. They would not lack for a thing.

A shudder went through him when he saw the pile of rubble in front of the mound. That had been a close call yesterday. If Rose had not been here . . .

But she had, so today his first concern was clearing a new opening. More rocks had fallen during the night, and the entry was nearly blocked. Plenty of work to do.

He handed his jacket to Rose, who gave him an anxious look.

"You're not planning on digging, are you? Let the men take care of that."

"I can't expect them to do my work for me." Adrian rolled up his sleeves.

She frowned, but said nothing more and settled herself in the shade of the cart, pulled out a book, and studiously ignored him.

The three men worked to shovel away the rockfall at the entrance to the tomb. That accomplished, Adrian insisted they widen the rest of the opening by hand. He didn't want an errant shovel to accidentally destroy a valuable artifact.

"Perhaps you should like to rest now?"

Rose's voice burst into his thoughts.

Adrian wiped the sweat from his brow and glanced over at Rose, who appeared enviously comfortable in her shady retreat. He looked back at their work—the entire end was nearly cleared away; the piled stone side walls of the tomb could be seen emerging from the turf.

He could not wait to get inside again and get a good look at what was there. But Roberts and Jacobs had already walked over to Rose, gratefully accepting the jugs of water she handed them. With a sigh at the delay, Adrian joined them.

"We're making good progress," he told her. "I will be able to get back inside soon."

"But what if the roof collapses? Shouldn't you tear down the entire mound?"

"That might destroy what's inside."

"I'll go in for you, Your Grace," Roberts said bravely.

Adrian clapped him on the shoulder. "It's good of you to offer, but this is something I must do myself."

"Promise you will be careful!" Rose exclaimed.

"Why, Sister dear, I didn't know you cared." Adrian flashed her a teasing smile, but it faded as he saw the apprehensive look in her eyes. She actually looked as if she cared what happened to *him*.

Yesterday, he thought she did. But he was not as certain today. She had other reasons to want him safe. Without him, her whole plan to fool London society and Lady Juliet would fall apart.

What was he to her? A needed employee—or a newly found friend?

He scrambled to his feet. "Time to get back to work."

Within fifteen minutes, the opening was wide enough to suit even Rose's cautious nature. Roberts lit a lantern, and Adrian held it before him, peering into the hole. The neatly stacked rocks along the side held the lintel stones forming the roof. Despite his reassurances to Rose, he had not been certain that the interior was stable, but it looked safe enough.

Someone jostled his arm. He turned around to find Rose edging closer.

"What do you see?" she asked.

He handed her the lantern. "Look for yourself."

She backed away, shaking her head. "You said there are bones inside."

Adrian laughed. "Afraid of ghosts?" He took the lantern from her and crawled into the tomb, pulling a bucket behind him.

Rose held her breath as she watched Adrian disappear inside the mound, fearing it would again collapse on him. She jumped at every sound he made and sighed with relief when he backed out again.

He sat at the entrance, bent over the bucket he'd taken with him, picking through the contents.

"Jacobs?"

"Your Grace?"

"Bring me that box in the cart—the large wooden one." The gardener ran to do his bidding and set the box beside Adrian.

"What's that for?" Rose asked.

"Bones," Adrian replied.

"You mean that"—she pointed a shaky finger at the blackened lump he held—"is part of a skeleton?"

He nodded. "Don't worry, I will rebury any remains I find."

She shivered. "It is not wise to disturb the dead."

"This fellow's been here a long time," Adrian replied. "I don't think he much cares."

"We could ask the vicar! He would be willing to preside over an interment." Rose suddenly remembered how old Adrian said this tomb was. "Was this person even a Christian?"

Adrian laughed. "I doubt it. More likely he worshipped stones or trees or some local god. I don't think we need to bring the vicar into it."

Rose agreed. The vicar might raise a fuss over reburying pagan remains.

With growing interest, she watched him sift through the remaining contents of the bucket. He put one or two fragments into the box, and tossed everything else aside. Rose looked at the growing heap of debris with disappointment.

"Is that all that is in there? Dirt and a few bones?"

"Have patience," he said. "I've barely started."

Exasperated by his slow progress, Rose went back to her shady spot by the cart and tried to concentrate on her book. But she kept looking up every few minutes, to make certain that everything was going smoothly. A pattern soon developed— Adrian crawled into the hole, and she held her breath until he safely came out again. He would sort through his bucket, then go back in. She heard no loud cries of triumph, so she assumed he was not finding anything of great interest—or value.

Why did he find poking about in a dark hole so fascinating? It looked to be a dirty, laborious, and horridly dangerous pastime. Yet for his sake, she hoped he would find something important; something he could use to impress the Antiquities

Society in London. She wanted Adrian to be a success, to earn the recognition he wanted, that he deserved.

When she next looked up, Adrian was sitting cross-legged on the grass, his head bent in concentration over an object in his hand. She saw the look of growing excitement on his face and hurried over.

"What did you find?" Rose plopped down beside him.

He handed her a small lump of metal, flat-sided and flared at one end. She examined the unusual-looking piece. "I have no idea what this is."

"It's an axe head—bronze, I suspect."

Rose turned the object over in her hand. "What happened to the handle?"

He looked amused. "The wood rotted away over the years."

"Oh." Rose felt foolish. "Is it an important find?"

He shrugged. "It's old. But not that rare."

Rose felt a surprising sting of disappointment at his words. She wanted him to find something really spectacular, like the torque in grandfather's glass cabinet.

"Is there anything else left in there?"

"I have only searched half the tomb," he replied.

"Well, then get back to it." Rose spoke more sharply than she intended, eliciting a laugh from Adrian.

"Why, *Sister*. Does this mean you are a tiny bit interested in what I am doing?"

"Of course I'm interested." She glared at him indignantly. "Why else would I spend the day out here? It is not for lack of anything else to do."

He bowed. "My apologies. I will try to hurry my pace to suit your enthusiasm."

"But carefully," she cautioned as he ducked back to the tomb.

Each time he disappeared from view, Rose's breath caught, and she did not breathe easily again until he reappeared. Each minute seemed like ten while he was out of her sight. When his head emerged from the hole, she let out a long exhalation of breath.

"I think I've found something you will like," he called to her.

Rose ran over. He handed her a curved metal ring, thick around as her finger, open on one side.

"It looks like a small version of Grandfather's torque," she said excitedly, her finger tracing the curved shape.

"I think it's a bracelet." Adrian took it from her and swished it in a pan of water, loosening the dirt, then scrubbed and polished it with a rag. The ancient metal, a mottled green and brown, began to give off a dull gleam.

Adrian took her hand and slipped the bracelet over her wrist.

"I only wish it was mine to give to you." He spoke softly, so only she could hear.

She threw him a startled glance. His grey eyes held her with a wistful look that sent a small shiver up her spine. Quickly, she looked away and ran her finger over the surprisingly smooth metal of the bracelet.

It *was* a gift. She never intended to lay claim to anything that he found. A gift she would value always, because it came from Adrian. Given not because he was trying to impress or entice her, but as a token of their friendship.

Friendship. That was what they shared, of course. From their uneasy relationship those first few days at the hunting lodge, she and Adrian had settled into a companionable existence. Like that of close friends.

Which was all they would—could—ever be.

"It's lovely," she mumbled. "Thank you."

Adrian felt decidedly unbrotherly toward Lady Rose at the moment. He dropped her hand and quickly turned back to other objects he'd pulled out of the mound. Wiping centuries of encrusted grime from an axe head would help clear his thoughts.

If she had not insisted on coming with him, or had not watched the work so eagerly, he might have been able to ignore her. But she had shown great interest in his work—and rejoiced in his find—demonstrating once again that she was not the arrogant aristocrat he once thought her. It had been easy not to like that person. But the real Rose, the one behind the aristocratic mask, was a very likable person.

Too likable. Adrian found it far too easy to think of her as a *woman*—an attractive, desirable woman, whom he admired and wanted for—

He shook his head. Adrian Stamford had no business thinking about the daughter of a duke that way, no matter how friendly she was to him. The outward barriers between them had come down, but the invisible ones were still there, as high and wide as ever.

He had to remember that. And remember that when his task was done, he would be going back to Buckleigh Manor, while she lived her life among the highest levels of society.

Two hours later, he finally finished searching through the tomb. To his earlier finds, he added two more axe heads, several metal rings, and some bits of metal whose purpose he could only guess at. The bracelet was the only piece of jewelry he found.

All in all, a minor excavation, but still important, because it was *his* discovery. Adrian felt certain that the tomb had not been previously disturbed. Already, his mind mulled over the words he would put on paper for the Antiquities Society.

He needed to make sketches of his finds tonight. Perhaps this evening, after dinner, if Rose had no plans for him.

When he finished putting every piece that looked like bone in the box, Adrian crawled back into the tomb one last time to leave it there.

"Shouldn't we say a few words?" Rose asked when he'd wriggled out.

Adrian cleared his throat and looked at the tomb. "We restore you to your eternal place of rest. May whatever gods you worshipped watch over you."

She arched a brow. "I suspect the vicar would *not* approve."

He grinned.

They rode together back to the house, parting in the hall. Adrian went upstairs to scrub off the grime from his explorations; Rose to change her dress.

* * *

Later, in the library, Rose watched with renewed interest while Adrian set out his finds on the large table and began to thoroughly clean them. She fingered the bracelet that still encircled her wrist while he chipped with a penknife at the centuries of encrusted dirt on an axe head.

"Do you have to do this to every piece that you find?" she asked.

"Usually. Some pieces are so begrimed that I have to soak them overnight before I can get anything off."

"What do you do with them afterward?"

"I sketch everything I find, then add them to my collection."

She shook her head. "Sketching is one thing I could never do. My governess despaired at my lack of artistic talent."

"You were taught by a governess?" he asked, looking surprised.

"You didn't think I went to Eton, did you?" She laughed.

"Would you have liked to?"

"Go away to school?" Rose wrinkled her nose. "Not at all. It was much nicer being at home."

"Didn't you find it lonely?"

She shrugged. "At times. But Simon was here often enough. What about you? Did you go to school?"

He grunted.

"Where?"

"Not Eton."

"Thank goodness. If you had, everyone would know about you and Simon, and we'd never be able to carry out this masquerade."

"What sort of things does a lady learn from a governess?" he asked.

"I can speak French, and a little Italian. And sew, and play the piano. I studied geography, history, and mathematics. Not a man's education, of course, but more than some other ladies I know."

"What?" He gave her a teasing look. "No Latin or Greek?"

"I never had any interest in learning either." She smiled ruefully. "You probably think that makes me woefully uneducated."

"Not at all," he replied. "I wish I had a European language. There are several antiquarians whose writings I would like to study, but I have to wait until they are translated into English."

"Tell me about your students. How many do you have?"

"Only two. The Topmore twins. Terrors, both of them."

"Only two?" Rose realized he must not make a great deal of money if he only had two pupils. She hated the thought of Adrian being, well, poor. Surely, if he was a good teacher, he could find a better job.

"Wouldn't you rather be teaching at a school, instead?"

"I do not want the restrictions of a full-time teaching position," he replied. "I would not be able to search for antiquities as often."

"But you must not earn very much . . ."

"I have enough to live on. I lead a simple life."

"Tell me about it. What is your house like?"

"Cottage is a better description." He laughed. "I remember the day I arrived at that lesser hunting box and realized it would swallow the place whole. But it is a nice size for one person."

"Do you do your own cooking and cleaning?"

He shook his head. "A woman from the village comes in and takes care of that. She cooks for me three nights a week, and I make do the other nights."

"Do you ever get lonely, living by yourself?"

He shrugged. "I have found that one can be just as lonely surrounded by other people."

Rose realized she had felt that way sometimes in London. The sudden feeling, even in the middle of a dance, that she was alone—the sense of isolation in the midst of a crowded theater box. The longing for someone with whom she could share her most intimate thoughts and dreams.

She looked at Adrian, head bent over his work. He may not have the luxuries she accepted as matter of course, but he was happy with his life.

Much happier, she thought, than she was with hers. She envied him that.

He finished cleaning the last piece from the tomb and set it aside, reaching for pencil and paper to start his sketch.

"I wish I could draw," she said wistfully. "I would like to be able to help you."

Adrian smiled at her. "How is your penmanship?"

"Excellent."

"Good. I will need you to copy my paper when I finish it. Everyone says my handwriting is abominable."

That confession, and the offer, brought a smile to her face. There was something she could do to help him. She only wished she could do more.

A strange restlessness plagued Adrian the next day. It was understandable that he would be somewhat downcast after the previous day's excitement, but that was not all. What really bothered him was his growing attraction to Lady Rosemary Devering. An attraction that was as foolish as it was inappropriate. They lived in two very different worlds.

They had been thrown together, alone, for too long. That was the reason. It would be better in London when they would be among company much of the time. All his concentration would be focused on playing Alston; he would not have time to dwell on thoughts of Rose.

Or so he hoped.

By the time he joined Rose for tea in the library, he had his emotions firmly in check.

As she handed him his cup, Markham appeared at the door. "Lord Felton is here, Your Grace."

Rose jumped to her feet and raced to her uncle, an anxious expression on her face. "Simon? Is there news?"

He shook his head.

Adrian's pulse quickened. They would want him to go to London now. The thought brought a brief flare of panic. He did not want to go; he wanted to say here, at Ashbridge, with Rose. Where it was peaceful—and private.

Felton marched over to the table, and Adrian rose to greet him. The earl's gaze raked him from head to toe.

"Well, you're looking a mite better than when I saw you last, Stamford. Taking to the ducal life, are you?"

Determined not to be intimidated, Adrian regarded him with disdain. "Really, Uncle, life at Ashbridge is tedious in the extreme."

Felton stared at him in stunned surprise, then guffawed loudly and turned to Rose.

"Sounds exactly like your brother, don't he? You've done a good job with the lad." He sat down. "It's a good thing, for we need to be off to town at once."

"What?" Rose stared at him. "What is wrong?"

"Oh, Ramsey's kicking up a dust—quietly, of course—about Simon ignoring his daughter. Thought I should come down and collect you two before he starts complaining openly."

Over his head, Adrian exchanged an uneasy glance with Rose. He still did not feel comfortable about fooling Lady Juliet.

"That was fine timing, having the lodge burn down like that," Felton continued. "Provided a good excuse for Simon staying in the country."

"You make it sound as if we burned it on purpose," Rose said with a shudder. "It was the most ghastly thing. Why, if it hadn't been for Ad—Mr. Stamford—we all would have burned in our beds."

The earl darted Adrian a skeptical glance. "Played the hero, did you? Well, I'll see that Simon offers you a suitable reward."

"That is not necessary," Adrian said.

Felton turned back to Rose. "So, my dear, can you be ready to leave on the morrow?"

"Tomorrow!" Rose shook her head. "Absolutely not. It will take days to pack. I should say it will be Friday, at the least, before—"

"The day after tomorrow and no later," Felton said. "Simon has to make an appearance in town as soon as possible. As do you." He gave her a pointed look. "I'm constantly accosted by your admirers, asking when you will be arriving."

Rose shrugged lightly.

Her uncle's eyes twinkled. "Don't you want to know who has been asking after you?"

"Not particularly." Rose stood. "I must tell Cook there will be another for dinner, and I will have the footmen bring the trunks down from the attic and set the maids to packing." She glared at her uncle. "Why do you always spring these surprises on me?"

Spine straight, she walked out of the room.

Felton gave Adrian a sheepish look. "She always complains, and then manages to get everything done in half the time." He looked around. "Any brandy about?"

Adrian retrieved the bottle and two glasses from the sideboard and joined the earl for a drink. He needed one. His world was about to be thrown topsy-turvy again.

"So, are you ready to take on London?" the earl asked.

Adrian shook his head ruefully. "I don't think I will ever feel ready. But can I manage? I think so."

"Well, if Rose thinks you are ready, you are."

"Does she?"

Felton snorted. "Of course she does. She would have tossed you out on your ear long ago if she didn't think you were up to the task."

"She has never told me what she thinks of my abilities," he said.

Felton laughed. "The fact that she ordered the trunks from the attic means you are off to London."

"You said Lady Juliet's father is chaffing at my—Simon's—absence. Will that create any problems?"

"Not once you come to town. He merely wants to show off his daughter's prize catch."

Adrian found it hard to imagine himself as a matrimonial prize. But the man would think he was the Duke of Alston, of course.

"Has there been any news from the duke?" Adrian asked hopefully.

Felton looked decidedly uneasy. "I expect we will hear news of his impending arrival any day now. Wouldn't it be a corker to discover he has beaten us back to London?"

"Indeed." Adrian was not at all reassured by Felton's words. He did not seem to have any more knowledge of the duke's plans than he had two weeks ago. Surely, with the wedding approaching, Alston would give them some hint about his intentions.

Rose returned. "Honestly, Uncle, things have been so peaceful here. Now you've thrown the entire house into a tizzy. I hope you are satisfied."

"You will manage," he said brusquely. "Now quick, my dear, no time for prevaricating. Is Stamford ready for this?"

Adrian deliberately avoided looking at her. Not because he feared she would say he was not—but because she would say he was. The thought of carrying on this masquerade in London, with the high stakes involved, suddenly terrified him. It was nothing to fool some servants. But a prospective bride—and her father?

But if he did not go to London, he would no longer be able to spend time with Rose. And that was worth any amount of discomfort.

"I think," she said slowly, and he listened anxiously for her words, "that he makes a much better duke than Simon."

Adrian flashed her a startled look, and she responded with a warm smile.

"Good, good." Felton patted her hand. "All thanks to your efforts, I'm sure." He heaved himself out of the chair. "All this travel has exhausted me. I plan to take a nap. I will see both of you at dinner."

"So," Adrian said when they were alone, "this is it. Am I really ready?"

"You will do fine."

"As long as you are at my side, whispering names in my ear

to match the faces." He sounded more doubtful than he wanted to.

"You will learn them soon enough."

"I still wish you would take Lady Juliet into your confidence. Your uncle says I am expected to be constantly at her side."

"That is good," Rose said. "It will keep you away from some of Simon's worse companions. Thank goodness Lowden is out of the country."

"Lowden?"

"He's been Simon's closest friend since they were in short coats," she explained. "But he is in North America, so there is no need to worry about him."

"I just hope your brother returns soon." Adrian grinned. "I would hate for him to miss all the festivities. It is his wedding, after all."

He thought a small shadow crossed over Rose's face, but then she said brightly, "Simon will be thoroughly downtrodden, I assure you. But it is his own fault, after all." She looked pensive for a moment. "I suppose we should go over the London house plans one more time. You must be absolutely perfect . . ."

The following evening, after dinner, Adrian took a final stroll in the garden. Tomorrow they left Ashbridge for London.

He should be more excited—after all, he was going to have the chance to present his findings to the Antiquities Society, with the backing of the "duke." Surely, this time they would express more interest.

London, however, meant he had to play his role of Alston in earnest. Even with Rose's help, he knew it would be a daunting task. There were so many things that could go wrong—a face ignored, a connection forgotten. He'd be in a constant state of apprehension.

But he could not quit, not now. Rose was depending on him. And Adrian knew he would do anything for her. By going to London, he would be able to stay at her side, acting the part of her dutiful brother, treating her in an intimate manner that would be impossible for Adrian Stamford. In the normal course of things, the daughter of a duke would have no reason even to speak to him.

But life had not been normal since the day Felton drove up in front of Adrian's cottage. And now he had to acknowledge that this project, which he'd undertaken as a lark, had become more of a bargain with the devil. Yes, he was living the life of a duke, with its luxuries and privileges, but there was a price to pay. A price that would be extracted from him when Alston returned and took his rightful place beside his sister. When Rose would once again become "Lady Rosemary" and he "Mr. Stamford." When the barriers of class and status would come down between them again.

He did not look forward to that day.

As Rose tucked the last personal items into her traveling bag, she felt a twinge of regret at leaving Ashbridge. She had always known they would go to London—that was the whole point of the masquerade, wasn't it, to protect Simon's interests with Lady Juliet? But she had enjoyed being here, alone, with Adrian. In London they would rarely have time for such intimacy.

Which was for the best, she realized. They had enjoyed an illusory existence this last week, ignoring the wider world outside, forgetting why he was here in the first place. Forgetting that she was Lady Rosemary Devering, daughter of a duke, and that he was Mr. Stamford, teacher of Latin to two small schoolboys.

When her uncle walked into the library this afternoon, she first prayed that he would tell her that Simon had returned, that Adrian need not go to London, that the masquerade was over. But then she realized that would mean that she would not see Adrian again. As long as Simon was still missing, Adrian had to come with her to London.

Yet even that would not last long. Simon couldn't stay away forever; he would return in time for his wedding. Then Adrian would go.

He had his own life, after all, his teaching and his ancient artifacts—something to go back to when this was all over.

Sadly, Rose realized that she was the one who had nothing to look forward to. Simon had his marriage, Adrian his work. While she—the best she could hope for was marriage to a man whom she could tolerate. A marriage that was all but a necessity with Simon's impending wedding. A marriage she must arrange this spring. A marriage that would take her away from Adrian forever.

She pretended not to notice when her vision blurred.

Chapter 10

∾

The London streets were jammed with carriages, and the lights twinkled in the deepening dusk when the Duke of Alston's burgundy traveling carriage pulled up in front of his impressive town house on Bruton Street, around the corner from Berkley Square.

Adrian took a deep, steadying breath as the coach came to a stop. Rose said he was ready. They would find out soon enough if she was right.

A footman opened the door, pulled out the steps, then stood at rigid attention, waiting for the duke to emerge. Adrian hesitated on the top step, then firmly planted a foot on the London cobbles.

The Duke of Alston had arrived.

The house before him was, appropriately, the largest on the street. Six double-square windows looked out of the stone frontage, and it towered a full story above its neighbors.

With Rose on his arm, Adrian walked up the steps, his stomach roiling with a mixture of anticipation and apprehension.

He wanted to turn tail and run when he saw the long line of servants assembled in the hall. Footmen in their burgundy-and-cream livery, housemaids in neat white aprons, even the stable lads in their newly polished boots stood at attention.

Markham stepped forward. "On behalf of the staff, welcome to London, Your Grace."

Adrian tossed Rose a nervous glance. Did they want him to

inspect the troops like a military general? She motioned him forward with an encouraging smile.

Hands clasped behind his back, Adrian slowly walked down the line, perusing the staff. He smiled at a tiny housemaid who curtseyed before she returned a shy smile. He stopped to brush an imaginary piece of lint off a footman's shoulder, and straightened another's wig.

By the time he reached the stable lads, Adrian struggled to keep a straight face. He wanted to tell them that he wasn't really the duke and they could relax; he did not care if shoes were unpolished or an apron bow askew.

But there were those in the house who did.

He glanced back at Rose. What was he supposed to do next?

She walked past him, heading for the stairs. "Come along, Simon."

Adrian turned to the assembled servants. "Thank you all. You may return to your duties now."

He heaved a silent sigh of relief and started up the stairs after Rose.

After living amid the splendor of Ashbridge, Adrian found it easier to ignore the gilt chandelier that hung beside the staircase, and he gave only a passing glance at the enormous paintings that lined the stairwell, or the three-foot-tall antique Chinese vases that stood on the landing. Instead, he found himself far more interested in watching the enticing sway of Rose's hips as she walked before him.

It was harder and harder to regard her in a brotherly manner. He was far too aware of her womanly charms.

"We will have a cold dinner in the drawing room in about an hour," Rose told him when they reached the family floor. "No need to dress. If it was not so late, I would have you send a note round to Lady Juliet, asking when you can visit, but that will have to wait until morning."

"I have to have *permission* to see her?"

Rose laughed. "It would be heartless of you to drop in without warning—she will want to look her best when she receives you."

Adrian came to a sudden halt. "You are not making me go there alone?"

"Of course not." She patted his arm. "I will go with you. Now, Roberts should be along shortly to unpack for you. Can you find your way to the drawing room later?"

Adrian nodded.

"Good. Be there in about an hour. We need to make plans." With a quick smile, she went into her room.

Adrian continued down the hall to the duke's bedchamber, halting for a moment at the door, wondering what he would find inside. Then he pushed open the door and took a good look. Like the room at Ashbridge, it was decorated in a plain, masculine style, and he breathed a bit easier.

Roberts must have already been there, for two trunks stood in the middle of the floor. Adrian sat in a chair and pulled off his boots, eager to get out of his traveling clothes before Roberts returned to help.

Tomorrow Adrian formally began the job for which he'd been hired—playing the Duke of Alston for people who knew him well, including his intended bride. People who would notice any odd behavior or strange mannerisms. People Adrian had never met before, yet whom he would have to treat as intimates.

He shook his head. If he stopped to think of all the things that could go wrong, he would never leave this room. He had to trust Rose's judgment—she said he could do it. And she would be with him, offering encouragement that he hoped would save him from disaster.

He thought longingly of the time they'd spent together at Ashbridge, wishing they could go back there. But Rose needed him here, and that was where he would stay.

Roberts returned before Adrian finished dressing, forcing him to submit to his valet's ministrations. Adrian realized he would have to endure this constantly, now that he was in London. It was expected of a duke.

He soon escaped and headed for the drawing room, where he

found Rose sorting eagerly through the pile of invitations heaped on her lap.

She gave him a welcoming smile, then held up a handful of paper. "I cannot believe how many entertainments we have missed already. Lady Grant's rout. And Lord Bleckner's masquerade ball. Thank goodness it is only the middle of the Season." She gestured at the invitation cards. "Look at all these! How am I going to decide which ones to accept?"

"Refuse them all?" Adrian suggested with a hopeful look.

She gave him a chastising glance. "It would cause gossip if you hid in the house like a hermit. I think we shall attend Lady Morning's rout on Friday—it is short notice, but will make no difference at a rout. Now, tomorrow night—the theater, I think. Or would you prefer the opera?"

Adrian grimaced. "The theater."

"The theater it is. You can escort Lady Juliet if she is not otherwise committed. We must consult with her about these invitations, to learn which ones she wishes to accept." Rose shook her head. "There is so much to do! I need a new dinner gown. And if Ramsey plans a ball . . ."

Adrian listened to her with growing dismay. She suddenly sounded like the old Rose again—the spoiled aristocrat concerned only with pleasure. What was happening to her? She had been in London for only a few short hours and already she had slipped back into her old ways.

What had he expected? That she would magically change because he wanted her to? In the country, at Ashbridge, they had slipped easily into a casual informality. But this was London— the center of the universe to a duke's daughter. She was in her element.

Yet it was the other Rose he wanted to see—the one he admired, teased, and thought about far too often. Somehow, he had to find a way to keep that Rose, even here in London, to show her that he valued that side of her.

He was not willing to give her up so easily.

*   *   *

Excited at being back in London at last, Rose found it difficult to sleep that night. There were so many things to do . . . and so many dangers ahead.

Once again, she admired the ease with which Adrian adopted his ducal mien. During the two-day journey from Ashbridge, he never once dropped his mask, whether dealing with innkeepers or stable lads. And today, while inspecting the staff, he paid them more attention than Simon ever had.

It boded well for the success of their venture. But she would not rest easy until after tomorrow's meeting with Lady Juliet. If that went successfully—and she felt certain it would—the *ton* would accept Adrian as Simon without question.

Their success would be assured.

In the morning, Rose penned the note for Lady Juliet. Accompanied by a large bouquet of flowers, it was taken round by a footman, who returned with the reply that the Duke of Alston and his sister would be most welcome to visit at half past one.

Rose breathed a sigh of relief. She had not been worried, exactly, but it was good to know that Simon's extended absence had not caused an irreparable breach. Adrian's visit would reassure Lord Ramsey and mollify Juliet.

"What am I going to say to her?" Adrian asked plaintively as he stood in the drawing room, while Rose inspected his attire one last time.

"Apologize profusely for staying so long in the country, tell her she is looking more beautiful than ever, and that you will be at her side as much as possible in the next weeks."

"She might throw me out on my ear."

Rose laughed. "No one is going to throw away a duke, least of all Lady Juliet. No, now that you are in town, she will be content. She'll want to go everywhere on your arm."

Reaching up, she straightened his cravat and stepped back to take one final glance. He looked exceedingly handsome in dove grey breeches and a charcoal coat. Juliet would be most pleased by the appearance of her future husband.

That is . . . Rose scrutinized him more carefully. She hoped it was her imagination, for it seemed as if Adrian was looking less and less like her brother with each passing day. Rose wondered now how she could ever have mistaken him for Simon—his eyes were a darker hue, and his mouth had a decidedly different shape. Even the way he stood—less rigidly and arrogantly than Simon.

Subtle differences—ones that she prayed no one else would notice—but they appeared so obvious to her now. In fact, she'd had to stop herself several times from calling him "Adrian" last night.

It had been a mistake to use his name while they were at Ashbridge. At least when she had been calling him Simon, she remembered who he was supposed to be. Now she had to think twice to call him by her brother's name. It did not bode well for her part in the upcoming masquerade, and she knew Adrian was depending on her.

Rose reminded herself just how important this was to Simon—and to her. Nothing must threaten her brother's marriage to Lady Juliet. Somehow, she had to try to forget that the man standing before her was Adrian Stamford. He was *Simon*.

"Is anything wrong?" he asked, his brow crinkling in doubt.

"You look very fine." Rose handed him his hat and gloves. Adrian set the beaver atop his head at a rakish angle and held out his arm to her. He looked far more confident than she felt, and she envied him that.

They walked to the waiting carriage.

"It seems ridiculous to take a carriage for a few blocks," he grumbled as the horses slowed in front of Lord Ramsey's house.

"You might be allowed to walk," she said, "but not I."

He turned in the seat and looked at her, apprehension finally showing in his eyes. "This is going to work, isn't it?"

"Yes," she said firmly. Her entire future depended on it.

Adrian found the interior of Lord Ramsey's town house, which was still far more ornate than Adrian's usual surroundings, was not nearly so lavishly decorated as the duke's home.

Somehow, he found this calming as he and Rose followed the footman up the stairs. The man halted, opened the door to what Adrian presumed was the drawing room, and stepped inside to announce the guests.

"His Grace, the Duke of Alston. Lady Rosemary Devering."

With a last glance at Rose for reassurance, Adrian took a deep breath and stepped into the room.

To his relief, there was no question which of the two women facing him was Lady Juliet. Rose had described her to an inch—the blond, curled locks, her pouty rosebud mouth and clear blue eyes. Blond was not his favorite color of hair—but she was strikingly good-looking.

Of course, he did not think Alston would settle for anything less.

Adrian went first to the older woman—surely Lady Ramsey—and kissed her hand, then presented himself to Simon's intended, taking her hand and bowing low.

"I have been remiss in staying away for so long, my lady. I pray that you will pardon me."

"We heard news of that dreadful fire," Juliet said in a soft and whispery voice.

"Thank goodness no one was injured," Lady Ramsey added.

"It was an unfortunate incident," Rose acknowledged. "Simon was so brave in fighting the flames."

"Oh, dear!" Juliet gasped. "You might have been hurt!"

"Only a slight twist of an ankle," Adrian said, hoping to explain his future reluctance to dance. "But I am here, to play your slave for as often as you will permit me."

From the corner of his eye, he saw Lady Ramsey smile at his exaggerated gallantry.

Juliet regarded him with less approval. "It has been so dreadfully dull in your absence," she said with a reproachful look. "Mama did not think it proper that I attend too many functions without your escort."

"I will endeavor to be at your side as often as she allows," Adrian said. "Will you allow me to escort you to the theater tonight?"

Lady Juliet smiled sweetly. "Oh dear, how unfortunate. We already have plans to attend Lady Gardner's dinner party."

The pointed look in her eyes told Adrian that she was not yet ready to forgive his—or rather Simon's—neglect of her.

"I am disappointed," he said, "but it is understandable, with my deplorable tardiness."

"Surely, you will wish to attend Lady Morning's rout on Friday," Rose said.

"Of course she will," Lady Ramsey spoke quickly. "Juliet, you can wear your lovely new dress, the one with the pink roses."

Adrian did not relish setting eyes on that dress. He preferred the darker, dramatic colors that Rose wore.

Rose began quizzing Juliet about the happenings in town, and Adrian was able to sit back and watch and listen.

Lady Juliet was not quite the widgeon Rose had led him to expect. Oh, he doubted she had a single serious thought in that pretty blond head, but she was the perfect ornament for an elegant drawing room. He wondered how long it would take for the duke to tire of her—or if he would. Adrian was not too confident about Simon's powers of discernment. The two might be deliriously happy with one another.

He casually glanced at the clock on the mantelpiece. According to Rose, even an intended bridegroom could not draw out his visit for more than half an hour. Their time would soon be over. He did not like the way Lady Ramsey eyed him with such avaricious delight, as if he were a delectable morsel of food.

Adrian saw Rose get to her feet, and he quickly stood, relieved that they were leaving early. But to his dismay, she shot him a cautionary look and followed Lady Ramsey out of the room.

Adrian felt a stab of panic. They were leaving him alone with Lady Juliet. His cravat suddenly felt restrictingly tight.

He tried to turn a reassuring look on Juliet, who was looking at him expectantly. What did she want of him? Why hadn't

Rose warned him about this? How was he supposed to know what to do?

Juliet moved to the sofa where her mother had been sitting, patting the cushion beside her. "Do sit down, Alston. Isn't it clever of Mama to have contrived to leave us alone?"

Adrian gingerly sat beside her. "Very clever."

"I own that I was a bit disappointed by your continued absence. What is the point of being an engaged woman if I cannot demonstrate my good fortune to the *ton*?"

"A regrettable lapse on my part," he said. "I assure you, I will be at your side until the wedding."

She glinted a sideways glance at him. "Aren't you going to kiss me?"

Adrian swallowed hard. Rose hadn't said a word about this. Now she had abandoned him, and he was facing his first crisis—alone.

He leaned over and planted a chaste kiss on Juliet's lips.

She giggled. "That wasn't the way you kissed me the last time."

How was I to know? Adrian thought with growing panic. But he dutifully put an arm about her shoulder, pulling her nearer, and kissed her with a bit more enthusiasm.

To his utter horror, she wrapped her arms around his neck and pressed against him, her mouth seeking his. Adrian wanted to disentangle himself and leap off the couch.

Instead, he tightened his arms around her.

And heard the door open behind them.

A faint cough sounded, and Juliet pulled away. Lady Ramsey was looking at them from the doorway, a satisfied smile on her face.

"You naughty ones! I feared something like this would happen if I left you alone too long." She shared a conspiratorial look with Rose. "Good thing we returned when we did."

Rose gave Adrian a surprisingly harsh look. "Simon, we must be going if I am to get ready for the theater tonight." She pressed a kiss on Lady Ramsey's cheek, and then did the same with Juliet. Adrian took her hands, kissed each one in turn, and backed out of the room, bowing, praying he hid his relief at leaving.

The footman handed him his hat and gloves; he waited while the man assisted Rose into her pelisse and bonnet, then led her out to the waiting carriage.

"What on earth were you doing in there?" Rose demanded the minute the door closed on them. "Have you no shame?"

"Me?" Adrian glared at her. "You were the one who left me alone with her. She practically attacked me."

Rose sniffed. "I hardly think a lady like Juliet—"

" 'A lady like Juliet'," he mimicked with unnecessary sarcasm. "Let me tell you, that baggage is no lady. Don't ever leave me alone with her again."

She fixed him with an icy stare. "A duke should know how to behave properly in every situation, no matter how awkward."

"Well, I am not a duke, and I am not accustomed to being mauled by elegant young ladies. And when your brother returns, I should demand to know how overtly familiar he has been with that girl. She certainly expected more than a chaste peck on the cheek."

"I will discuss that with him," Rose replied coolly. "But in the meantime, I expect you to behave with proper decorum at all times."

To her annoyance, he grinned impishly. "Of course I will."

Rose turned away and looked out the window.

He probably *was* speaking the truth about Juliet, but when she'd stood beside Lady Ramsey in that doorway and seen Adrian with his arms wrapped around that widgeon, Rose wanted to throw something—anything—at his head. She had felt a spurt of pure, raw . . . jealousy.

Rose shook her head. *Nonsense.* Juliet thought she was kissing Simon, not Adrian. There was no reason for Rose to be upset; he'd only been playing at—

Rose sat up suddenly, smothering a gasp at her thought. She had been *jealous* at the sight of Adrian kissing Juliet.

Which was foolish. She and Adrian had developed a closer

friendship during their days at Ashbridge, but that did not mean that she had . . . feelings for him.

Or did she? Why else would she be so rattled?

With a sinking heart, Rose realized she wanted to know what it felt like to be held in Adrian's arms, to receive his kisses. She envied Juliet that experience.

She dared a glance at him through lowered lashes. He looked so masculine, so handsome as he lounged on the seat across from her, one leg casually crossed over another, with a self-satisfied smile on his face. Despite his protestation, he looked as if he had enjoyed himself.

He had played his role perfectly today. Lady Ramsey and Juliet had not expressed a moment of doubt. If they accepted Adrian as Simon, the rest of the *ton* would. Rose should be pleased at his success. She should tell him so, in fact.

But the words stuck in her throat. Because she could not forget the image of his lips on Juliet's and the deep, burning pain that had shot through her heart.

Adrian anxiously paced the drawing room that evening, waiting for Rose to come down. He was not nervous, exactly—attending the theater was not a terrifying prospect, now that Juliet was not coming, but it was his first public appearance as the duke. He prayed all of Alston's friends were elsewhere this evening.

He heard the door open, and he whirled around, ready to gently berate Rose for her tardiness. But the words would not come.

She looked exquisite—and not a single pink rose in sight.

Her dress was fashioned from a shimmery green fabric that caught both light and shadow in its web, making him think of sun-dappled gardens in the country—the country where they had spent so much time together.

Then his attention focused on the low-cut décolletage and the swell of her breasts rising above the fabric.

At that moment he did not entertain a single brotherly feeling about her.

"You look lovely tonight," he said, and meant it.

Her eyes widened in surprise, then she smiled. "How kind of you to say so, *Brother*."

That one word neatly dampened his pretensions. A needed reminder that even if Rose was not his sister, he had to pretend she was. And had to remember that she was the daughter of a duke, and he only a humble schoolteacher.

They picked up Felton at his club, then joined the swelling traffic. The streets approaching Covent Garden were crowded with vehicles, and Adrian's impatience grew as they slowly inched their way forward.

"It would be easier to get out and walk," he grumbled.

"For you, perhaps." Rose flashed him a teasing smile. "It would strain my delicate nature to be forced to walk."

Adrian smothered a smile. This, from the lady who'd dug him out from a pile of rubble with her bare hands. Rose might feign delicacy in society, but she was strong enough to brave the crowds in any London street.

He patted her hand. "Of course. I forget that the ladies must be cosseted and protected."

Rose shot him a withering look.

At last their coach halted in front of the porticoed entrance. They were hailed before they even took two steps toward the entrance.

"Alston! Lady Rosemary!" A short, dark-haired young man with shirt points that reached nearly to his ears came dashing down the steps.

"Boxey!" Rose held out her hands in greeting.

Boxey? Adrian recognized that name—Lord Boxham, possessor of a considerable fortune and, according to Felton, one of Rose's more persistent suitors, even if he was only a viscount.

"When did you arrive in town?" he demanded, drawing both her hands to his lips. "I've been looking for you everywhere."

Before she could reply, two other men approached. They gave Adrian perfunctory greetings, then turned their attention to Rose. She laughed gaily, basking in the attention of each new addition to her court.

Adrian did not find it nearly so entertaining.

Felton elbowed him gently. "See? What did I tell you? Half of London's been waiting for your sister to come to town."

Adrian stood on the stairs, uncertain what to do. If they did not hurry, they wouldn't reach their seats before the first act began. But Rose showed no inclination to move and chatted with her admirers, as if she were content to stand on the steps all evening.

"Perhaps we could move a few paces toward the door," he whispered in her ear. "We are blocking the entry."

Rose gave him a startled look, then laughed when she saw how a group had formed around her. "Of course."

"I'll escort you inside," one of her gallants offered.

"No, Alston has that honor tonight," she said. "But you may come and visit me during the intervals."

They groaned in disappointment, but stepped back and let them walk into the theater. Once inside, their progress was impeded by constant interruptions. Adrian began to think that every man in the theater was bent on speaking to her tonight.

He looked behind him, but Felton had already disappeared—no doubt preferring the calmness of the ducal box to the crush in the corridor. Adrian was trapped here with Rose and forced to endure their slow progress across the foyer and up the first set of stairs.

He suspected the first act would be over before they reached their seats. Still, Rose was in no hurry, stopping to chat cheerfully with everyone who called her name. Her arms were laden with flowers, and she finally passed several bouquets to Adrian, who accepted them awkwardly.

When they reached the first landing, he heard muffled applause from within the auditorium. He glanced at Rose, who seemed oblivious to the sound. What was the point of going to the theater if you weren't going to watch the play?

He laughed. The answer was obvious—these people weren't here to see the play. They came to see and be seen, exchange gossip, and encourage or discourage admirers. The rarified world of the English aristocracy.

He thought he had known what this experience would be like, but nothing could have prepared him. Watching Rose now, surrounded by men with titles, wealth, and backgrounds suitable to her own, Adrian realized just how wide lay the gap between them.

A gap that looked unsurmountable.

Chapter 11

Rose sat back against the carriage seat, her face flushed with excitement. The evening had been a triumph. She had never enjoyed the theater so much.

She smiled at Adrian. "Wasn't tonight marvelous?"

"Was it?" She heard the lack of enthusiasm in his voice.

"Of course." Lifting a nosegay of violets to her nose, she inhaled their fragrant scent. "You should be pleased. You did a fine job of playing Simon."

"Do you think anyone even noticed?"

"Goodness, what is wrong with you? Did you not like the play?"

"How could I enjoy what I could not hear?" Adrian scowled. "The constant parade through the box was *slightly* distracting."

Rose laughed. "I am sorry, Adrian. I had no idea it was going to be like that."

"Was it really necessary to speak with every single gentleman in the theater?"

She laughed. "I did not speak with *every* gentleman there."

"Are you certain?"

In the now-darkened interior, she could no longer see his face, but from the tone of his voice, she could imagine his disdainful expression.

"You wanted to listen to the play, and we disturbed you," she said. "I'm sorry. I had not realized—"

"It's not that."

She caught a glimpse of his face as they passed a street lamp.

He looked exhausted, and she suddenly realized the evening had been a strain for him. He must have been uncomfortable the entire time, worrying that he might make a slip. And she had been so intent on enjoying herself that she had not even noticed.

"Normally, it is not so hectic," she said. "Visitors come and go only during the intervals. But tonight . . ." She held out her hands helplessly.

"I'm glad *you* enjoyed yourself."

Later, as she retreated to her room, and Mary helped her out of her dress and brushed her hair, Rose thought about Adrian's words. Had the evening really been as wonderful as she first thought?

Rose stared back at her reflection in the dressing-table mirror. There was no reason she shouldn't have enjoyed herself. She had drawn a great deal of male attention, ranging from puppies like Boxham to more eligible men like Devonhurst. If she once feared they would forget her after such a long absence, tonight had shown she had no worry in that regard.

Then why did she feel this niggling doubt? The evening should have been a personal triumph. Why did it now seem so flat?

Because of Adrian Stamford.

Somehow, while she taught him the ways of her world, he'd drawn her into his—a world where people talked about things that mattered, where titles and status meant little, and social conventions were not important; a world where people listened to a play, instead of smooth male flattery. Along the way, he had shown her an entirely new way to look at the world.

The realization frightened her.

She had always been secure in society, confident of her place in it and the role she played. But Adrian had made her question that role when he accused her of being an arrogant, spoiled aristocrat. And however unjustified that charge, he had hit a nerve. She no longer felt comfortable with the way she had enjoyed being on display at the theater tonight—the side of her that enjoyed receiving the adulation of her male court, the side that, until a month ago, would have dismissed Adrian Stamford as an unimportant country schoolteacher.

But while he had shattered her illusions about him, he had shattered her illusions about herself, as well. She felt as if she was hovering between two worlds—London and the *ton*, and something different, a life she did not understand and knew little about—a world she had caught a glimpse of at Ashbridge, watching Adrian dig for artifacts with such enthusiasm. Enthusiasm was denigrated, not admired, in society, where it was far more fashionable to display bored discontent. Or later, when he had talked about his life at his cottage. It sounded peaceful, cozy, romantic.

But she did not live in his world. Her place was among the *ton*, an elite society with its own rules and manners. She could not allow Adrian to spoil it for her. He had his own life to live; she had hers.

And they were very, very different.

"Lord Boxham to see you, Your Grace." Markham stood at rigid attention at the library door.

Annoyed at the interruption, Adrian glanced up. He was putting the finishing touches on his article for the Antiquities Society. Whatever did Boxham want from him this early in the morning?

"Send him in," Adrian said and slid his manuscript into the desk drawer.

Boxham sauntered jauntily into the library and plopped into the chair facing the desk, displaying a waistcoat in an eye-straining shade of puce. Adrian tried not to wince and waited for his guest to speak.

"I daresay you know why I'm here," Boxham began.

"No," Adrian replied.

Boxham swallowed hard. "It's your sister. I've come to ask for your permission to pay my addresses to her."

Adrian stared at him, incredulous. This . . . this fribble wanted to marry Rose? The thought was laughable—wasn't it?

"Do you have reason to believe she will welcome your suit?"

Adrian could not believe Rose would consider marriage to Boxham.

"You saw how energetically she greeted me last night," Boxham said, leaning forward eagerly. "I think she's finally ready to accept my offer this time."

"This time?" Adrian raised a brow. "You asked her before?"

Boxham regarded him with indignation. "I certainly did— last fall, if you recall. *With* your permission."

Adrian winced. He'd blundered there. But he could not believe that Simon would be willing to let Rose marry this man. Apart from being far too young and idiotic, the viscount had execrable taste in clothing.

Or had Simon granted his permission as a way to plague his sister?

"How did she phrase her rejection?" he asked.

Boxham colored. "She did not tell you? She said she was not . . . interested. But that was before your own engagement. I thought perhaps now . . ."

Adrian frowned. Boxham was right; Rose's situation had changed. She herself had said she intended to make a match while she was in London this spring.

But Boxham?

Adrian shook his head. The man was clearly delusional. Rose would no more marry him than a pig farmer. Adrian opened his mouth to send Boxham on his way when he recalled how annoying he had found last night's visit to the theater. While he had suffered in boredom, Rosemary had reveled in the fawning tributes from her suitors.

Surely, she would not want him to discourage any of her admirers.

He waved his hand. "Go ahead. You have my permission to speak with Lady Rosemary."

"Is she at home?" Boxham's eyes widened with hope.

Adrian jerked the bellpull. "Let's find out."

Markham reported that Lady Rosemary was, indeed, at home, and Adrian sent Boxham off to find her.

He had a sudden, clutching fear that every single gentleman

they had seen at the theater last night was going to show up on his doorstep, begging for Rose's hand. If it was up to Adrian, he would send each and everyone of them packing.

But it wasn't up to him. He might pretend to be her brother, but he was not in a position to say whom she could and could not marry. In truth, he wondered if even Simon had that power. Rose was old enough to wed where she wanted. He needed to have confidence in her ability to know what was best for her.

With a weary sigh, Adrian pulled out his article again and began reworking the corrections on the third page.

He was on the last page when the library door crashed open, and Rose stormed into the room.

"Was that your idea of a joke?"

Adrian looked up. Anger flashed in her eyes, turning them a vivid, storm-sky blue. She looked so lovely when she was in a temper. He set down his quill. "Is there a problem?"

"Problem?" She paced the room with quick, angry steps. "Yes, there is a problem. You gave permission for that idiot to ask me to marry him. How could you ever think I would consider Boxham?"

Adrian disguised his relief. "You seemed to be fond of him. I assumed he was one of your favorite beaus."

"Favorite?" She shuddered. "I cannot abide the man. He has the brains of a pea. And he's only a viscount."

"Perhaps you should give me some guidance, then." Adrian suppressed a laugh. "Am I to turn down all offers from viscounts? And men with puce waistcoats? Please, you must tell me your requirements."

She glared at him for a moment, then the corners of her lips curved up in a smile. "You are teasing me, aren't you? I should have known."

He grinned. "Alas, you've seen through me. But if you do not want me making any more jokes at your expense, you must give me some guidance."

"That's easy." Rose sat down. "First, do not—"

A knock sounded at the door, and Markham entered. "Lord Arlington and Lord Debham to see Lady Rosemary."

Rose stood and held out her hand to Adrian. "Come along, Simon. We can finish this discussion later."

He groaned. "Can't I stay here?"

"And allow me to entertain two male guests without a chaperon? What can you be thinking?"

Reluctantly, Adrian got to his feet. It was going to be a repeat of last night all over again. The men would lay themselves at Rose's feet, and he would be forced to listen to their effusive praises. Was he doomed to spend his entire time in London watching other men fawn over Rose?

It was not fair.

"Don't you have some aged relative to call on for chaperonage?"

She giggled. "You find that duty onerous?"

"We will go out each day," he said, deciding instantly. "If you are not at home, you cannot accept callers."

"Of course we will go out—I have my own calls to pay."

"I was thinking of more *educational* destinations—such as the British Museum."

Rose laughed and took his arm and pulled him toward the drawing room. "You are such a jokester, Simon."

Adrian steeled himself for the upcoming tedium.

The following evening, Adrian stood in the drawing room, checking his cravat one more time in the mirror. Tonight was Lady Morning's rout party—his first opportunity to escort Lady Juliet in public. Rose assured him that it would be a pleasant task—no dancing, just talk and refreshments.

He wished he had her confidence. He had felt lost that night at the theater, where all those faces and names blurred together. He would not remember half of them if he saw them tonight; he still desperately needed Rose's help to get through this.

When was the real duke going to return?

He prowled the drawing room, waiting for Rose to come down. This had all sounded so easy when they'd first proposed it to him. Of course, they hadn't told him everything then— Lady Juliet, for example. He did not like the idea of deceiving her. But Rose insisted that it was necessary, and he trusted her reasons.

Would he ever find out what they were?

He heard the door open, turned, and sucked in a breath. Tonight Rose wore a dark blue gown that reminded him of her angry eyes this afternoon. But now her eyes were a calm, reflective blue, like the sapphires around her throat and wrists and dangling from her ears.

Adrian realized she must be wearing a small fortune in jewels. One earring would probably pay his wages for several years.

Seeing her like this, dressed in her elegant evening gown, was a painful reminder of her position in society. He might be wearing the duke's clothes, but it did not change the fact that underneath, he was a lowly Latin teacher.

A teacher who grew more and more regretful that he had agreed to this job, one that he no longer regarded as work, just as he no longer thought of Rose as his employer. No, she was . . . a woman. A woman who was far too often in his thoughts these days.

And no matter how well he played his role, Adrian would never be her equal. In her world, birth was the only thing that counted. And while his was respectable, it did not match the level of hers.

"You seem quiet tonight," Rose said in the carriage on the way to Lord Ramsey's house. "Nervous?"

He nodded. "It was easy not to talk with people at the theater. What if someone traps me in a corner tonight?"

"I shall keep an eye on you," she promised. "And you will have Juliet's help as well. She will keep the conversation light."

"It is Lady Juliet who puts me into a quake," he confessed. "What if she lures me into a dark corner?"

Rosemary laughed. "If you need my advice on how to handle that situation, I fear you are in trouble."

"You mean no ungentlemanly suitor has ever lured you into a secluded tête-à-tête?"

She peeked at him over the top of her fan with the look of a practiced flirt. "Not against my will."

Her answer did not please him. Adrian stared glumly out of the window. What had he expected her to say—that she was never more than two feet from a chaperon at all times? Of course not. She was a grown woman, not a young girl fresh from the schoolroom. She had probably traded kisses with several men.

He wanted to know where, and with whom.

Lady Juliet kept them waiting in the drawing room for a full twenty minutes, increasing Adrian's nervousness.

Adrian strangled a cough when she finally made her entrance. She looked as if she had been attacked by a flower seller. Bright pink faux roses covered the bodice of her dress and littered her skirt like bright splotches of . . . measles.

He shot Rose a quick glance. She caught his gaze, then quickly looked at her toes, but not before he had seen the mirth in her eyes.

Adrian took Juliet's hand and brought it to his lips. "You look exquisite, my dear."

Her girlish giggle grated on his ears.

"This is so exciting," Juliet said when they were in the carriage. "This is the first time I have gone out without Mama."

"You do not need your mother any longer," Adrian said, patting her hand. "You have me now."

He saw Rose put a gloved hand to her mouth, smothering a laugh.

"Dinner was *so* dull the other night without you there," Juliet said, pressing closer. "Did you enjoy the theater?"

"How could I have enjoyed it without your presence?"

"Several people asked about you," Juliet said. "They wondered at your long absence from town."

"Do not worry. I will be at your side every day until the wedding."

"Where shall we go for our wedding trip?" Juliet looked at him through lowered lashes. "I would love to see Paris."

"Whatever you desire, my love."

Juliet flung her arms around him. "Oh, Alston, thank you. I cannot wait to tell Mama."

"I shall order the carriage to turn around this very minute," Adrian said.

A look of sheer dismay washed over her face. "Oh, no, please. I can tell Mama later."

Rose leaned forward. "My brother loves to tease. You soon will grow accustomed to his manner."

Adrian coughed. He had been perfectly serious.

Juliet laughed lightly and tapped him with her fan. "I knew you were teasing me."

"Simon," Rose said. "You really should not tease your wife the same way you tease your sister."

"Of course not," Juliet agreed. "A man teases his wife in a loverlike way."

Her words were like a splash of cold water in his face. *The way he wished to treat Rose.*

Adrian felt a rush of relief when the carriage finally halted. He needed to get out of these close confines. He reached for the door, but Rose put a hand on his arm. "You might wait until we arrive at Lady Morning's door," she said. "I have no intention of tromping the entire length of the street."

Adrian glanced out the window and saw that they were last in a long line of carriages that stretched down the block. It could be half an hour, at least, before they reached the house. He glanced at Rose, and she gave him a warning look. With a resigned sigh, he settled back in the seat.

At long last, their carriage arrived at the head of the line. A liveried footman pulled open the door, and Adrian helped the two ladies down. Then they joined another long line on the stairs leading to the house.

"It looks to be a sad crush tonight," Rose observed. "Lady Morning considers her parties a failure unless one or two guests suffocate."

"Then she will not notice if we leave early," Adrian said in a low whisper that only she could hear.

Rose rapped him on the forearm with her fan.

Inside, the scene was as bad as he imagined. The long line of guests snaked through the entry hall and into a drawing room that was so crowded he did not see how it could hold one more person.

"Is it always like this?" Adrian did not bother to keep his voice low. In the surrounding din, no one else could hear him.

She nodded. "Stay close so we do not get separated."

He couldn't imagine how that could happen in this mob. Adrian glimpsed a doorway on the far side of the room, but a solid mass of people blocked their way. He feared they might spend the entire evening in this room—except that still more people pushed in behind them. Somehow, they would have to move.

Rose and Juliet chatted amiably with the two ladies standing next to them. Adrian merely directed a pained smile at anyone who caught his eye. The men would understand that look.

An impatient guest jostled Adrian, and he stepped back to let the woman pass. He turned back to complain to Rose, but she was gone.

Panic flashed through him. Where was she?

Grabbing Juliet's arm, he dove into the crowd, frantically looking for a flash of blue. He had to find Rose.

"What are you doing?" Juliet demanded.

"Trying to find my sister," he muttered.

She halted, a stubborn set to her mouth. "It was not necessary for you to bring your sister tonight. We are engaged, after all. I no longer need a chaperon."

"You have it the wrong way round," Adrian said. "I am chaperoning Rose."

Juliet giggled. "Just think! Once we are wed, I can be her chaperon."

Adrian could only guess what Rose would say to that. But he would never know unless he found her. And he could not make it through the evening without her help.

Where had that blasted woman gone?

He saw a flash of blue on the far side of the room, and his spirits lifted. That had to be her. He threaded his way through the throng. But halfway there, he realized it was not Rose after all. Frustrated, he halted and looked around again.

Juliet tugged at his arm. "Look, there's Lord Sanders. We must say hello."

Before he could stop her, she pulled him toward a tall, red-faced man near the door. Adrian wanted to run. Who was Sanders? How was he going to find out, without Rose's help?

Sanders's face broke into a smile as they approached.

"Lady Juliet." He took her hand. "Such a pleasure to see you." He switched his gaze to Adrian and nodded briefly. "Alston. I see you finally arrived in town."

Juliet possessively curled her fingers around Adrian's arm. "Yes, he has been a very wicked boy, staying away for so long."

"And how nice for you, my dear, that he has finally returned." Sanders did not look the least bit pleased.

Juliet giggled loudly, and Adrian suddenly realized why she had insisted on speaking to Sanders. No doubt he had been paying court to her before the engagement. Was she trying to deliver a subtle message to Alston? That if he did not behave, she could look elsewhere for a husband?

Too bad she hadn't delivered the message to the right person.

A space opened up near the door. Adrian placed a proprietary hand on Juliet's shoulder. "Come along, my dear. I see our chance at last." He nodded farewell to Sanders and propelled Juliet forward through the doorway and into the next room.

She turned to him in annoyance. "Really, Alston, you might let me finish a conversation."

"Haven't I warned you about my overwhelming jealousy?" he asked. "I cannot bear to see you speaking to another man."

His remark drew a laugh. "Oh, Alston, you are such a tease."

He looked at her sharply. "Do you think I am teasing?"

A flicker of doubt entered her eyes, then she laughed again, less confidently this time. "You know you have no cause for concern."

"Indeed?" He raised a brow. "That is gratifying to hear."

"Alston!" A voice called to him from across the room.

Adrian froze. Someone wanted *him*. Rose was not at his side, and he must face one of Simon's friends alone, unprepared. Slowly, he watched a stern-faced man approach. Adrian gulped; the man looked angry. But when he reached Adrian, his face broke into a smile, and he slapped him genially on the back.

"Alston, you old dog. Where have you been hiding yourself? Thought you'd be to town long before this."

"I had some family matters to attend to," Adrian said.

The man looked around. "Speaking of family, where's your sister? Surely, you didn't leave her in the country."

Adrian laughed in relief. He should have known. No one wanted to talk with him. They all wanted Rose. "What, you did not hear about her triumphal appearance at Covent Garden two nights ago?"

"Is she here tonight?" the man asked eagerly.

"Somewhere," Adrian said. "I lost her in the other room."

"I will go find her for you," the man offered eagerly. "Don't want her to get lost."

"You do that," Adrian agreed. "Tell her I'm frantic with worry."

The man gave him a bemused look, then smiled. "Will do." He pushed his way through the crowd, intent on his mission.

Adrian let out a relieved sigh. That had gone well, although he still had no idea who the man was. But he knew others would approach him tonight, and it was only a matter of time before he said something wrong. He needed Rose!

"It is so warm in here," Juliet said, waving her fan. "Let us talk a walk in the garden."

"I have to find my sister," Adrian insisted. "You stay here."

Juliet pouted.

He would go back and search for Rose in the other room again. She could not be far away. He spun toward the door, and collided with a servant carrying a heavy tray of tall champagne flutes, which crashed to the floor.

Chapter 12

~

Rose anxiously scanned the room, looking for a sign of Adrian. Where had that man gone?

She tried to reassure herself. He was not completely on his own; Juliet was with him. But Rose needed to find him fast, before he found himself in a situation he was not prepared to handle.

Bringing him to Lady Morning's had been a mistake. There were too many people here; finding him quickly was difficult.

The whispered murmurings around her grew louder and louder, and after Rose heard the name "Alston" mentioned three times in a row, her breath came quicker.

What had Adrian done?

Everyone was looking at the door leading to the other drawing room. Ignoring the people who stood in her path, Rose plunged forward until a mass of bodies blocked the doorway. She stood on tiptoe, trying to see over a shoulder, but her view was blocked.

She poked the man in front with her fan. "Excuse me," she said when he turned around. "I must get through."

"It's Lady Rosemary," someone whispered, and her name spread across the room. In an instant, the crowd pulled back, and she had a clear path into the room.

And a clear view of Adrian—the man everyone thought was the Duke of Alston—on his knees helping a servant clean up a spilled tray of drinks. Every person in the room stood staring at the sight.

Rose did not know whether she wanted to laugh or cry. Adrian had been so worried about remembering everything she taught him—yet he had been tripped up by a simple act of kindness.

The liveried footman took a glass from Adrian's hand. "I'll take care of this, sir."

"Oh, this was entirely my fault. Let me help you." Adrian gingerly picked up a shard of broken glass and set it on the tray.

The room was so quiet Rose clearly heard the clink of glass.

She had to rescue him from this fix. Stepping forward, Rose put her hands on her hips and gave Adrian her sternest look. "Simon! What are you doing?"

A look of pure relief washed over his face as he looked up at her, replaced quickly with a flush of chagrin.

"I bumped into this poor fellow," he said. "I thought I should help."

"That is very considerate of you," she said. "Do you need my help?"

The hushed murmurings of the crowd stilled again. Rose knew that all eyes were on her, wondering if both Devering siblings had lost their minds. But her words had deflected attention away from Adrian.

He waved her away. "No need—I am almost finished here. What we really need is a mop."

Rose glanced at the crowd. "Could someone please summon another of Lady Morning's servants?"

Several guests looked at her as if she had grown wings, but one enterprising gentleman sprang into action. He gave the bellpull a vigorous tug, then knelt beside Adrian, using his handkerchief to start mopping up the spilled liquid.

His actions galvanized the room. As if deciding the unusual sight no longer held any interest, they turned as a body and either resumed their conversations or drifted off into the other rooms.

When the second servant arrived, Rose motioned for Adrian to retreat. He smiled weakly at her, then followed her to where Juliet stood against the wall. She looked stunned.

"Say something to her," Rose hissed at him.

"I am sorry." Adrian flashed Juliet an apologetic smile. "I seem to be particularly clumsy tonight. Perhaps I would do better if I sat down. Shall we look for the supper tables?"

"Lady Morning has a new French cook," Rose said, glancing at Juliet. "I hear he has a wonderful way with sauces. I cannot wait to try them. Shall we?"

Juliet glanced uneasily between Adrian and Rose, then nodded. The color returned to her face.

"Do you like the French style of cooking?" Adrian took Juliet by the elbow and steered her toward the exit. "Perhaps we should hire ourselves a French cook?"

Rose breathed a silent sigh of relief. Adrian had said exactly the right thing. If anything would divert Juliet's attention, it was talk of her upcoming life as Duchess of Alston. She might even forget about Adrian's attack of helpfulness in the drawing room.

Not that the rest of the *ton* would. But when one was a duke, one could get away with a great deal of eccentric behavior— even helping the servants. But Rose dare not let Adrian out of her sight again, to make certain there were no more mistakes. Too many odd incidents would cause talk.

Rose recovered her composure in the supper room, and the rest of the evening passed without incident as she stayed close to Adrian's side. Finally, at half past one they left Lady Morning's. Adrian escorted Juliet to her door, then rejoined Rose in the coach.

He slumped in the corner. "I made a mull of things, didn't I?" he asked. "I am sorry."

"Do not worry," Rose said. "You have to expect to make some mistakes. Thank goodness it was relatively minor."

"It seemed the most natural thing to do—after all, I knocked the tray over."

"Perhaps you will start a new craze among the *ton*—by next week everyone will be helping their servants."

Adrian laughed. "That I doubt. But thank you for coming to

my rescue." He cast her a questioning glance. "Would you really have helped clean up the mess if I had asked you?"

She smiled mysteriously. "You will never know."

He shook his head ruefully. "I guess this only shows that I am not cut out to be a duke, after all."

"I think you would make a marvelous duke." Rose blurted the words out before she could stop herself.

"Do you?"

She tried to laugh off her declaration. "A rather eccentric one, to be sure."

"I hope Lady Juliet agrees with you."

"Juliet wants to be a duchess," Rose said. "She will overlook a great deal to achieve that."

"What is so wrong about offering assistance to another person?" he asked, stretching out his long legs. "If you dropped a glass, I could pick it up. But if a servant drops it, I cannot?"

"That is their job," she explained.

"And all this business about opening and closing doors for me. I am not a helpless infant."

"No, but you are a duke."

He grinned. "I would think that a man with such an exalted title would be considered more capable, not less."

"An exalted title gives one more privileges, as well."

"Such as being crushed with a hundred other people into a room meant for fifty?"

Laughing, Rose nodded. "Exactly."

"I think I would prefer to be a plain 'mister,' rather than endure *that* again. At least I could breathe at the theater."

"Even a duke must make sacrifices."

"Has there been any news from your brother? He must be on his way home by now."

Rose was glad she was sitting in shadow, for she didn't want Adrian to see the look on her face. They knew no more about Simon's whereabouts now than they had a month ago, before Uncle came up with the scheme to use Adrian to play the duke.

"He will be home in time for the wedding," she said firmly, as if saying the words would make it so. She did not want to worry Adrian. "When are you planning to talk with the Antiquities Society about your find at Ashbridge?"

"My article is finished," Adrian said. "If you would be so kind as to write the supporting letter . . ."

"I will do it right away—but you have to tell me what to write."

"Oh, nothing very complicated. Just tell them that I unearthed some interesting artifacts on your estate and that they should talk with me."

She could not resist the urge to tease him. "You don't want me to praise your bravery in risking your life in the pursuit of history?"

"I would rather you did not mention that unfortunate incident."

"Unfortunate incident," indeed! Adrian could have been killed. She would write the letter the way she wanted.

At last, the carriage pulled up before the house. A footman opened the coach door and let down the steps; as soon as Rose and Adrian reached the stairs, another footman flung the front door open and stood at attention until they were inside.

It was such a part of her daily life that Rose had never paid it much notice. But now, she saw it through Adrian's eyes, and for a moment she realized how silly it all was. It was helpful to have assistance getting out of the carriage, but she was perfectly capable of opening the front door to her house.

Yet, if she could do that for herself, why couldn't she do other things? Dressing without help was impossible, but what about carrying water for her bath? Or preparing meals? She could haul coals, clean the fireplace, and do the washing.

Her head swam at the thought. It was all well and good to be aware and appreciative of the work done by the servants, but to take on those tasks for herself . . . ? It was inconceivable. She had been tended by servants all her life; it was what she was accustomed to.

And it was not as if the servants were ill-treated—they were well-fed, housed, and clothed. Working in a ducal household

was a sought-after privilege, for servants carried the status of
their masters.

Still, she could not stop looking at Mary with new eyes as
she helped Rose undress and prepare for bed. Rose was tempted
to ask if she was happy working here, if she minded being a servant, but she held back.

She was afraid to find out.

Damn Adrian for making her think about such things. He
was a man, after all, and accustomed to looking out for himself.
And even he was not so independent as he maintained. He
might not have a valet, but a woman came in to cook and clean
for him. Servants were a necessity, even for a country teacher.

Rose pushed the confusing thoughts away. No matter what
Adrian thought or said, this was her life. There was no point in
dwelling on things that would not change.

She went to her desk, deciding to write her letter to the Antiquities Society tonight. She would rather praise Adrian's discoveries in the tomb than dwell on the differences between
them.

Adrian sat in the morning room the next day, buttering his
second piece of toast, when the butler announced Lord Dudley
was calling.

"Shall I have him wait in the drawing room?"

"No, send him in." Adrian did not recognize the name; no
doubt it was another of Rose's suitors. He really needed to have
that talk with her. How else was he to know whether he should
talk to the fellow, or show him the door?

When Dudley walked in, Adrian's first thought was that he
had been mistaken—this man was not here to talk about Rose.
He was old enough to be her father, at least.

But to Adrian's horror, Dudley's first words confirmed his
first guess.

"I've come to ask for your sister's hand," Dudley told him.

"Do you have reason to believe that my sister is interested in
your suit?" Adrian asked. The best thing he could say for Dudley was that he dressed better than young Boxham.

"Why wouldn't she be?" Dudley demanded. "She's not getting any younger. Too fussy, girls are these days. Marry 'em off young, or they start getting all sorts of ideas. They need someone to look after them, guide them."

Guide Rose? Adrian doubted that this overconfident fool was strong-willed enough to accomplish that.

What should he do? He feared if he showed Dudley the door, he'd later discover that Rose was panting to get her hands on his London house or his country estate.

No, Rose was not *that* mercenary. Adrian didn't think there was a single thing about Dudley that would attract Rose. But until she told him otherwise, he felt obligated to pass along all her suitors.

"You have my permission to speak to my sister," Adrian said, with great reluctance. "The decision, is, of course, hers to make."

Dudley shook his head. "That's the problem with you young fellows. Now if your father—God rest his soul—was here, you wouldn't hear any talk about letting Lady Rosemary make up her own mind. He'd tell her whom to marry and that would be that."

All the better that the sixth duke was dead, Adrian thought.

After assuring Adrian he would return later to speak with Rose, Dudley left, leaving Adrian to wonder if he was doing the right thing.

Would Alston allow Rose to make her own choice, or would he choose a husband for her? If so, Adrian was doing her a favor by letting her pick her own husband quickly, before Simon returned. Yet if her brother had any say, wouldn't he have already arranged a marriage for her?

The whole situation was making his head ache. Adrian resolved to talk with Rose *today*. He wanted clear directions on what she wanted him to do when her suitors applied for his permission.

Walking into the library, he found Rose's letter for the society on the desk. A smile crept over his face. She must have written it last night. He wondered what it said, but she had sealed it with Alston's crest. The contents would remain a secret—until he wormed the information out of her.

Perhaps now, the society would pay attention to him at last.

An hour later, Adrian stood on the sidewalk outside the offices of the Antiquities Society, Rose's letter of recommendation clutched in his hand, his article and drawings in a portfolio under his arm. Now that he was finally here, he felt strangely reluctant to go inside. What if they turned him down again? His dreams would be permanently dashed.

Taking a deep breath, he strode up the stairs and opened the door. The paneled entry hall was narrow, with doors leading off to either side and a staircase at the far end. Adrian went to the nearest door and knocked.

"Come in."

Adrian walked into a small room, filled floor to ceiling with bookcases and glass-fronted cabinets. A short, bald man with spectacles sat at a table, taking notes from a book.

"May I help you?" he asked without looking up.

"My name is Adrian Stamford. I have written to the society before about some of my findings. I've made a new discovery—an undisturbed tomb from the early Roman period, I believe. I hoped that the society would consider my article for print."

"Leave it on the table." The man turned back to his book.

Adrian stared at him, dumbfounded. They were going to dismiss his work just like that? Ignore him, as they always had in the past?

Then he remembered Rose's letter.

"Are you the society's secretary? I have a letter from the Duke of Alston. The tomb was found on his estate, and he is eager to have the discovery promoted."

The balding man looked up with an annoyed expression and held out his hand for the letter. Adrian waited with growing apprehension while the man read and reread it. Finally, the man took off his spectacles and examined Adrian more carefully.

"The duke seems to think you have found something of significance."

Realizing he had his chance at last, Adrian grabbed the portfolio and pulled out his drawings, spreading them out on the table. "This is a rendering of the tomb, showing its construction, and these are the objects I found inside, and approximately where they were located."

The secretary picked up each drawing and examined them carefully.

"The composition is bronze?"

Adrian nodded. "They have the typical greenish brown patina."

The secretary held up the drawing of the bracelet Adrian had given Rose. "This looks like an interesting piece. Was it in good condition?"

"Excellent," Adrian said.

"Does the duke have these relics at Ashbridge?"

"He was kind enough to permit me to bring them to London," Adrian said.

The man smiled. "Perhaps you would like to give a short talk about your discoveries at our monthly meeting. I believe our members would be interested in hearing about your findings."

Adrian could hardly believe his ears. Finally! They were interested in his work. "I would be pleased to do that."

"We would be delighted to have the duke attend as well."

Adrian swallowed hard. "The duke is a busy man. I cannot promise that—"

"Do talk with him, will you? Impress upon him the importance of his support, and that the society would like to personally thank him for it."

"I will ask him."

The secretary glanced again at Adrian's article. "I will read through this. Perhaps we can consider it for publication in our next journal."

"Thank you."

Adrian left the office, feeling as if he were walking on clouds. Not only were they going to consider his article for publication, he was going to actually speak at the society's monthly meeting. Finally, he had the opportunity to present his findings to the eminent men in his field.

And all because they thought he was supported by the Duke of Alston. Without that letter, they would have ignored him again.

For a moment, it rankled that Alston's letter had made such a difference. But however unfair, it was the way of the world. Alston's name had gotten him in the door. Ultimately, it would be Adrian's work that they accepted or rejected, whether he came with a recommendation from the duke or not. The rest was up to him.

He returned to the house in time to find Dudley stomping down the front stairs in high dudgeon.

"You've got to do something about that sister of yours, Alston," he said. "Far too independent for my tastes—and a lot of others, I'd wager."

Adrian felt such relief to discover that Rose had turned Dudley down that he didn't even bristle at the insults. Smothering his urge to smile, he held out his hands in a helpless gesture. "What can I do? I'm only her brother."

Dudley harrumphed loudly and marched off.

The footman had barely taken the hat from Adrian's hand when Rose's voice came from the top of the stairs. "Simon? Is that you?"

"My very self."

"Would you be so kind as to come up here? Now."

Adrian heard the annoyance in her voice, and he gave the footman a rueful shake of his head. "Looks like I'm in trouble now."

Rose waited outside the library. She grabbed his arm and pulled him into the room, shutting the door firmly behind her. The look on her face could only be described as fury.

Adrian raised a brow. "Dudley?"

"Why did you tell him that he could speak with me?" she demanded. "How could you even think that I—"

"I don't know what to think," Adrian said. "If you want me

to protect you, you have to give me a list of names of the men you are willing to see. Or unwilling—whatever is shortest."

"Use your imagination," she said. "How could you even think I would consider Dudley?"

"What qualities are you looking for in a husband?"

Her eyes flashed angrily. "Certainly not middle age."

"He claimed his maturity would be a good influence on you. Says you are too independent."

Rose gave an unladylike snort. "If I wanted to be truly independent, I would marry someone on his deathbed. Then at least I would end up a young widow."

"A *rich* young widow."

She smiled mischievously. "That goes without saying. Where were you this afternoon? Did you go to the Society? Did they talk with you?"

"Yes," he replied, feigning nonchalance.

"What did they say?"

He gave a deep sigh. "They were not impressed."

"What?" Her expression turned indignant. "How dare they treat you—"

"Until I brought out your letter."

A smile slowly spread over her face. "Which convinced them of your remarkable talents."

He shrugged, still hiding his excitement. "They are going to consider my drawings and the article for publication."

"That's wonderful, Adrian." Rose's eyes glittered with excitement. "I am so happy. Did they tell you when they will decide?"

"I imagine it will depend on how well the talk goes."

She looked puzzled. "What talk?"

He could not hold back any longer, and grinned at her. "The talk I am giving at their next meeting."

Rose stared at him in silence for a moment, then let out a shriek of joy. "Oh, Adrian, that is wonderful!"

"All thanks to you." Adrian grabbed her hands and twirled her around the room in dizzying circles. "My lady patroness."

She laughed along with him, her head thrown back, looking

joyful and happy and all the things he himself felt. He owed her so much. Without that letter, this never would have happened. Without Rose—

He suddenly realized the impropriety of his behavior and brought their impromptu dance to an end. He stood there, her hands clasped in his, while he gazed into her eyes for a long, slow minute.

If he was not careful, he was going to fall in love with this woman. If it was not already too late.

Adrian let his hands fall from her side and coughed, trying to hide his sudden discomfort. He did not want Rose to think that anything was amiss. "I guess I am more excited about this than I thought."

She squeezed his hands. "So am I. It is even more than you hoped for. Is the meeting open to the public? May I come and listen?"

"I suspect that when the time comes, you will be thoroughly sick of hearing my remarks," he said. "I intend to make you my practice audience."

"Gladly," she replied.

"They are hoping that the duke will attend, as well."

"The duke?" She looked confused for a moment, then laughed aloud. "You mean Simon! I should like to see how you arrange *that*!"

"I explained that Alston was a very busy man."

"Well, you can tell them that the duke's sister would be more than willing to be there—and the duke's uncle—who will both applaud enthusiastically throughout the speech."

"I wish I had your confidence. Now that I stop to think about it, I am terrified. What am I going to say to all those learned men that they do not already know?"

She put her hands on her hips and stared at him, a smile twitching on her lips. "Is this the same Adrian Stamford who gallantly fought the fire at the lodge? The same Adrian Stamford who called me a spoiled, arrogant brat and threatened to leave me in an inn yard? I did not think you were afraid of anything."

He shook his head. "I was far more frightened last night when I lost you at the rout."

"I promise that you will not lose me again."

Adrian turned away. If only that were true.

What really terrified him was knowing that once her brother returned, she would be lost to him forever.

Chapter 13

Rose was truly thrilled for Adrian. She knew how much this chance meant to him. And surely, after those learned men heard him speak, they would recognize his talents and shower him with praise. Adrian Stamford would become a respected name among antiquarians. Why, he might even head the society one day. His discoveries would be on display in the British Museum.

She wanted him to be a success. Rose cared about his future, cared what would happen to him once he finished masquerading as Simon. She wanted to know that he would be happy and successful.

And if he became a respected antiquarian, she might even have the opportunity to read about his activities from time to time.

Rose wanted to celebrate Adrian's wonderful news, but how? Their evenings were filled with dinners or rout parties or trips to the theater. Celebrating at lunch did not seem particularly festive.

She would present him with a special gift—something that would mark his achievement, like a watch or a penknife, a gift that would always remind him of the giver.

And she could order him some new clothes to replace the ones he lost in the fire. Everything he wore now belonged to Simon. He needed to have some of his own.

She wondered what one wore to address the Antiquities Society? Certainly not formal evening wear. But breeches or pantaloons? Plain or embroidered waistcoats? Perhaps Simon's tailor would know. She wanted Adrian to look perfect.

It was late the next afternoon when she finally returned to the house. Her shopping excursion lasted longer than she had intended, and as a result packages were heaped on the seat of the carriage. It took three footmen to carry them all into the house.

Rose had not expected to buy quite so many things for herself, but she had spotted that lovely hat in the window next to the stationer's store. And she could not resist the jet bracelet she saw at the jeweler's. Before she knew it, she'd bought more things for herself than she had for Adrian. Realizing that simply would not do, she retraced her steps and purchased some additional gifts for him.

As she hoped, Adrian was in the library, seated at the desk, looking very scholarly with his head bent over a book. She directed the footmen to take the packages inside.

Adrian's mouth dropped open as a parade of footmen entered the library. He could barely see them behind the towering stacks of boxes and paper-wrapped packages in their arms. What was going on?

He saw Rose trailing behind the last footman, still in her bonnet and pelisse. Adrian realized this was her doing.

Eyes sparkling, she greeted him with a wide smile. "How was your day, Simon?"

"Quiet, until now."

She laughed and motioned for the footmen to set down their burdens. After they left, she removed her bonnet and sat in the armchair facing him.

"I am exhausted. I spent the entire day shopping."

"So I noticed," Adrian observed dryly. "The London merchants must be even more pleased than your beaus to have you back in town."

She shrugged off her pelisse. "I had not intended to buy quite so many things . . . but you must see!"

Rose took the lid off a hat box and drew out a bonnet, fluffing out the plumes. Setting it on her head, she tied the ribbons in a jaunty bow and looked at Adrian.

"What do you think?"

Adrian thought she would look lovely in anything, but he nodded appreciatively. It was a dashing hat.

Pulling the paper off another package, Rose pulled out a delicately fringed shawl and wrapped it around her shoulders. "I shall wear this to dinner tonight."

As he watched her model her purchases, Adrian wondered how much money she had spent on this "little" shopping expedition—probably more money than he spent in several years. That shawl alone must have cost several guineas.

She tore open another wrapping and held up a pair of men's bedroom slippers. "For you."

Surprised by the gift, Adrian took them from her. They looked to be of the finest calfskin—far more suited to ducal feet than his. "Thank you."

With a giggle, she turned back to her hoard. "That's not all."

To his growing dismay, it seemed half the packages she had bought were for him—linen handkerchiefs, socks, cravats.

"You did not need to do this for me," he said when she presented him with a silver inkstand that would have looked superb on the desk of a duke. He had trouble picturing it sitting on his scratched dining table, where he did his writing.

"I want to," she replied simply, before she handed him a pocket watch with the initials "A.S." engraved on the cover.

"Rose." This time he gave her a stern look. "You cannot buy me all these things. It is not right."

She glanced over her shoulder. "Why not?"

"Because . . . because . . ." His voice trailed off.

Because he could not reciprocate.

He wanted to be able to shower her with feathers and bonnets and gowns and jewels—all the things a wealthy husband would buy her. All the things he never could.

And she had probably not given a second thought to the amount of money she spent today.

"I particularly thought you would like this," she said, handing him a brass-bound box. He lifted the slanted lid, exposing a portable writing desk.

"You can take it with you to your digs and do your drawings while you're there," she said.

"Thank you," he mumbled.

Yet once again, she went back to the chair. "I saved this for last—it was the only thing I could find on the topic." She handed him a slim, leather-bound volume.

Adrian opened the cover and read the title page: *Mona Antiqua Restaurata : An Archaeological Discourse on the Antiquities Natural and Historical of the Isle of Anglesey.*

Rowlands. She had actually found a copy of Rowlands.

He stared at her in stunned amazement. "Wherever did you find this?"

"At a bookseller's. It was the only book he had about antiquities. Is it something you can use?"

"Use?" Adrian stared at the book in his hands, still wondering at her marvelous luck. "I've been aching to get a copy of this. It was privately printed, and there are only a few copies."

"Oh, good. I hoped you would like it."

Reason overcame him at last. He remembered how much the one copy he had ever seen cost. "How much did you pay for it?"

She smiled mysteriously. "Didn't someone ever tell you that it is not polite to ask the price of a gift?"

"But it must have cost a fortune! I know it did. I will not allow you to spend that kind of money on me."

"Oh, pooh," she said, waving away his protests. "It did not cost *that* much."

Accepting all these gifts from her made him feel . . . useless, dependent. "I cannot accept this." He gestured at the other gifts on the table. "Or these either."

She looked confused. "Why ever not?"

"It is not proper."

"Do not be silly." Rose laughed. "You are my *brother*, remember? I can buy you anything I want."

"I am not your brother, Rose." Adrian picked up the book and gave it a wistful look before setting it down again. "Why did you buy all these things?"

"I wanted to do something for you." Her voice was soft. "I wanted to celebrate."

"Celebrate?"

"Your speech for the society."

Adrian sighed. She had meant well, but she had no idea how her generosity made him feel. How it highlighted the difference between their lives.

"It was thoughtful of you to think of me, but I cannot allow it."

She looked at him, bewildered, and he saw the glint of tears in her eyes.

"Rose—"

"You are an ungrateful wretch, Adrian Stamford." Rose ran out of the room.

Adrian grimaced. Now he had hurt her, which was the last thing on earth he wanted to do. He needed to go after her, to explain the problem was his, not hers. That he had his pride.

But he remained in his chair. It was no use; it would not change anything. He had an adequate income, but it would never provide the luxuries to which Rose was accustomed. No apologies would ever change that.

Adrian sat back and looked over the gifts she had given him. He picked up the watch, turning it over in his hand, then flipped open the lid. There was another inscription inside: "For Adrian, May 1816, R.A.D."

He felt a strange tugging at his heart. Rosemary Alicia Devering, daughter and sister of the Duke of Alston, his friend—a woman he wanted more than anything.

A woman he could never have.

In the privacy of her room, Rose wiped her eyes. Why was Adrian being so horrid? She only wanted to please him.

She had given a great deal of thought to everything she bought him. She envisioned him dipping his quill into the inkwell, then bending his head to cover a page with his scrawling handwriting. Thought of him sitting on a pile of rocks, sketching a new discovery atop his portable desk.

And when he consulted his watch, to know if it was time to dismiss his students, it would be the watch she bought him. And perhaps he would think of her for a moment.

Each morning she awoke with a mixture of hope and dread. Hope that her brother would return, and dread that he would, for then Adrian would have to leave—leave so suddenly that she might not even be able to say good-bye to him.

She would miss him when he left. Miss the way he teased her, yet treated her with a tenderness she never received from her brother. Rose wanted him to know that she considered him her friend.

Now he was angry, and she did not know how to make amends. Yet the more she thought about it, the more irritated she grew. It was highly unfair of Adrian to be angry with her.

Certainly, she had become carried away and bought him far more than she originally planned. But she had a generous allowance. It was hers to spend as she wished, and if she wished to spend it on him, that was her choice. Why would he object to that?

She thought back over his reactions, his growing dismay as she pulled out each new present, his shocked comment about the price of the book.

The price. Money.

Now she knew why he had been upset. He did not want her spending money on him, but he was too full of pride to tell her. She was wealthy, and he was not.

Why should it matter?

Because in the normal course of things, a man like Adrian would not have dealings with the daughter of a duke. By hiring him to play Simon, she had forced the contact on him. He was living the life of a duke right now, but when it ended, he would go back to his snug little cottage and those unruly twins. While she remained in her world.

She had given him a glimpse of another world, one to which he could never belong. And her largesse today had only emphasized that fact.

She shook her head. He was being silly. She did not mind

that he was not of her class. He had demonstrated over the last weeks that the real differences between them were minor—in her eyes, and his, but not society's.

An ineffable sadness overcame her. Why could she not find a man from her own circle whom she could like and respect? Someone like Adrian.

Rose gasped and pressed her hand over her mouth, as if trying to take back the words she'd uttered only in her head.

Someone like Adrian.

A man about whom she dare not have such thoughts. A man she could only look upon as a friend, and nothing more. Because that was the way the world was.

The air between them was strained that night. When she came down to the drawing room, she wanted to tell him that she understood his dismay, wanted to convince him that it was not important, but she did not know how to broach the subject.

And Adrian gave her no opportunity. He said nothing on the drive to Lord Ramsey's, and remained icily polite after they collected Juliet and continued on to their dinner party. The journey home at the end of the evening was equally silent. The moment they entered the house, Adrian disappeared into the library.

Saddened by it all, Rose went to her room. Why did there have to be this gulf between them? Could he not forget for a time who she was—and who he was, as well? Pretend that it did not matter, at least until he was gone?

Adrian knew his behavior was churlish, and by morning he was eager to make amends with Rose. She had not meant to hurt him. She simply did not understand. He searched her out in the drawing room.

"I want to apologize for yesterday," Adrian said. "I sounded ungrateful, and you were being very generous."

"It is all right," Rose said. "I bought more things than I should have."

He pulled out the watch and held it in his palm. "This was very nice."

"I wanted you to have something to remind you of our time together."

Her words stabbed at his heart. Adrian wanted to pull her into his arms, to hold her tightly and tell her how he felt about her. But pride held him back.

Instead, he gently brushed her cheek with his fingers. "I will never forget you, Rose."

He looked into her eyes, searching for a sign of her thoughts. Dare he hope—?

A knock sounded on the door, and they sprang apart.

"Lady Ramsey and Lady Juliet are here, Your Grace." Markham stood at attention.

Adrian had forgotten that they were coming this morning to examine the house. Entertaining those two women was the last thing Adrian wanted to do right now. He still had not eased the awkwardness between himself and Rose—an awkwardness that was all his fault.

But his job was to play the duke, and the duke would graciously display his home to his future wife.

He tossed Rose a pleading look. "You will join us, won't you?"

She remained silent for a moment, then nodded.

Markham escorted the two women into the drawing room. Adrian smothered a grin at the sight of the enormous bonnet atop Juliet's head. Laden with both flowers and feathers, it looked so heavy he wondered how she could keep her head up. Not at all like the tasteful hat Rose had modeled for him yesterday.

He greeted Lady Ramsey and her daughter with feigned enthusiasm.

"It is so thoughtful of you to give Juliet the opportunity to survey her future home," Lady Ramsey simpered.

Adrian took Juliet's hand and brought it to his lips. "I want my wife to be happy here."

Juliet giggled. "I certainly hope I will be."

A footman entered and took their wraps.

"Lady Rosemary." Juliet's mother held out her hands in greeting. "How nice of you to join us."

"Simon insisted that I help. He feels he knows so little about household matters."

A slight frown creased Juliet's face. "I do not wish to bother you, Rosemary. I am sure you will find it dreadfully dull to walk through your own home."

As if he would not, Adrian thought. "Rose will be a far better guide than I. She knows so much more about these things."

Juliet looked annoyed, but did not object further.

Adrian noticed the calculating expression with which Lady Ramsey examined the contents of the drawing room, from the gilt-framed paintings on the wall to the Louis XVII table beside the door.

"Such a lovely room," Lady Ramsey said. "Look Juliet, how the draperies pick out the green in the carpet."

"I abhor that shade of green," Juliet said.

Adrian groaned inwardly. This was not going to be an easy day. He pasted a false smile on his face. "Shall we get started?"

Between Lady Ramsey's effusive praise of each and every thing she saw, and Juliet's condescending dismissal of everything as being the wrong color or the wrong style or not quite suitable for such an exalted household, Adrian was ready to wring both their necks.

He admired Rose's tact in ignoring Juliet's snide comments.

His patience had worn thin by the time they reached the bedrooms. He opened the door to the duchess's chamber and escorted the ladies inside.

Juliet took one look around the room with its maroon and gold appointments and made a moue of distaste. "How awful! I must have this room redone before the wedding. It would give me nightmares to sleep here."

Adrian pinned her with a cold stare. "This was my mother's room."

Juliet had the sense to look embarrassed.

"Juliet has never been overly fond of the darker colors," Lady Ramsey said, trying to smooth over the tension.

"Juliet does not seem to be overly fond of much," Adrian said. "Perhaps you think we should gut the interior and start from scratch. Or better yet, shall I sell this place and build you a new one?"

She looked at him eagerly. "Could we?"

He glared at her. "You may decorate your own rooms as you like, but as for the rest of the house—"

Rose laid a hand on his arm, and he caught himself.

"Simon so hates change." She leaned forward and spoke to Juliet in a conspiratorial tone. "You have to sneak the changes past him. As long as you don't draw his attention to them, he rarely notices."

Adrian silently thanked her for salvaging the situation. "What changes have you worked that I have not noticed?"

She smiled mischievously. "Oh, nothing, nothing."

"I am eager to see your room, Lady Rosemary." Lady Ramsey smiled politely. "I am certain it is decorated in exquisite taste."

"I imagine Juliet would prefer to see the ducal chamber," Adrian said quickly. He wanted to spare Rose from any more of Juliet's critical comments.

Juliet giggled. "I would like to see your *room*, Alston."

Adrian saw Rose roll her eyes, and he barely stifled a laugh. He was starting to feel sorry for Simon, saddled with Juliet for a wife. Adrian would be doing him an enormous favor if he insulted her to the point that she called off the engagement.

But the duke's future had been arranged years ago. It was not up to Adrian to alter it for him, no matter how much he wanted to.

However, he was not going to stand by and listen to any more criticisms of Rose. The moment he found himself alone with Juliet again—as horrifying as that thought was—he would tell her so in no uncertain terms.

The ducal bedchamber apparently met with Juliet's approval. Adrian noticed how her eyes kept straying to the bed. Anticipating her wedding night? He shuddered at the thought. Thank God that was Alston's responsibility.

Assuming the duke actually showed up for his own wedding. There still had been no word of him. Rose showed little concern, but Adrian was worried. There was a time limit to his masquerade, and that day was creeping ever closer.

What kind of fellow was Alston to stay away for so long? Or did he know Juliet well enough to know what he was getting into, and wanted to put off the day of reckoning as long as he dared?

That was a motive Adrian could understand.

At long last, Juliet and her mother departed. Adrian went immediately to the library and poured himself a large glass of brandy. Rose followed him there.

"Does your brother know what a featherhead he is marrying?" Adrian asked, settling into a chair. "If she were my wife, I would strangle her within a week."

"She is young and arrogant, and her mother does not help," Rose observed. "Simon will manage to deal with her."

"I am beginning to understand why he is staying away."

He saw a brief flash of uneasiness cross Rose's face. "He is coming back, isn't he?"

"Of course!"

"You have never told me the whole story—why it is so important for me to play your brother." Adrian leaned forward. "Why didn't you just tell Ramsey he was out of the country?"

Rose glanced at her hands. She was clutching them so hard her knuckles showed white.

"Rose?"

"We dared not give Ramsey any reason to break off the engagement." She spoke so softly he had to lean forward to listen. "There is a provision in my grandfather's will that if Simon does not marry Juliet, the greater portion of the holdings are diverted away from him."

Anger filled him. Why did parents—and grandparents— think they had the right to rule their children's lives with such an iron hand? Dictating the woman Simon must marry was abominable.

"That's ridiculous. I would not stand for it."

"You are not a duke," she said. "You have seen this house, and Ashbridge. They cost a fortune to maintain. Without Juliet, Simon would lose nearly all the ready cash."

"So this entire masquerade is all about money?"

She nodded.

"What happens to you if Simon does not marry her?"

"My dowry is tied to Simon's income," she said. "I lose as well."

Adrian stared at her. No wonder she had been so involved in carrying out this impersonation. "That is why you want to find a husband. You need one safely in hand in case Simon's circumstances change."

"You have seen Juliet—I cannot continue to live here or at Ashbridge after they are wed. I have to find a husband."

"And better to do so while he still thinks you have money."

She looked down. "Yes."

Anger surged through Adrian. Not at Rose, but at her grandfather.

He saw the apprehensive look in her eyes. Did she think he would think less of her, now that she had confessed the truth?

"I pray that your brother returns in time for the wedding," he said. "He deserves to have Lady Juliet tied around his neck for life after putting you through this."

"Thank you, Adrian. I was afraid . . ."

"That I would blame you?"

She nodded. "I should have told you why this was so important."

"It does not matter. I will still do all I can to help. As your brother, it is my responsibility to find you a husband."

She sighed. "I suppose I must settle on someone, mustn't I? Has anyone else approached you besides Boxey and Dudley?"

"Only those two."

She gave a mock shudder. "That is not much of a choice."

"It's early yet," Adrian said. "Do you have any particular men in mind?"

She shook her head.

"If you can't give me names, how about requirements? Age?"

"Not above five and thirty," she said. "And no more youngsters like Boxey. I want a husband, not a younger brother."

Grabbing a piece of paper from the desk, Adrian settled himself into the chair and dipped a quill into the inkwell. With a grand flourish, he labeled the list "Rose's Requirements," and wrote "Age—25–35."

She giggled when she saw what he'd done. "Oh, stop being silly."

"I am serious," he said. "How can you settle on anyone if you don't even know what you want." He dipped the quill in the ink again. "Now, what about a title?"

She pretended to ponder the question. "I would consider a viscount, I think—if he was handsome enough."

"Money?"

"Of course." Rose gave an emphatic nod of her head. "I want a very generous settlement—and a huge clothing allowance."

"How about personal characteristics? Height? Hair color? Or does that matter?"

Rose giggled. "Those are very important matters. Not too tall—your height is about right. And lean—I do not want someone who looks like the Prince Regent."

"Should he have musical abilities?"

"I don't care."

"A sportsman? Or a scholar?"

"Either would be fine, as long as he doesn't bore me with too much talk about it. I want someone who will make me laugh, and who is interested in something—like you and your antiquities."

"A pity," he said, shaking his head.

"What?" Her brow puckered.

"If I had money and a title, I would fit the bill perfectly."

He said the words in jest, but as he looked at her, seeing

those deep blue eyes widening with surprise, he suddenly realized he hadn't been jesting at all. He liked the idea of spending the rest of his life with Rose—without having to pretend to be her brother.

She looked taken aback at his words, then laughed lightly. "Then you should be able to find exactly the right man for me. Look for someone like you."

He hadn't expected her to pretend he was serious, but her lighthearted words left him feeling strangely deflated. Merely someone *like* him. One who had title, and money; who belonged to her own class.

Not him.

Rose glanced at the clock and jumped to her feet. "Goodness, look at the time! I will be late for Lady Tattenham's dinner if I do not start dressing." She walked toward the door. "Do not linger too long—you need to dress also."

Adrian nodded.

Just at those moments when he thought the barriers were down between them, when he thought that there might be some way to resolve his hopeless longings, he was brought up short with a reminder of the gulf between them.

Aristocratic marriages were first and foremost business arrangements, after all.

He hated the thought of Rose being condemned to that sort of marriage. He wanted her to be deliriously in love with her husband, and he with her. To have the kind of marriage that would shock and scandalize the *ton* for its sheer, unbridled joy. To have the kind of marriage his parents had given up everything to have.

Had Rose once wanted that kind of love? Or had she never even considered the possibility? Worse, what if she once dreamed of such a thing, but had discarded it in the face of reality and now, with Simon's upcoming marriage, necessity? That would be the worst thing of all. To long for love, and have to settle for amiable toleration.

No, there was one thing worse. To be in love, and know that your situation was hopeless. To know that no matter what you said or did, you could never be a part of that person's life. That was the worst thing.

All he could do was watch from the side and pray that she made a choice that turned out well for her. And try to forget his own painful longings.

Chapter 14

❦

"The Earl of Lowden to see you, Lady Rosemary."

Rose, enjoying a quiet morning in the drawing room, jumped from the sofa at Markham's words. Lowden? Here? He was supposed to be an ocean away, in North America.

Lowden. Simon's closest friend; the one person who would notice that Adrian was not the duke.

The disaster she had long feared was here.

She had to get him out of the house, quickly, before he asked to see Simon. Rose glanced out the window. The grey clouds looked ominous, but they would not stop her. She would ask Lowden to take her for a drive or a walk or anything to get him away from the house.

Wiping damp palms on her skirt, she struggled to compose herself before the earl came in.

"Rosemary!" Lowden walked through the doorway, hands outstretched. The tall, blond earl looked pale and thin—yet still highly dangerous to Adrian.

"Hello, Lowden." She took his hands. "This is a surprise. I thought you were far across the ocean."

"Do not mention the word 'ocean' to me." He groaned. "I never want to see a body of water larger than the Serpentine again."

She laughed. "Did you have a rough crossing?"

"Abominable."

"But how wonderful that you are back. I have been sadly bored. Now you can entertain me."

He smiled. "I am always at your disposal."

Rose stood. "Good. Did you come by carriage or on foot?"

"On foot."

"Then we shall go for a walk—unless you wish me to order the landau brought around."

"The weather is not the best—"

"Nonsense. I could do with a bit of fresh air. Give me a few minutes, and I shall—"

"Rose, whatever did you do with the rest of my speech?"

She froze and stared in dismay at the doorway, where Adrian stood, papers clutched in his hand.

"Alston!" Lowden was across the room and pumping Adrian's hand. "You're a sight for sore eyes." He slapped him on the shoulder. "What is this I hear about you being caught in the matrimonial noose?"

Adrian smiled. "It is true."

Rose stepped between the two men and grabbed Lowden's arm, eager to get him away from Adrian. "Simon, if you will excuse us, Lord Lowden and I were just leaving for a walk."

"Oh, no," Lowden protested. "I want to hear more about the upcoming nuptials. Fell into Ramsey's snare, did you?"

"Now that you are back, I guess we will have to invite you to the wedding." Adrian turned to Rose. "Do you think we can find room in the church for one more?"

Rose felt limp with relief. Adrian had recognized the name and remembered who Lowden was.

Lowden looked taken aback for a moment, then he laughed. "Don't put on that ducal starch for me, you rogue. I expect one of the best seats in the house."

"Lowden." Rose tapped her foot with impatience. "I believe I do have a previous claim on your time."

He reddened. "You are right. Say, what do you two have planned for the evening? Can I invite you to dine with me?"

"Oh, I am certain you would rather spend your second evening in town with more enlivening company." Rose grabbed his arm and pulled him toward the door.

"Come to the theater with us tonight," Adrian said. "Rose needs an escort."

"This is my lucky day," Lowden said, smiling at Rose. "I presume Lady Juliet will be with us as well?"

Adrian nodded.

Rose stared at Adrian, wondering if he had lost his mind. Did he not realize the risk Lowden posed?

"I will meet you here this evening," Lowden said.

Rose pulled him out the door before Adrian made an even more outrageous suggestion. How was she going to keep Lowden from growing suspicious if he spent time with Adrian?

"Simon seemed rather subdued," Lowden observed as they walked toward the park.

Rose laughed lightly. "Oh, he has been in a daze ever since the engagement was announced."

"Finally realized what it means to give up his bachelorhood, eh?" Lowden's eyes twinkled merrily.

"I think so." She gazed intently into his dark eyes. "Now, please, tell me all about your journey. How did you find America?"

A wave of exhaustion passed over Rose when Lowden finally took her home. It had taken every ounce of her energy to keep the conversation focused on him, and away from Simon. And tonight would be even worse. Why had Adrian invited Lowden to join them at the theater?

She wanted to make up an excuse and beg off. But that would be of little use—and it was Adrian and Lowden she had to keep apart. Adrian was the one who should fall prey to some loathsome ailment and be forced to stay home.

Chilblains? The weather was too warm.

Gout? He was too young.

She thought brain fever was the appropriate illness, but that was a bit too drastic.

Rose found Adrian in the library, immersed in the book she had given him.

"What were you thinking earlier?" she demanded after she closed the door. "Did you forget who Lowden is?"

"Your brother's close friend," he replied.

"Then why did you invite him to go with us tonight?"

He leaned back in his chair. "Think on it, Rose. He will grow suspicious if I try to avoid him."

"But you have to avoid him. He will know you are not Simon."

Adrian shook his head. "What chance will we have to talk at the theater?"

She realized he was right. They could not avoid Lowden, or else he would suspect something odd was going on. The theater was a safe, public setting. Juliet would demand Adrian's constant attention. He would be safe enough.

But what would happen tomorrow—or the next day?

When would Simon be back?

Now that Lowden was here, Rose realized that every day her brother stayed away increased the danger to Adrian. Simon *had* to be back soon; the wedding was almost upon them. She only had to keep Adrian safe from discovery for a few more days.

Rose glanced over at Adrian, who was watching her intently.

"Everything will be all right," he said. "If Juliet talks as much as usual, no one will be able to get a word in edgewise."

She wished she could be so confident. Rose felt as if she were enmeshed in a nightmare from which there was no awakening.

"Tonight, I will leave early to get Juliet, and then come back here for you and Lowden," he said. "That will help."

"And I will insist on sitting next to Juliet at the theater, which will keep you and Lowden apart. He will not have the opportunity to speak more than two words to you."

"The person I want to speak with is your uncle," Adrian said. "Surely, he can get information from someone in the government who knows when your brother will return. I do not want you in this constant state of worry."

If only it was that easy. She hesitated, wanting to confide in him, but feared to do so. How would he react when he learned the truth, learned that no one knew where Simon was? Learned that the situation was far more desperate than she had let on. "I will suggest that to Uncle."

He smiled. "Good. Now, I want your opinion about this section of the speech. Do you think I should . . . ?"

By that evening Rose's confidence had flagged. She found it more and more difficult to act as if everything were going well. There were too many things to worry about—Lowden and Adrian, Simon's whereabouts.

Where in God's name was her brother?

The thought that had been hovering in the back of her mind for days now pushed its way into her consciousness.

What if Simon was not coming back? What if he was dead?

She balled her hands into fists. Rose refused to believe that her brother was dead. Injured, perhaps, stranded somewhere, but not dead. He would be found, eventually.

But if that did not happen within the next week, it would be too late. Why hadn't they gone to Ramsey with the truth? The wedding could have been delayed. Juliet wanted to be a duchess badly enough; she could have persuaded her father to be patient.

Now, after using Adrian to play Simon, Rose and her uncle would have to tell Ramsey that Simon was backing out of the wedding. It was their only choice—she could not confess that the man who had been dancing attendance on Juliet was an impostor. Society would be scandalized at the news; Rose would be ruined.

In four days Adrian would give his talk to the society. That would be their deadline. If her brother had not returned by then, "Simon" would have to mysteriously disappear, the wedding canceled. Ramsey would rightly be furious. Juliet would not quite be left at the altar, but near enough.

At least things would go right for Adrian. If his talk went well, he would be well on his way to achieving success with his antiquarian work. Rose sighed. It was the one good thing that would come out of this whole mess.

*   *   *

That evening, Adrian departed for the Ramsey house far earlier than he needed to, in case Lowden came early. He agreed with Rose, the less he spoke with the earl, the better. Rose was already dressed and waiting; she could deal with Lowden when he arrived.

Mercifully, Adrian did not have to wait too long for Juliet this night.

"Your sister is not going with us?" she asked as he helped her into the carriage.

"We are going back to get her."

Juliet frowned. "Are we never to be alone, Alston?"

He patted her hand. "We will be alone often enough once we are wed."

She slid closer to him on the seat. "I can barely wait until that day."

"It will not be long now," Adrian said.

Juliet lay her hand on his thigh. "I am particularly looking forward to our wedding night."

Adrian laughed uneasily. Thank God it was only a short trip to Bruton Street. He began to think even Lowden was a safer companion than Lady Juliet.

"Do I shock you?" Juliet asked.

"No, not at all." Adrian forced a smile. "I cannot wait for that night, myself."

To his dismay, she started stroking his thigh. "We are alone now, Alston."

He swallowed nervously, then leaned over and planted a chaste kiss on her lips. "It would not do for you to arrive looking . . . mussed."

Juliet moved away. "Really, Alston, I begin to think your reputation is sadly exaggerated."

"What reputation?"

"All that talk about your fancy ladies. Did you spend all your time discussing politics?"

Adrian remembered Rose's description of her brother's interests: horses, gambling, and women. Adrian had not indulged in a single one of the duke's vices since coming to London. Was Juliet growing suspicious?

"I am to be a married man," he said. "I can no longer indulge myself with the pleasures of bachelorhood."

"You could at least kiss me with a little more enthusiasm."

"Juliet, dear, I dare not." Adrian decided lying was his best option. "I fear that if I start to show you the depth of my desire for you, I will not be able to stop. I do not wish to dishonor you before the wedding."

She sniffed, but the excuse seemed to mollify her.

Adrian was thankful when the coach finally pulled up outside the ducal mansion, and he jumped to open the door. Lowden and Rose were already coming down the steps, and he sat back down.

"They are coming."

"They?" Juliet looked puzzled.

Adrian realized he had neglected to tell her about Lowden. "Did I not tell you? Lord Lowden is joining us as well."

"I had not heard he was in town." To Adrian's relief, she did not sound irritated.

"I believe he returned only yesterday."

Rose climbed into the coach, followed by Lowden.

"Lady Juliet!" Lowden took her hand and brought it to his lips. "I salute you. You are an exceptional woman to have captured Alston."

Juliet giggled coyly.

"Lowden just returned from the Americas, and he has the most marvelous stories." Rose smiled at him. "Tell her about the bear."

"I am certain Lady Juliet has seen a bear."

"But not such a ferocious one." Rose shivered. "Merely listening to the tale frightened me."

Adrian grinned to himself. Rose had matters well in hand already, as he knew she would. With little prompting, she managed to keep Lowden talking until they reached the theater.

He saw that Rose's arrival tonight did not garner the attention that her previous visit had. Was it because she had an escort other than her brother? Whatever the reason, he was glad. He needed her help in keeping Lowden distracted during the evening, and she would not be able to do that if she was surrounded by adoring men.

Once in the box, it was easy enough to sit Rose and Juliet together, with the men on either end. Adrian would not be able to say a word to Lowden, even if he wanted to. Juliet demanded his undivided attention.

She chattered away during the entire first act, noting the people she recognized in the audience, commenting on the actors' costumes, and critiquing their performances. If it had not been for Lowden's presence in the box, Adrian would cheerfully have stuffed the Duke of Alston's elegant, monogrammed handkerchief into her mouth.

"I am so dreadfully thirsty," Juliet announced when the lights rose during the break. "Do get me some lemonade, Alston."

"I will join you." Lowden stood up. "I am certain that Lady Rosemary wishes something as well."

"You can get drinks for both the ladies," Adrian said quickly. "I will stay here."

"Both of you may go," Juliet said. "Then Rosemary and I can have a nice coze."

"Alas, your mother would never forgive me if I left you here without male protection," Adrian said.

Juliet giggled. "Such a gallant!"

Lowden gave Adrian an odd look before he went to get the lemonade.

Adrian had just enough time to share a look of relief with Rose before Juliet began talking again.

"Where are all your suitors tonight?" Adrian asked Rose, when Juliet stopped to take a breath. "Has Lowden scared them away?"

She laughed. "I certainly hope so."

"Lowden is a very respectable catch," Juliet said. "You should pay more attention to him, Rosemary."

"I think my sister knows how to deal with the men in her life, my dear." Adrian patted Juliet's hand to take some of the sting out of his words, even though he was seething. How would Rose endure having this woman for a sister-in-law?

Only moments before the curtain rose, Lowden returned with the lemonade.

"It was a regular crush out there," he said.

Adrian was glad he had been delayed. Between his irritation at Juliet's constant talk, and his worries about Lowden, Adrian felt as if he were perched on the edge of his seat for the remainder of the evening. And matters were only going to get worse. Avoiding Lowden in the days to come was going to take all the ingenuity he had.

When the curtain came down for the final time, they joined the queue leaving the theater.

"Shall we go over to the club after we take the ladies home?" Lowden suggested to Adrian before they climbed into the carriage.

He shook his head. "Not tonight. I'm fagged."

"You're becoming a regular dull dog," Lowden complained. "Do not tell me that you plan to be one of those staid and proper husbands?"

"But of course, " Adrian replied with a wry grin.

Lowden frowned. "Something has happened to you, Alston. You do not seem to be the same person you were when I left."

"I am finally facing up to the responsibilities that I have to bear." Adrian hoped he was not doing permanent damage to Alston's friendship with the earl, but he had to keep the man at arm's length. He must never guess that Adrian was not the real duke.

"You are going to invite me in for a drink, at least," Lowden said after Adrian escorted Juliet to her door.

"I am rather tired tonight, as well," Rose said. "Perhaps another time."

Lowden's expression turned impassive. "I see. Well, I suppose I should be grateful that you allowed me to spend a few hours in your presence tonight. There is no need for you to see me home—I can walk from here. Good night, Lady Rosemary. Alston." He climbed out of the carriage.

"He is angry," Adrian said as the coach pulled away.

"I know," Rose replied. "But we cannot be too careful. You have to keep away from him."

Adrian pressed a hand to his brow. "I feel a strange illness coming on."

Rose sighed. "I hate to admit it, but that may be the best solution. Juliet will be annoyed, but it will keep Lowden from growing more offended."

"To what malady shall I succumb? One, of course, that will miraculously cure itself in time for the wedding."

"Brain fever would at least explain your erratic behavior."

"Why, thank you," Adrian retorted. "And here I thought I was behaving quite normally."

"I am teasing you," Rose said. "A simple catarrh will do. No one will wish to be near you."

"Catarrh it is."

The coach stopped at Bruton Street. Adrian helped Rose down, and they walked toward the door.

A man jumped out at them from the shadows.

"Lady Rosemary!" he cried.

Adrian grabbed Rose and shoved her behind him before he recognized the man.

"Boxham! What are you doing here?"

Rose stepped to his side. "Boxey? You nearly frightened me to death."

"Beggin' your pardon, Lady Rosemary. It was not my intention. I just had . . . I must speak with you."

"Well, speak then," Adrian said. "The night air is cold. You do not wish Lady Rosemary to catch a chill."

"I wish to speak to her *privately*," Boxham said.

Rose groaned. "Boxey, not again. What did I tell you last time? I am honored by your tender feelings for me. But I know that we will not suit."

"But we will!" he cried. "You must give me the chance, my lady. I can show you that I will be the most perfect husband. I intend to worship the ground you walk on, kiss the hem of your dress."

"I do not think that groveling appeals to my sister," Adrian said.

"Do you mind?" Boxham snapped at Adrian. "I meant for this to be private."

Adrian laid a companionable hand on the man's shoulder. "Boxham, I sympathize with your plight. But you need to find a woman who returns your feelings. Besides," he continued, with a smirk, "my sister is far too old for you."

"I beg your pardon!" Rose exclaimed.

"Think on it, Boxham. You are what—nineteen?"

"Twenty next month."

"*Nineteen.* Rosemary is nearly three-and-twenty. She is well on her way to thirty. You do not want a wife who is that old, do you?"

"Alston!" Rose shot him an indignant look, but Adrian merely grinned.

Boxham looked troubled. "It is not that great a gap . . ."

"But it will seem longer with each passing year. Just think of all those fresh and dewy-eyed young ladies making their debut this season. Why, Rose is nearly hag-ridden compared to them."

He felt a sharp jab to his side. "Ow!"

"I am not going to stand here and be insulted." Rose turned and marched into the house.

"Now you have made her angry," Boxham said.

"I merely deflected her anger away from you," Adrian explained. "Now I suggest you toddle on home and stay out of her sight for a few days. She will forget all about this."

"But—"

"Rose is not going to marry you, Boxham. Accept that. I do not want you to speak with her about this again."

Boxham's whole body sagged. Adrian gently patted him on the shoulder.

"There must be a score of young ladies who would be

thrilled to catch your eye," Adrian assured him. "Just open your eyes. The possibilities are endless."

"I do not think I can look at another while my heart still pines for Lady Rosemary."

Adrian leaned closer. "Believe me, you are being saved from a fate worse than death. The woman is a harridan. I pity the poor fellow who finally marries her. She will make his life a living hell."

"Really?" Boxham already looked more cheerful.

Adrian nodded. "Count yourself lucky that you escaped. One day, some poor fellow will not be as fortunate. Now—go home. I am going into my house, and I do not want to see you out here again."

Boxham nodded and sauntered away.

Shaking his head at the follies of youth, Adrian walked inside.

Yet he felt a pang of sympathy for the lad. Adrian knew what it was like to love without hope.

Chapter 15

⚘

Rose met him at the drawing room door, a concerned look on her face.

"Did you finally persuade him to leave?" she asked.

He nodded. "I told him you would make him miserable."

"You are *too* kind."

He followed her into the room. "I had to discourage him *somehow*."

"You might have done it with a little more thought to my feelings. Too old indeed. Now I feel as if I should be walking with a cane."

"Oh, I think you have a few more good years left on you."

Rose sat on the sofa while he poured them each some wine. "Poor Boxey. I thought I had made myself clear the last time we spoke."

"Some people are not willing to take no for an answer." Adrian handed her a glass and sat beside her. "And I get the impression that Lord Boxham is not the brightest star in the galaxy."

She giggled. "No, he is not. But he is sweet. He would make an adorable brother."

Adrian tried to look indignant. "And I would not?"

"*Younger* brother. I shall have to take a closer look at the young ladies making their come-out this spring. Perhaps I can find the proper one for him."

"He's too young to get married," Adrian said. "Give him a chance to live a little."

"I think Boxey needs someone to look after him." Rose sipped her wine.

"Just so long as it is not you."

She nodded in agreement.

"I have to admit I feel some sympathy for the fellow," Adrian said.

"Sympathy?" Her eyes widened. "For Boxey?"

"The poor man is suffering from a broken heart."

"Boxey is too young to know what being in love is like," she said firmly.

"And you are not?" He gazed at her intently.

She met his eyes for a moment, then looked away. "No."

"Is that why you have not married?" he asked gently. "Some stupid fool did not recognize the prize he was being offered?"

Rose studied her wineglass. "It is not that. More a matter of . . . not even being aware."

"Do not tell me even Boxham has more courage than you! Why have you not spoken to the fellow?"

"It is not a woman's place to speak . . ."

"Balderdash. I've yet to see you shrink from any opportunity to speak your mind."

She smiled ruefully. "Yes, I know. You have seen me at my worst."

"Then tell the poor man what you feel."

"It is not so easy as all that," she said. "There are . . . complications."

"Because of your brother's absence?"

Rose smothered a laugh. "That is the least of the problem."

"Don't tell me he is unsuitable?"

"Yes—I mean no. I am the one who is unsuitable. His life is very . . . different, and I do not think I would fit in easily."

He could almost imagine that she was talking about someone like him.

Someone like him.

Adrian trembled. Could she possibly?

"I cannot imagine any situation that would not be graced by your presence." He took her hand and ran his thumb across her palm. "You are the most remarkable woman I have ever met."

"But set in my ways . . . and spoiled."

"At times," he admitted with a fond grin. "But you can also be selfless and caring beyond all imagination."

"You make me sound like a saint."

"Not a saint, just a flesh and blood woman who enjoys life."

"Rather a cowardly soul who is afraid to take a deep look at who she really is," Rose said. "Because she fears what she will find there."

Her words puzzled him. "What could you possibly be afraid of?"

"Myself. And you."

"Me? What makes me such a fearsome fellow?"

"It is not you, Adrian, but what you do to me. You make me look at things differently, make me think in new ways. I am not certain I want to."

He slipped his arm around her shoulder and drew her close. "Wasn't it Plato who said the unexamined life was not worth living?"

"I do not know. Remember, I do not have Greek—or Latin. That makes me feel stupid."

"You are not stupid, Rose. You merely do not have a gentleman's education. Which is not necessary for a woman like you."

"An idle, spoiled aristocrat?"

He sighed with exasperation. "Do you think years of Latin and Greek have done much good for Boxham—or your brother? They have no use for it—nor do you."

"But I cannot even talk with you—"

He placed a finger on her lips. "Do you really think I wish to discuss the conjugation of Latin verbs with you?" Adrian wrapped his other arm about her waist and drew her even closer. "That is the very last thing I wish to do."

Their lips were so close, barely a breath apart. Her blue eyes were wide, dark, uncertain as they gazed into his.

"What do you wish to do?" she asked breathlessly.

"This." He brought his mouth down on hers.

Her lips were warm and soft, softer than he could ever have imagined, and sweet to the taste.

Like roses.

Her fingers grazed the back of his neck, and he uttered a moan of sheer pleasure.

Adrian drew back and gazed at her, watching as her eyes flicked open with surprise. He trailed soft kisses down the line of her jaw, and she closed them again, a faint smile curving her lips.

"I love you," Adrian whispered.

In answer, she cradled his face in her hands and pulled his mouth back to hers.

This cannot be happening, he told himself. It is all a dream— a marvelous, wonderful dream. And at some point he was going to wake up and it would end. But until it did . . .

Everything about Adrian was wonderful. Rose breathed in the faint hint of sandalwood that clung to his skin, felt the silk-iness of his hair between her fingers, his hard muscles beneath his clothing. She even liked the rough stubble that dotted his chin.

The feeling of being held in his arms was indescribable. And his kisses—

"What is going on here?"

Adrian jerked away so quickly that Rose would have fallen back if her hands were not wrapped around his neck.

Felton stood in the doorway, an incredulous expression on his face.

"What does it look like?" Rose demanded irritably.

Adrian gently disengaged her hands and placed them on her lap.

Felton snorted. "Highly improper behavior, that is what. You are damn lucky I was the one at the door. Else neither of you would ever be able to show your face in society again."

Rose glared at him. "What are you doing here at this hour?"

"I need to talk with Mr. Stamford."

She jumped up. "Is Simon on his way home?"

Felton looked uneasy. "Why don't you go up to bed, my dear? I can explain matters to you tomorrow."

She sat down again. "I am not leaving."

Felton half filled a glass with brandy, tossed it off with two long swallows, then refilled his glass before finally sitting down.

"I just received a report from the man I sent to look for your brother," he said.

"And?" Rose prompted him.

"He has disappeared, Rose. There is no trace of Alston anywhere. Gone. Vanished."

Rose gripped the arm of the sofa. Simon was not dead. He could not be. She clenched her fingers. *He could not be.*

Adrian put his arm around her shoulder. "Surely, the government must know where he is."

Rose went rigid. It was going to happen now; the entire truth was going to come out, and Adrian would discover that they had lied to him from the start. Discover that they never knew where Simon was, or when—or even if—he was coming back. Lied, because they were afraid he would not help them if he knew.

What would he think of her when he found out?

Rose could not bring herself to look at Adrian, but stared instead at the empty fire grate. "Simon was never working for the government. He disappeared while on holiday in Switzerland."

Adrian jerked his arm away, and she felt his burning gaze. "You mean that you did not know if he was ever going to return?"

She shook her head. "We hoped . . ."

"I see." Adrian's voice was hard as he looked over at Felton. "And now you have to tell Ramsey the truth—his plans for a ducal son-in-law are shattered."

Felton took another huge gulp of brandy. "No one can say for certain that Alston is dead. There is no body—there is no proof."

"That might satisfy the solicitors, but I doubt it will mean much to Ramsey and Lady Juliet," Adrian said.

"Only one thing that can save us now," Felton moaned.

"Unless Simon walks through that door tonight, I would not hold out much hope," Adrian said.

"We will pay you anything you ask if you continue playing the role," Felton said. "For a bit longer. I want to go to Switzerland and search on my own."

"You could not possibly get to Switzerland and back before the—"

Rose saw a look of pure disgust cross Adrian's face. "Oh, no. I am not going to play Alston at the wedding."

"But think on it—once we find Simon, he can slip into your place with no one the wiser. If not . . ." Felton shrugged. "You can live like a duke for the rest of your life."

Rose buried her face in her hands, ashamed of her uncle, ashamed of herself. She never should have asked Adrian to play Simon, never involved him in their tangled web of lies.

"I would not allow Lady Juliet to think she was marrying Alston. A marriage like that would be completely invalid if anyone discovered the truth."

Felton waved off his protests. "Who would ever know?"

"Adrian is right, Uncle," Rose said. "We cannot ask that of him. You are going to have to speak to Ramsey."

"We still have a week before the wedding," Felton insisted. "I will not give up hope until the last minute."

"It would be cruel to keep Juliet looking forward to a wedding that is not going to happen," Rose said. "We have to tell her."

"What will you tell her?" Adrian demanded. "That the man she thought was Alston was really a country schoolteacher?"

Rose heard the bitterness in his words. She could not blame Adrian. They—she—had lied to him as well.

"We will tell Ramsey that Simon has . . . changed his mind about the wedding," she said. "He can tell everyone that Juliet cried off at the last moment."

"That's right; you have to protect your brother's reputation—and your family's." Adrian's sarcasm was biting.

"It protects Juliet," Rose said heatedly. "She would be in disgrace if people thought Simon called off the wedding."

"So the poor Duke of Alston will take his broken heart to some faraway country, never to be seen again." Adrian shook his head. "I have to admit, you planned this beautifully."

"I thought Simon would come home," Rose said, fighting back tears. "I would not have lied to you if I thought otherwise."

"Then it's all settled?" Felton looked at them hopefully. "You will talk with Ramsey next week, Rose?"

"*You* will talk with him," Rose said.

"I feared you would say that." Felton stared glumly at his glass.

Rose turned to Adrian. "Will you stay a few more days—until we can untangle this web?"

"I don't know."

Felton looked at Rose. "Take yourself off to bed, my dear. No use you looking haggard in the morning. I'll talk with the lad and see if we can come to some arrangement."

Rose glanced at Adrian. His face was hard, emotionless.

What must he think of her now?

"I will talk with you in the morning," she said, and fled into the hall.

How was it possible for her life to go from wonderful to a complete disaster in only a few short minutes?

Adrian would never forgive her for this. She had lied to him, out of pure self-interest, confirming all the things he once accused her of. She was selfish, and spoiled. Pure greed had led her to hire Adrian, because she wanted to make certain that Simon married Juliet and did not lose his—and her—money. And to ensure Adrian's cooperation, she had not told him the entire story.

Now she had to face up to her sins.

Even then, she still intended to avoid the complete truth. They would not tell Ramsey that "Simon" had been an impostor; no, she would lie again and tell him that Simon had changed his mind rather than reveal the masquerade they had carried out. All because it would reflect badly on her.

She really was a horrible person.

How could Adrian have ever thought he loved her? She did not deserve it.

Hurt, bewilderment, anger, all warred within Adrian as he confronted Felton.

Rose had lied to him from the first day they met. Lied about Simon. She knew he was missing, knew there was no guarantee he would return for his wedding. Yet she had led Adrian to think that all was well and the duke's return was only a matter of time.

What else had she lied about? Had she really meant the words she said earlier tonight, the kisses she had shared? Or were those mere lies as well, to keep him complacent?

Felton cleared his throat. "The wedding is not until next week," he said. "We need you to stay until then."

"I thought you intended to give Ramsey—and Juliet—a few days' notice?"

"We need you here for several more days. Think how foolish we would look if we went to Ramsey and Simon returned at the last minute."

"Yes, how foolish." Adrian frowned. "My inclination is to leave tomorrow. You should go straight to Ramsey with the truth—or as much of it as you are going to tell him."

Felton shook his head. "No, you cannot do that. We need you."

"For what? You can't believe that Simon will make a miraculous appearance at the last moment? Face it Felton, this is over. He has to be dead."

"If you won't do it for me, do it for Rosemary." Felton gave him a smirking glance. "You appear to be *fond* of her."

"Postponing the inevitable is not going to do her any good."

"She needs time to contract a marriage of her own, with

someone who won't cry off when word gets out about Simon and Juliet."

"You think she can arrange that in a few short days?" Adrian demanded sourly, but he knew it was true. Why, Rose could send word to Boxham, and he would come running. No doubt there would be other equally willing suitors if she gave them encouragement.

He sighed. If that was what Rose wanted him to do, he probably would agree. But he wanted to talk with her first. He had to know if she had been speaking the truth earlier tonight, when she said she was afraid of him, because he made her take a deep look within herself?

Had she grown to regret her part in this? Enough that she would be willing to make a clean break with this life—forever? Adrian knew she had the ability to do whatever she wanted. The question was—did she have the courage? The safe route would be to entice one of her beaus into a quick offer of marriage. Even with the change in the family fortunes, and the questions about her brother's strange disappearance, she would still live among the *ton*.

Despite everything he had learned this evening, Adrian still loved her. Loved her for what he knew she could be if given the chance to live away from the mindless frivolity of London society. She was smart, eager, interested in the world around her. Rose's talents, her sensibilities, were wasted on the *ton*.

He wanted her with him, in Wiltshire, where he could watch that side of her flourish.

But would she go with him?

He had to find out.

"I must talk with Rose." Adrian stood. "I will decide then."

Felton nodded.

Adrian left the drawing room and slowly walked up the stairs. Everything was happening too fast; he needed time to think about what he wanted to say, to rehearse his words until they seemed right. But there was no time. He, Rose—even Felton—all had decisions to make now. And his decision, at least, depended totally on what Rose planned to do.

He hesitated outside her door, then knocked softly.

"Come in," she called.

She must have expected him, for she was still in her gown, sitting at her dressing table. She glanced at him briefly before turning away. Her face was pale, drawn, with a hint of redness around her eyes. Had she been weeping?

"Did Uncle persuade you to stay?" she asked.

"I wanted to talk with you first," Adrian said. "He thinks I should stay a while longer, to give you time to find a husband."

Rose laughed mirthlessly. "A pity you sent Boxey away. He would accept the job."

"Is that what you want? Marriage to whatever man will have you?"

"What other choice do I have?" Her tone was bitter. "I told you what happens if Simon does not marry Juliet. Now, if he is . . . if he is . . . gone . . . my situation is even more awkward."

Adrian took in a deep breath and exhaled slowly. "Rose, earlier tonight I said I loved you. I—"

"Please, Adrian, do not say anything more. I know what you must think of me."

"I still love you."

She turned in her chair and looked at him, her expression sad. "I do not deserve your love."

"It is not an easy thing to fall out of love with someone," he said. "I know you said you were uncertain, but would you . . . could you live with me in Wiltshire? I know it is not what you have here. There will be no fancy balls and evenings at the theater and new bonnets bought on a whim. But I have enough to provide for you. You can have a maid, and even a housekeeper."

"It is sweet of you to offer, Adrian, after everything I have done." She shook her head. "I cannot accept."

"Why?" He was not willing to give up; he wanted to make sure that she was saying no out of conviction, not some misguided sense of honor.

"I would make you miserable."

"Don't you think I should be the judge of that?"

"Adrian, I do not think . . . it will not work. I am not suited to be your wife. Your entire life is so . . . foreign to me. I could never become accustomed to it."

"I think you give yourself less credit than you deserve. I have seen you, Rose; I know what you can do when you put your mind to it. Nothing is impossible for you."

She looked up at him, pain etched on her face, moisture glistening on her lashes. "I am not as strong as you think I am, Adrian."

"Yes, you are," he insisted. "You simply do not believe it."

"We could never be happy," she said. "Our lives are too . . . too different. I would not be happy, and I would make you unhappy as well."

"Do you think you would be any happier married to Boxham?"

"We come from the same world," she said.

"Do you really love all this"—he waved his hand at her room—"so much? Do you require luxury to be content?"

"I do not know," she said, her voice a whisper. "But I am afraid to find out."

Adrian clenched his fists at his sides. If she had told him this earlier today, he would have argued with her. The woman who had dug him out of that pile of rubble in Hampshire was not easily cowed. She was far stronger than she believed.

If she would only let him, he knew he could make her happy. But he realized, with a flood of sadness, that she did not intend to give him the chance.

Her fingers twisted nervously in her lap. "I would like you to stay, Adrian. For a few more days? It would make things . . . easier. Just in case . . ."

"I am finished acting as your brother."

"What about your talk at the society?"

The society. He had forgotten all about that. Three days from now, he was scheduled to present his findings at their monthly meeting. The chance he had been waiting for . . . He could not leave London now.

But he was through pretending to be Alston. He would stay in town, but not in her employ.

"I will remain in London until the meeting. That can be your deadline for telling Ramsey."

She bowed her head. "Thank you."

"I won't be staying at this house, however."

Her head snapped up. "But—"

"Tell everyone I was unexpectedly called out of town. I know you can write a pretty apology to Juliet."

"But if we need you—"

"I am sure that Lady Rosemary Devering will have no further use for Adrian Stamford."

"Will you let me know where you are staying?" she asked.

"Yes. And do not worry—I will be careful about where I am seen. I have no desire to be mistaken for Alston again."

"Uncle can get a draft from the bank tomorrow, to pay you for your work."

"Do you think I want your money?"

Rose's eyes regarded him sadly. "We hired you to perform a job, and you did your part. Now it is time that we do ours."

He nodded. "All right, you may pay me. May I borrow a trunk, to pack my things? I will return it."

"Keep it—and anything else you want. Simon's clothes—they are all yours."

"I do not think I will have much use for black silk breeches in Wiltshire."

"No, but you can use his other clothing. Take them, Adrian, please. They've been altered to fit you—Simon could not wear them anymore."

He stood awkwardly. There was nothing more to say—but he did not want to leave. This might be the last time he ever saw her.

Adrian reached out and touched a shaky hand to her hair. "I wish you would believe in yourself."

Her fingers brushed against his hand. "Take care of yourself,

Adrian. And be careful when you are digging in ancient tombs."

It was a dismissal. Adrian pulled his hand away and let himself out the door, quietly closing it behind him.

Chapter 16

❧

Rose buried her face in her hands and wept.

She wished she could share Adrian's faith in her ability to change, but she knew herself better. What if she married him and went to Wiltshire, only to discover that she was wrong, that she could not endure life in a quiet village. She would be miserable, and soon she would make Adrian miserable as well. There would be no escape for either of them.

Perhaps, just perhaps, she might be happy. But it was better not to take the chance at all, than to make a grievous mistake. It was better this way for Adrian, better for her.

Even if it hurt.

Was this what love truly meant—caring so much for another person that you were willing to sacrifice your own desires to keep him happy? If so, she must love him desperately. Adrian's happiness was the most important thing in the world to her. If walking away from him was the way to ensure it, that was what she must do. In time, he would forget about her and find someone else to love—someone who was certain to make him happy.

She knew it would not be so easy for her. Memories of Adrian—and her lost dreams for what might have been—would stay with her for the rest of her life.

Rose slept fitfully that night, and awoke early, but she stayed in her room. She did not want to risk meeting Adrian on the stairs. She ate breakfast in her room and did not venture out until well after noon, when she was certain he would be gone.

She could not stop herself from going to the library. She had grown so accustomed to seeing him there at the desk, his head bent over his papers, that it was a shock to find the room empty, the desk free of clutter.

How was she going to stay here without him? Every time she heard a footfall, or a voice, she jumped, thinking it was him, until she remembered he was gone.

Rose wished she could get out of the house, out of London altogether. But that was impossible—not while there was still a chance, no matter how slim, that Simon would return. It would only be three days, after all. If Simon was not here by then, she and Uncle would go to Ramsey and give him the discouraging news.

Then she could leave. But where would she go? Ashbridge provided no refuge. That place was as filled with memories of Adrian as the London house. No, she would have to go somewhere else, somewhere far away, where she would not see Adrian's shadow in every room, hear his voice in every sound.

She feared she would never find such a place.

And today, in the midst of her pain, she had to write to Juliet, to tell her that Simon had been called out of town for a few days. Rose prayed that she would not demand a more detailed explanation, for there was none to give.

Juliet would be furious. What bridegroom left town this close to his wedding? Rose prayed that neither Juliet nor her father recognized this as a sign of what was coming. Rose had to keep them complacent until Adrian was safely out of London. She did not want his part in all this revealed.

Then she had the more frightening task of telling Lord Ramsey and his daughter that her brother had abandoned his obligations.

Until then, Rose had to keep up the pretense that nothing was wrong. Which meant she must go for a drive in the park, and attend tonight's musicale at Lord Redding's, and smile and laugh as if she did not have a care in the world.

*   *   *

Adrian stared at the four walls of his tiny room at the King's Head Inn in Southwark. The mismatched furniture, plain white curtains, and uncarpeted floor were very different from the ducal splendor of Bruton Street, but he felt comfortable here. It was far removed from Alston's world.

He did not intend to hide for the next three days, but the places he intended to visit were unlikely to be patronized by anyone who would recognize Alston. Out-of-the-way book-shops, obscure museums, and historical sites did not attract the *ton*. He would be safe enough, one more anonymous Londoner.

And the morning after his talk to the Antiquities Society, he would be on the mail coach, heading toward home.

A home where he had hoped—dreamed—that he could take Rose. A home that would never be filled with priceless objects of art, gilded plasterwork, or fine carpets underfoot. But a home that would be comfortable, where she would never want for anything she needed—a home filled with love.

But he had not been able to convince her that she could live there, happily, with him. If only he had more time . . . he might have persuaded her that she could be happy with him, that she would find a whole new world that would engage her and give her far more to do than the arid environs of the *ton*. They could have worked together, searching for artifacts, writing about their adventures.

Adrian pictured her organizing his collections, packing up pottery scraps and axe heads and arrow points in neatly labeled boxes, bringing a needed order to his life. He would teach her Latin, not because she needed it, but because it would make her feel more a part of his world. She could teach him French and translate articles for him.

Yes, they could have been happy, but she was afraid to take the chance. And he did not know how to show her how wrong she was.

After enduring two days of feigned gaiety, Rose wanted nothing more than to remain at home today. Adrian's speech to the society was tonight; tomorrow he would leave London. She wanted to sit in her room and mourn.

But she had promised Lowden he could drive her in the park. And she knew if she stayed home, she would only grow more morose. On public display in the park, Rose would have to put on a cheery front.

She felt a twinge of guilt at continuing to deceive Lowden. He was Simon's closest friend, and he would be as shocked as anyone when news of the canceled marriage became public. Even then, she would be able to tell him only that Simon had gone away, not that they did not know where he was, or feared he was dead.

Simon dead. Uncle felt certain he must be, since he had not returned by now. Without irrefutable proof, she refused to give up hope. But her optimism would not appease the solicitors. She was not familiar with the laws regarding missing persons, but Rose knew it could be years before someone was legally declared dead. Her life would be lived in a strange limbo until the matter was resolved.

Her uncle had dropped by just this morning, reminding her that time was running out and she needed to wring a proposal of marriage out of someone this very day if she had any hopes of a decent match. Rose had laughed and told him he was being silly, and sent him on his way. All her talk about finding a husband this season had been just that—talk—she now realized. She was not willing to marry without love.

Lowden arrived promptly at the appointed hour.

"You look rather peaked today," he said after he helped her into the open landau.

"That is not very chivalrous of you to say."

"But it is true. Something is wrong, Rose. Can't you tell me what it is? Does it have to do with Simon's absence?"

She shook her head. "I merely danced far too long into the night and am tired."

Lowden still looked at her suspiciously, but did not press.

The park seemed more crowded than usual, and Lowden stopped the horses often to chat with friends. Rose did her best to seem normal, but after half an hour of enforced cheerfulness, her strength was at low ebb.

"I really am rather tired," she said in a soft undertone. "Do you think we could go back now?"

Lowden did not hesitate, but turned the horses around.

He was all solicitous concern when they returned to the house, escorting her inside, sending a servant for tea. Rose wished to be left alone, but she could not bring herself to ask him to leave. She would let him stay long enough to have a cup of tea, at least.

Lowden joined her on the sofa. "Rose, I know something is wrong. Why can't you—or your brother—confide in me? We have been friends for ages."

"I am not free to speak about Simon's private matters." She had given him a hint; by the end of the week he would better understand her meaning.

"The fellow's been acting deuced strange," he agreed. "Is he really in such a pelt over the wedding?"

"Lowden, do not ask me to explain. I cannot." He might doubt her, but it certainly was the truth.

"When he returns, I am going to have a stern talk with him." Lowden spoke with growing irritation. "He has no right to cause you such distress."

"Do not blame Simon," she said softly. "It is as much my fault as his."

He took her hand. "I doubt that. Rose, I hate to see you upset like this. Can't you bring yourself to tell me?"

She shook her head.

"Perhaps I can earn the right to offer you my help. You know I hold you in the highest esteem. I have often hoped . . ."

Rose knew what he was going to say, and for an instant she wanted to hear it. It would be so easy to accept his offer, to let him take her away from all this, to protect her from the disaster that was about to fall around her head.

So easy. But so wrong. Lowden was a good friend, one she had known for years. She admired and respected him, but she did not love him. Until this instant, she had not realized how much that mattered. He was a suitable partner; society would label it a good match.

But now, because of Adrian, she knew what love was. And even though his departure had left a gaping hole in her heart, she could not settle for a marriage that would bring her only companionship—and safety.

Lowden deserved to have a wife who wanted more than that from him. And Rose could no longer give it.

"It is not possible," she said.

"Is that not for me to judge?"

She saw the disappointment in his eyes, and she wished she could tell him otherwise, but it would be far too cruel.

"I am deeply honored," Rose said at last, "but I cannot accept. Someday, you will realize that I am doing you a great favor by saying that."

"When I am dead and in my grave?"

She winced at the bitterness in his voice. "When you find a lady who wants more than friendship from you," Rose replied.

Lowden sighed and stood. "I think, under the circumstances, that I will not stay for tea. I can show myself out."

She nodded and sat quietly while he left the room.

Uncle would be furious if he discovered she had rejected Lowden, saying she had thrown away her best chance to come out of this debacle relatively unscathed. But she was not going to use Lowden to save her own skin. That would be unnecessarily cruel.

Perhaps Adrian was right—she did have more courage than she thought. Courage enough to turn down a good man who offered her safety and security in the face of an otherwise uncertain future.

But not courage enough to take a chance on love.

She propped her elbow on the arm of the sofa and rested her chin on her hand. When had life grown so complicated? She had been raised with a sure knowledge of her status and place in society. She was the daughter of a duke, the highest rank of the aristocracy. A secure future should have been hers as a matter of course.

But now her whole world was tumbling down around her. Simon was gone; perhaps dead. She might never see him again.

Rose refused to believe that. Because deep down she did not think Simon was dead. He would come back one day. It would be too late to fix everything, but as long as she did not lose him, that did not matter. Her life would go back to a semblance of normalcy.

Except that her life could never go back to the way it was. Because of Adrian. Adrian, who had forced her to recognize what an idle, frivolous life she led—a life that had no purpose beyond being the first one to share the latest *on-dit*, or owning the most expensive bonnet, or hosting the season's most talked-about party.

She had been perfectly content with such a life until a few weeks ago. Now, she knew that no matter what happened, she would never be able to enjoy it with the same sense of pleasure. That was what had given her the strength to refuse Lowden. Few marriages among the *ton* were based on love. It was not fashionable.

Rose no longer cared. She knew that she could not marry without love.

But was love enough for marriage?

She heard a noise at the door and looked up. Uncle walked in.

"You're looking the gloomy puss," he observed.

"Is there a reason why I should not?"

He shrugged. "Tell me again where that Stamford fellow is staying. I want to speak with him one more time, to see if I can persuade him to stay. Checked with the banker—you have access to plenty of Simon's funds. We can offer him a princely sum."

"No!"

Felton raised an eyebrow. "I did not think it would hurt to try one more time."

"I do not want you bothering him tonight," she said. "He has a very important speech to make."

"I can talk with him in the morning then."

"You would be wasting your time. He will not help us again."

Felton lowered his bulk into a chair. "You are determined to go to Ramsey tomorrow?"

"We must. The news will devastate Juliet. I wish to tell her as soon as possible. That will give them time to undo some of the arrangements. We are honor-bound to pay for their expenses, you realize."

"Knowing Ramsey, he's run up a good deal of them. Still, you're right. The girl's got a right to know. I suppose you're planning on going down to Ashbridge after we talk with them?"

She shook her head. "I want to be much farther away than that. Across the channel."

"Travel that far?" He snorted. "Too much trouble."

"I want to go to Switzerland and look for Simon."

Felton coughed. "Probably a good idea, that. Not that I didn't hire reputable fellows, but there is nothing like doing a job for yourself."

"How soon can we leave?" she asked eagerly.

"Not above a week."

"I want to be gone before the date of the wedding."

"Impossible."

She shook her head. "I will make the arrangements if you are not willing."

Felton sighed. "And you always said you hated to be rushed."

"This is a rather delicate matter," Rose reminded him. "Our quick departure will add credence to the story we give Ramsey."

Felton heaved himself out of the chair. "If we are going to leave in that short time, I have work to do. When do you wish to go see Ramsey?"

"I shall send him a note tonight, asking for an appointment at ten tomorrow morning. If that is not agreeable, I will inform you."

"Very good. Switzerland it is."

As soon as he left, Rose went upstairs to her room. Now that she had decided on a course of action, she felt better. She could keep herself busy with packing for the next few days, occupy her mind with the arrangements.

She pushed open the door to her room and saw a suit of clothing draped over her dressing-table chair.

The clothes she had ordered for Adrian, to wear to the Antiquities Society; she had forgotten all about them. Rose glanced at the clock. There was still time to get them to him before his speech, if she hurried. She rang for a footman.

"Have the carriage brought around at once," she said. If traffic was not bad, she should be able to get to Southwark in time.

Hesitating, she wondered if she should take one of the footmen with her, but decided it was too great a risk. It was not proper for a young lady of her breeding—or any breeding—to visit a public inn alone, but it could not be helped. This was a respectable inn, after all. The innkeeper could deliver the clothing to Adrian.

Rose laughed wryly. She did not want to do that. She wanted this chance to see Adrian one more time.

She flew out the front door the instant the carriage pulled to the curb. The coachman looked startled when she gave him directions to the King's Head, but he was too well trained—and paid—to question any whim of his employers.

The carriage ride to Southwark seemed to take hours. Rose perched on the edge of her seat, fearful she would arrive too late. She wanted so much to see Adrian, to wish him well.

They crossed the Thames at Westminster and drove past rows and rows of newly erected houses. The streets were crowded, impeding their progress.

Just as she despaired of ever reaching her destination, the coach pulled into the yard of the King's Head. Rose jumped out and ran to the entrance, hoping to find the innkeeper quickly.

The hostelry was not busy, and a strange carriage was an uncommon appearance, so she was barely in the door before the man greeted her.

"You have a guest staying here, Mr. Adrian Stamford," Rose said. "I need to see him."

The innkeeper gave her a dubious look.

"I have a package to deliver to him." She held up the bundle of clothing.

"I am afraid Mr. Stamford went out some time ago."

"Oh." Her heart sank. She was too late, after all.

"Do you wish me to put these in his room?"

"No. I mean yes." She handed him the clothes and pressed a shilling into his hand.

"Who shall I tell him these are from?"

Rose shook her head. "It does not matter."

She walked slowly back to the carriage. Her effort had been all for naught.

In the privacy of the coach, tears dripped down her cheeks. She was not going to see Adrian before he left. She dare not go to the Society meeting, even if women were admitted. This was Adrian's night; she wanted it to be perfect for him. Her presence would only cause a stir and detract from what he had to say.

But she wanted to know how the Society received his talk, if they were pleased with the work he had done, and if they planned to publish his article. She would have to write him a letter. Rose hoped he would write back and tell her. He might toss the letter on the fire, unread.

No, Adrian was not that cowardly. He would read it, and most likely reply. But she would be out of the country then, and would not get the news until much later.

She envied Adrian for having a place to go to when he left London. She did not know how long she and Uncle would be searching for her brother. It could be months before she was back in England again. It was nearly summer; Adrian would be free from his pupils for the next few months. It would give him time to find new sites to excavate, new treasures to unearth.

Rose ran her finger along the bracelet that lay beneath her sleeve. She had taken to wearing it constantly since he left—her one tangible reminder of him, and the excitement of that dig.

Rose sat up straighter. She realized she wanted to be there when he was digging, to make certain he was safe, and to share in his joy when he found something ancient and unusual. And to watch while he struggled over the rudiments of Latin grammar with the Topmore twins and endured their mischievous pranks. She wanted to see his tiny cottage and his collection of spear points and axe blades and bits and pieces of broken pottery.

She wanted to be with him.

A chill of . . . fear? . . . anticipation? raced up her spine. It would be far different from the life she had led up until now. But that old life no longer held her. Now that she had seen it through Adrian's eyes, it would never look the same to her again.

He had asked her to come with him, to be his wife, and she had told him no, she was too afraid, afraid she would disappoint him.

But now, she was suddenly more afraid not to.

Rose rapped on the roof of the carriage, signaling the coachman to hurry. She had a great deal of packing to do if she intended to leave for Wiltshire in the morning. She would to deposit herself on Adrian's doorstep at the King's Head before the mail-coach left. She prayed he would take her with him.

Chapter 17

~

Adrian tugged at his cravat for the tenth time while he waited in the hall at the Antiquities Society. In a moment, he would be called in to give his presentation.

He had already met several of the members earlier, at dinner. They were polite, but not overly friendly, and Adrian feared his speech would be received with only lukewarm enthusiasm. Several men had expressed disappointment that his patron, the Duke of Alston, had not accompanied him.

Shrugging, he glanced down at the papers in his hands. He had to win them over with his talk.

It was nearing eight. He wondered, not for the first time, or even the hundredth over the last three days, what Rose was doing now. Was she already in the box at the theater, surrounded by her coterie of admirers? Setting out for dinner at another noble household? Or still dressing for an elegant fete?

He wished she were here tonight; her presence would have given his confidence a boost. She had helped him mightily with his speech; she deserved to hear it. Several times today he started to pen her a note, urging her to come, then tore it up. There was no point in prolonging his agony. She had made her choice, and it did not include him.

The door at the end of the hall opened, and the society's secretary stepped through.

"Mr. Stamford? We are ready for you."

Adrian straightened his cravat one more time and followed the man into the meeting room.

* * *

The moment she arrived home, Rose rang for Mary and sent her after the trunks. She had little time to get ready if she was going to leave with Adrian in the morning.

She could not possibly pack everything tonight, but only the things she needed right away. The challenge was deciding what was to go in the trunk now, what could be set aside to pack later, and what should be left behind. She would not need more than one—maybe two—ball gowns in Wiltshire. And riding habits—did Adrian even own a horse? Perhaps he would let her bring two of Simon's horses from Ashbridge.

How many day dresses would she need? Rose did not know a thing about the society in the neighborhood; the horrible twins' parents might be their only near neighbors. She set out her simplest, plainest gowns to pack. She did not want to look out of place in Adrian's world.

To her surprise, she did not feel a single twinge of dismay as she sorted through her clothes, choosing one dress, discarding many others. What was a dress when she could have Adrian?

Rose suddenly realized she had forgotten one small detail. They were not married—nor could they be until the banns were read three times. She could not possibly go to Wiltshire with him tomorrow.

She smiled. That was one problem that could be solved easily. They could delay their departure in the morning long enough to obtain a Special License. Uncle could help them.

Uncle. She needed to tell him what she intended to do and let him know he was going to have to deal with Ramsey alone.

Tossing the dress she held to Mary, with instructions to finish packing her nightclothes, Rose hurried out of the room and down to the library. She would send a footman in search of her uncle.

Rose grabbed a candle from the hall table and went into the room. She rummaged through the drawers until she found ink, quill, and paper and sat down to pen her note. At this time of the night, Uncle might still be at his club. If not, the poor footman would be all over London, trying to track him down.

Deciding it was best not to give Uncle any details, she merely told him to come to the house immediately and left it at that. She would explain everything when he arrived. She folded the letter and looked for a seal.

The library door opened; the footman was here. She glanced up, and her breath caught in her throat.

"Adrian!" she gasped.

"Adrian? Who the deuce is Adrian?"

With her legs threatening to collapse beneath her, Rose stepped from behind the desk and tottered toward the man standing in the doorway.

"Simon?"

"Who else would it be? Why is the house so dark? It looks like a mausoleum in here. And what are you doing home at this hour of the night?"

"Simon!" She shrieked and raced to him, arms outflung. He grabbed her in midstride and swung her into the air.

"Steady, girl. Glad to see me, are you?"

"Where have you been? I've been worried sick. Uncle was sure you were dead, but I knew you weren't." She hugged him tightly. "Oh, Simon, thank God you are home."

"Well, I did cut it a bit closer than I planned. But you did not think I would forget my own wedding, did you?"

"Forget? We were going to tell Ramsey tomorrow that you had cried off."

He laughed uproariously. "Cried off? Oh, that is rich. With all that money at stake? I would be there if they had to carry me in feet first."

"Where have you been all this time?"

"In Switzerland."

"But Uncle sent people there—no one could find a trace of you."

"That's because I was laid up with a broken leg—tripped over some blasted rocks while climbing and damn near fell down the side of an Alp. Fortunately, someone found me and took me in."

"I knew it! You found yourself a Swiss milkmaid!"

"Rather a Swiss goatherd. But he tended me all right, and I finally was able to get down off the mountain. Then I had a deuce of a time getting here—roads washed out, carriages broken down, horses lamed. Nothing went right."

She held him at arm's length and then hugged him again. "Oh, Simon, I am so happy you are back. Everything is going to be all right now."

He stepped back himself and eyed her quizzingly. "Now, who is this Adrian fellow?"

Rose laughed. "Let's go to the drawing room, and I will pour you a glass of brandy. You are going to need it when I tell you what has happened."

Simon displayed outrage, amusement, indignation, and horror, often all at the same time, as Rose began to tell him what had transpired during his absence.

"This fellow has been posing as me?"

"And doing an excellent job of it, too. No one suspected a thing."

"Not even my future bride?"

Rose giggled. "Her least of all. She has that ducal coronet firmly in her sights."

"Well, where is the fellow now? Squiring my lady about town, no doubt."

Rose shook her head. "Oh, Simon, I have been such a fool."

"No one may call my sister a fool—not even you."

"But it is true. We—Uncle and I—were afraid that Adrian would not help us if he knew that you were really missing. So we pretended you were on a mission for the government."

Simon grinned.

"It is not amusing." She shot him a chastening look. "We began to panic when the wedding was only a week away. Uncle actually asked him to go through with the wedding."

"What? Marry my wife?"

"She is not your wife—not yet. Adrian would never agree to such a thing—indeed, he was very angry Uncle even suggested it. That is why we were going to Ramsey tomorrow. Adrian refused to act as you any longer."

"And we are well rid of him, I am certain."

"Simon! You have no idea how much you owe him. He tried to save the hunting lodge, and he discovered all sorts of antiquities on the north field and—"

He held up his hand. "All right, all right, he is a paragon of virtue. One day I shall have to pay him a visit and suitably express my thanks."

She stood up and grabbed his hand. "You can do it right now. Tonight."

"He is still here?"

"Not at the house, but at an inn in Southwark." She squeezed his fingers. "Oh, Simon, this is perfect. You can get the Special License for us."

"Special License?" His expression darkened. "What are you talking about?"

"So we can get married. Adrian is leaving for Wiltshire in the morning, and I intend to go with him."

"Married?" Simon stared at her. "You want to marry a school teacher and live in a cottage? Are you mad?"

"It is what I want," Rose insisted.

"You will be bored in a week."

"I will not. It is London that bores me, Simon. I am tired of living such an aimless life. With Adrian, I can—"

"Starve with dignity?"

"Be happy," she retorted. "And now that you are back, there will be no trouble getting my money. We will not starve."

Simon pulled his hands free and sank back into the chair. "Get me another glass of brandy."

By the time he had drained that glass, and listened to her story, she had overcome some of his opposition.

"Do you really think you will be happy living in a cottage in the country?" he asked doubtfully.

"At first I feared I would not. That is why I sent Adrian away. But after Lowden proposed, I—"

"Lowden asked you to marry him, and you turned him down?"

She gave him a withering look. "Let me finish. When he asked me to marry him, it made me realize that it is not the place or the status of the groom that makes a happy marriage, but the person himself. I do not love Lowden. I do love Adrian and know I can live with him anywhere."

"What is Juliet going to say about having a Latin teacher for a brother-in-law?"

"Frankly, Simon, if I never have to spend another minute in that woman's company, I shall be overjoyed."

He frowned. "That bad?"

"Yes. She is rude, spoiled, arrogant, and far too forward for a gently bred young lady. She kept kissing Adrian!"

Simon chuckled. "It sounds like I will have to take her in hand once we are married."

"You have to. But come. Adrian should be back to his room by now. We need to speak with him."

"How are you so informed of his whereabouts if you have not seen him for three days?"

"Tonight he spoke at the Antiquities Society's meeting about the things he found in the field. They were very eager to hear what he had to say, and they will probably even publish his article in their journal! You must become a patron of the Society, so you can help him."

Simon shuddered. "Sounds dreadfully dull."

"It is quite fascinating. You will have to come on a dig sometime."

He shook his head. "Are you certain that I am in the right house? In the right city? In the right country? Are you really my sister, Rose?"

She laughed and pulled him into the hall. "Do come along, Simon. We must talk to Adrian."

While she pulled on her cloak in the front hall, he looked in puzzlement at the trunk by the door. "What is this?"

"I told you. I am going to Wiltshire with Adrian."

"Not until you are married," he said firmly.

"Which can be accomplished in the morning," she replied.

"Don't you think you should consult with the prospective groom before you make all your plans?"

Her eyes widened in sudden horror. What if Adrian no longer wanted her? He might not, after all; might have come to believe her insistence that they were not suited.

She had to go to Southwark to find out.

During the drive, Rose tried to finish telling Simon all that had gone on during his absence, but he asked more questions than she had time to answer. He only knew the bare outlines of the tale when they pulled up outside the King's Head.

"Perhaps you should wait here," Rose said. "I want to talk with Adrian privately."

"Not a chance," Simon said, climbing out of the carriage. "You're not walking into an inn at this hour of the night by yourself." He grabbed her arm to keep her at his side.

The innkeeper looked surprised to see Rose again, and stared with puzzlement at Simon, but after Simon slipped him some coins, he was more than willing to show them to Adrian's room. Rose's heart thumped loudly in her ears as they went up the stairs and down the hallway.

Did he still want her?

Adrian felt in a celebratory mood when he returned to the inn. His talk had been well received, several members of the Society had spoken to him personally and expressed an interest in hearing about his other findings, and more important, indicated they were interested in sponsoring him for membership. He had plenty to celebrate.

But no one to celebrate with.

He ordered a mug of ale and took it up to his room. He thought the innkeeper gave him an odd look, but Adrian dismissed it as his imagination.

He understood that look when he entered his room. A suit of clothing—breeches, waistcoat, jacket—lay across the bed, and he had a very good idea where it came from.

Rose.

He looked carefully, but there was no note, no message of any kind. Had she meant for him to wear it to the Society meeting, and sent it too late?

The thought cheered him immensely. It meant she was thinking about him, still.

He slipped off his jacket, rolled back his cuffs and sat down to enjoy his ale. There was little else to do except wait for the coach to leave in the morning.

A knock sounded on his door.

"Come in," Adrian called.

The knock sounded again, louder. Scowling, he crossed the room and pulled open the door.

"Yes, what is—" He stared dumbfounded at Rose. She stood before the door, looking nervous, uncertain.

"Hello, Adrian," she said.

"Hello."

"May I come in?"

Feeling like an idiot, he nodded and stepped back to let her in. It was then that he saw the man behind her—a man he had seen only once before, in the public room at a small country inn.

"Alston?"

The duke stepped forward and shook Adrian's hand. "I hear you've been going by that name as well."

"Is it not wonderful?" Rose's eyes danced. "Simon came back tonight!"

"And from what she says, not a minute too early." Alston glanced around the room. "Mind if I order up some brandy?"

"Fine." Adrian ran a hand through his hair, surprised, puzzled and uncertain all at the same time. What were they doing here?

Alston left to look for the tapman.

"Simon is nothing but tactful," Rose said.

"I am glad, for your sake, that he is back," Adrian said.

"Yes, it will make things a bit easier, won't it?"

He watched while she prowled the room, carefully examining every piece of furniture. Why had she come? Merely to tell him that her brother had returned?

"Did your speech go well?" she asked.

He nodded, impatient to discover her purpose. "Why are you here, Rose?"

He saw the nervousness in her eyes. "I wish to go to Wiltshire with you. That is, if you will still have me."

Adrian sucked in his breath, wondering if he had heard her correctly.

"But you said—"

"Any number of foolish things." She stepped closer and placed her palm against his chest, and he felt the heat from her hand through his shirt. Raising her head, she looked into his eyes.

"I love you, Adrian. And I finally realized that is the only thing that matters."

"Are you certain? Do you wish to have more time to think about it?" His words came in a rush.

"Kiss me, Adrian." She tilted her head to meet his.

He kissed her tentatively, then with growing confidence as they wrapped their arms around each other. Rose, his Rose, was willing to marry him. He wanted to shout the joyous news from the rooftops.

Instead, he kissed her until they were gasping for breath.

"Ah, Rose, I will do everything in my power to make you happy."

"Just be yourself," she whispered. "The man I fell in love with."

A loud cough sounded from the doorway. Alston stood there, looking uncertain.

"Have you two had time to discuss matters?" he asked.

Adrian looked down at Rose's glistening blue eyes. "I believe so."

"Well, you may have won Rose's heart, Stamford, but you do not yet have mine." The duke regarded him sternly. "I must look out for my sister's interests."

"I don't need your permission to marry," Rose said.

"I wish to have it," Adrian said, squeezing her hand to silence her. "I will not lie, I do not have a duke's income. But I am not dependent on teaching for my livelihood. My parents left me some money."

"And a house," Rose prompted him.

"Two houses. The manor house is far too large for only one person. I rent it out and live in the cottage."

A look of disappointment flashed across Rose's face. "But I wanted to live in a cottage!"

Adrian laughed. "I am sure you will manage to endure the manor house. It has its own discomforts. I will take extra care to make certain that each and every chimney smokes." He looked squarely at Simon. "And although I do not have a title, my mother was a lady. She refused the marriage her father arranged for her and followed her heart. You need not fear that your sister is stooping too low."

Rose took a step back and stared at him. "Whyever did you not tell me this before?"

He grinned. "You have to admit, it was rather amusing the way you treated me like a country bumpkin at the hunting lodge."

"Only because you acted the part," she retorted. "Or have you forgotten that night at dinner when—"

"Enough, enough." Alston held up his hand. "Stop squabbling. You sound like an old married couple already. Take her, Stamford, with my sympathies."

"You withdraw your objection?" Adrian asked.

"I learned a long time ago never to object to any of my sister's wishes. Safer that way."

"I assure you, I will take excellent care of her." He drew Rose into the crook of his arm.

"Rose can afford to support the both of you," Alston replied. "Her marriage portion is substantial."

"I do not wish to—" Adrian began.

"We can discuss that later." Rose pressed a finger to his lips.

"Where have you been all this time?" Adrian asked the duke.

"Recuperating from a broken leg in the Swiss Alps," he explained. "I sincerely thank you for taking my place"—he shot a dark glance at Rose—"although I am not certain that I would have approved had I known beforehand what my sister was planning."

"Simon can get us a Special License in the morning," Rose said. "We can still leave for Wiltshire tomorrow."

Alston shook his head. "Out of the question. What will people say when you are not at my wedding, Rose? You have to wait."

"But Adrian cannot stay in London now that you are back!"

Alston circled Adrian, examining him carefully. "Oh, I don't see why not. We'll pass him off as a distant cousin."

Rose looked thoughtful. "And if we darken his hair . . ."

Adrian started laughing. "Not another masquerade, please. It is better that I go home."

"No." Rose's mouth was set in a firm line. "I want to be with you."

Alston shrugged. "Let him stay as himself, then."

"Won't people wonder when they see the two of you together?"

"What is there to wonder? No one is going to suspect that you had the audacity to set someone up in my place and fool the entire *ton*," Alston said. "They will merely accept the resemblance as an interesting coincidence."

Rose turned to Adrian. "Will you stay?"

"This is a comfortable enough inn. I do not mind."

"Here?" Rose looked aghast. "Not at all. You have to come back to the house."

Adrian grinned. "And be relegated to one of the lesser bedrooms? I am accustomed to being treated as a duke, you know."

"Well, you must at least move to an inn closer to Bruton Street. I do not want to have to drive all the way over here each time I want to see you."

"Fair enough."

She flung her arms around him and hugged him close. "I am so happy, Adrian. And I will make you happy, too. I promise."

"I know you will."

Epilogue

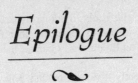

Everyone who attended the wedding of the Duke of Alston to Lady Juliet Ramsey declared it an unequivocal success. The bride looked radiant, the groom handsome, and the rest of the bridal party suitably elegant.

And if anyone had any doubts, the lavish reception that followed at Lord Ramsey's London town house was the talk of the town for weeks.

The duke and his new bride presided over the head table at a banquet for two hundred. Every conceivable delicacy was laid before the guests and Champagne flowed like water.

Sitting beside Adrian, Rose glanced down the table and caught Lowden looking at her. She wiggled her fingers at him, and he pushed his chair back and walked over to her.

"Enjoying the festivities?" he asked.

"Oh, yes. Are you?"

He groaned. "Your brother and I did the town two nights ago, and I still have not recovered."

Rose laughed. "You poor thing."

"I hear felicitations are in order."

Rose turned to Adrian, who was chatting with the guest on his right, and tapped him on the shoulder.

"Let me introduce you. Adrian, this is Lord Lowden. Adrian Stamford."

An expression of sheer disbelief crossed the earl's face as he stared at Adrian, then back at Rose.

"My God! He looks just like—"

"No one," Rose said firmly, holding his gaze.

Lowden's eyes widened in confusion, then filled with growing amusement. "You little minx! I cannot believe you had the nerve to do this."

Rose smiled sweetly. "Why, Lowden, I have no idea what you are talking about."

Shaking his head, he shook Adrian's hand. "I wish you well, Stamford. You are going to need it."

Adrian looked at Rose and grinned.

Adrian could still barely believe that Rose was going to be his. He had not been able to take his eyes off her all day, even when she stood next to the bride in the wedding procession. She was by far the loveliest woman in the room.

"Do you dislike the idea of spending the summer at Ashbridge?" he asked her. "It will not be an exotic honeymoon."

"Not at all. I think Simon's idea is marvelous. Who knows how many more sites you might find on the property?"

"There is a good chance of that," he admitted. "But I fear that staying there will only remind you of what you are giving up."

"It is Juliet's house now," she said firmly. "Mine is in Wiltshire. I cannot wait to see it."

"Do not be fooled by its grand name—even the manor house is small."

"Which will make it that much more wonderful," she said, snuggling closer. "Besides, I imagine that we are going to find ourselves in all sorts of unusual places while you carry out your excavations. It will be nice to have a place to call home in between."

"You talk as if my future is all settled."

"You are well on your way to become a respected antiquarian," she said. "Membership in the Society, an article in the next publication. They adore you."

"They *adore* the patronage of the Duke of Alston."

"It is silly, isn't it, that they accord him so much respect just because he has an exalted title."

Adrian laughed. "You are sounding more and more like a republican every day."

"Well, it is true! They never would have listened to you if it had not been for that letter. It only shows how foolish they are. When you are president of the Society, that will not happen."

"And I suppose you expect me to take on that position next year?"

"Not at all." She grinned. "I will not be ready to share you."

He gazed into her eyes again. "And I never want to share you with anyone."

"You will have to, you know—unless we have no children."

"Well, I will share you by day. But at night, you will be mine."

"Always," she said. *"Amo, amas, amat."*